The Mad Professor

The Mad Professor

by

Hermann Sudermann

Translated by

ISABEL LEIGHTON
and
OTTO P. SCHINNERER

Volume Two

New York
Horace Liveright
1928

CONTENTS

CONTENTS

The Mad Professor

CHAPTER XVII

"THE THREE FATES"

FOR the time being nothing of any consequence happened. The term began and every one met in the Faculty Room except those whose work took them to clinics and laboratories.

The greetings which were accorded Sieburth were as cordial as they had ever been. Scarcely a suggestion of hesitancy or embarrassment preceded the handshakes that were exchanged with him, and here and there a good-natured, indulgent smile that savored more or less of malice depending on individual disposition, manifested itself.

Only Hildebrand seemed disconcerted and tried to avoid him, and after his overly noisy, "Hallo, there you are!" turned quickly to one side without wasting any further mark of friendliness on him. He did not even give him time enough to inquire after Herma's well-being.

"So I suppose I cannot count on seeing her again," he thought, and for the moment it was with difficulty that he suppressed the grief that welled up within him.

The behavior of Hagemann, his favored rival, to

I

whom he had never attributed many good qualities, was much to be appreciated. He came towards him, making a special point of it and involved him in a lengthy conversation about the apportionment of subject matter for next term's lectures; one should get together in time, he felt, so as to avoid any undesirable duplication.

It was clear that this subject only served as a subterfuge, for weeks, even months could have elapsed before the time for this discussion was ripe.

One could not decide whether this was done out of pure goodness of heart or whether it was simply an opportunity to radiate esprit de corps and display himself before the others in the light of one who believes in suspending judgment.

Pfeifferling behaved as drolly as ever. That old "blowhard" was the only one of them all to allude definitely to the incident. He drew his little pig's eyes together until they formed two roguish slits and said, slapping Sieburth jovially on the back, "Well, you little lady-killer!"

All in all, the pain could be endured and was only disagreeable in so far as in the past, in spite of existing enmities, he had always been sought after and had had the upper hand and now he suddenly saw himself in the rôle of one who had to wait upon the whims of others.

Moreover, a harmless and natural view of the matter seemed to be in a fair way of gaining ground and thus the occurrence, being regarded lightly, would gradually fade into oblivion.

One thing, however, was certainly essential and that was to meet every one with the merry laughter of complete unconcern, and he devoted himself to this obligation with a zeal precluding any inclination to retreat, and worthy of a better cause.

He was undecided on only one point, i.e., whether or not it was politic to pay a formal autumn visit on the families with whom he had been associating; but since, up to the present time, he had always considered this social duty unnecessary and had always been invited everywhere in spite of his attitude, he decided to make no change in his procedure if for no other reason than to show that his conscience was not troubling him.

He also avoided stopping ladies with whom he was well acquainted and with whom he used to chat when he ran into them on the street, and contented himself with observing the nature of their greeting as they passed.

Some were embarrassed, others officious, but none so far were noticeably distant. They more frequently approached him with more than ordinary warmth, even though it lacked the note of sincerity.

An example of this kind of thing was the wife of Privy Councilor Kemmerich, who, being as she was one of the famous "Three Fates," was of very great importance. . . .

At the home of this selfsame Privy Councilor's wife on this particular Friday afternoon, while their husbands conducted classes or attended meetings from which they could not be excused, sat the other members of this friendly circle, the wives of Professors Ehmke and Vallentin, gathered around the coffee table as usual for a cozy chat.

Much as these coffee parties were feared, one did well not to underestimate the spirit that governed them.

Mrs. Kemmerich was a woman who jokingly said of herself that she had seen better days. She had been previously married to an art historian whose reputation outlived him. She had associated with all sorts of artists and patrons of art on the most friendly of footings and wore as a final memento of that Apollonic period a glorious auburn wig which, arranged in fantastic rolls and ringlets, framed the persistently youthful face of the matron. She had also retained a merry laugh from her younger days which lost itself in a melodious gurgle, the unexpected outbreaks of which often offended the sense of propriety of her more austere companions.

Her two friends were very differently constituted. They had eked out a wretched existence with their husbands during the long stages of an instructor's career and still carried the marks of the accompanying virtues and privations of their froglike perspective around with them.

The one, Mrs. Ehmke, dabbled in philosophy of life. She considered the new Feminist movement a sin against the "Spirit of the German Family," a phrase which she used constantly, and she was wont to praise, for the purpose of contrast, the simple dignity of the Roman women, having the time of Republicanism in mind.

Whereas Mrs. Vallentin was satisfied, with modest self-sufficiency and without the use of scholarly standards, to devote herself to a thorough study of current events in the families at *The Albertina*.

But even she would have been highly indignant had one called by the simple term of "gossip" the quality with which she was endowed, that of an astounding memory which enabled her to rehash antiquated stories from the life of each and every one, one right after another, and her ability if necessary to assist facts by leaps into the realm of phantasy.

She could understand and forgive and was proud of it, which, however, did not prevent her listeners, whenever she regaled them with all the pertinent facts, from interpreting her much-vaunted forgiveness in the spirit of pitiless condemnation.

Even so, taken all in all, the name and destiny of an individual were not in such grave danger at the hands of these "Three Fates." Yes, one could even go so far as to say that in this or that case they would have worked blessings if their labors had not been interfered with by blindness or defiance.

Sieburth had been one of their favorite charges for a long time and their inability to give their so-called maternal blessing to a union with Cilly Wendland, the impending advent of which he himself had given them reason to suspect, caused them much mental anguish.

However, their recent reëstablishing of their previous relationship had revived old hopes and they were all but preparing to announce the news of the betrothal to a waiting world when that horrible notice appeared and threatened to destroy their unselfish endeavors.

For what man with such a stigma attached to his reputation could dare to approach a girl who had clean hands to offer and could demand the same.

"Undoubtedly a long time would have to elapse," Mrs. Vallentin thought, "before former relations could be resumed. Cilly would only lower herself if she were to accept him now while the whole world is wagging its tongue about him."

And Mrs. Ehmke added a bright remark about the sanctity of German family life which might tolerate mistakes but could never stand for their publication.

"I don't know," said the wife of the Privy Councilor while her gurgling laugh threatened to topple the tower of curls, "but that if I were Sieburth I should go straight to Cilly, make a clean breast of it and promise never to indulge in any more such foolishness."

"Foolishness you call it? I call it scandal!"

"Scandal is only that which you damn by giving it that name," replied Mrs. Kemmerich, "and we are here to prevent such a verdict if only in the interest of the University which is close to our hearts. If we shrug our shoulders and let it take its course, deeming it a matter of little consequence, the rest of the world will do the same, and in a few months it will have been forgotten, or will have become converted into a harmless anecdote which our dear friend"—and she took Mrs. Vallentin's hand—"will be able to tell the wives of the newcomers over the coffee table and over which all of us will have a hearty laugh."

"Please except me," Mrs. Ehmke interjected. "It will always be a source of sincere sorrow to me if the very foundation of the German family is repudiated."

"But this feeling of grief will not, I hope, prevent you from turning a seemingly friendly face to the future Professor and Mrs. Sieburth," parried the wife of the Privy Councilor.

"If there should be such a couple—most assuredly not," said Mrs. Ehmke.

"And if that shouldn't work out, surely then to him?"

Mrs. Ehmke reflected. "I don't know. Mine is a very straightforward nature. It would be very difficult for me, to say the least."

"I think I have it!" said Mrs. Kemmerich. "I'll ask Sieburth to come here and I'll talk to him really openly and maternally. I'll bring home to him in what an embarrassing position he has placed himself and that he had better make an end of the philandering habits of bachelorhood as quickly as possible . . . in case he should like me to, I would even prepare the way with Cilly . . . Cilly is no goose, on the contrary, she knows more about life than all of our young women put together . . . and if she loves him—and I am sure that she does—she won't hesitate a moment about throwing herself into the breach for him, particularly if that breach is upholstered with the down of a featherbed."

She laughed her gurgling laugh and Mrs. Ehmke made a face that indicated how little this rather broad joke merited her approval. But she did not contradict her friend further.

Mrs. Vallentin was willing to be convinced on the condition that in Cilly's interests a probationary period should elapse, which need not necessarily be of long duration, only of such length that the engaged couple could be spared having to run the gantlet of public opinion.

This was the only matter which had not been unanimously adjusted but otherwise everything seemed settled in Sieburth's favor and even if the expected engagement to Cilly should not materialize, ways and means would be found to divert his position once again into the proper channels.

And at that moment the maid announced an unexpected caller.

Mrs. Follenius was here and asked to be received.

"She comes just at the psychological moment," said the hostess. "She is a friend of Sieburth's of long standing and will be very useful to us in the working out of our plan. She has always made a great effort to unite those two. At her spring dinner—do you remember?—she put them next to each other with a distinct purpose in mind."

Marion Follenius entered dressed in black silk and glowing with the affability of her blond type.

She modestly accepted the congratulations for the blessings the Kaiser's visit had bestowed upon her and her husband. Of course, the honors conferred on a poor merchant's wife naturally could not compare with the aureole of glory that at all times surrounded the wives of famous scholars, she said, and the three women bowed their heads gratified.

Just as business men, who assemble for an important conference, speak first of the weather or the next club dinner or an especially good brand of cigars, never losing sight, however, of the matter which brought them together, so they discussed with assumed interest the favors the Kaiser had conferred in which others also had shared, but each one of them was ready to inject the subject of Sieburth into the conversation.

The Privy Councilor's wife was the first to find the courage to put an end to this dallying with subterfuges.

"We were just in the midst of formulating a plan of conduct towards our friend by which to nullify the consequences of that perfidious advertisement."

Marion Follenius sighed with relief.

"I, too, am engrossed with that problem, and would be happy to receive a guiding suggestion from women I respect as I do you, for I must admit I see no possibility of maintaining social relations as heretofore."

The three women were taken aback.

If a woman as worldly and as slow to pass judgment as the commerce councilor's wife was ready to turn against him, perhaps they had been too lax in their estimate of the indiscretion and every softhearted comment would only reflect on their spotlessness.

The Privy Councilor's wife allowed herself to be swayed least of the three.

"Well, well," she said in a quieting voice, "we don't want to spill the child along with its bath water. If we were to banish from our sight, on account of occasional indiscretions, every man who kisses our hands, there would be no one left for us to associate with except our own husbands, and we can't even be definitely sure of them until—well, until we are certain of another condition which we anticipate with very little pleasure."

She had unfortunately overstepped the mark with this argument. Mrs. Ehmke made a disapproving remark in which the words, "sacredness" and "lifting the veil" were audible and Mrs. Vallentin stiffened in silent protest.

Marion Follenius, on the other hand, smiled knowingly.

"Well, well," she also began, "when it comes to experience, I can't begin to measure up to you ladies but I really believe that in this instance, we should disregard the men, especially our own husbands, for all of them have been bachelors and at times behave as such even now, by which I, naturally, don't refer to ours. But they are all under one cover and if we listened to them we would let even this scandal go by uncensured."

"Do you see?" Mrs. Ehmke cried triumphantly. "Mrs. Follenius calls it scandal too."

And Mrs. Vallentin who only now was able to speak again added severely, "My husband agrees with me in all such cases!"

But Mrs. Kemmerich did not surrender so easily.

"Children," she said, "be sensible! What should such poor bachelors do?"

"They should marry," cried Mrs. Ehmke. "They

should acquaint themselves with the duties German family life imposes on a man of decent morals."

"They do that most of the time," said Mrs. Kemmerich, "but until that time arrives they have to live too, and how they go about it is their own business as long as they do not break like wolves into the enclosures we have set up about ourselves and the homes of our friends."

Marion Follenius smiled again—this time not only knowingly but mysteriously.

"Now the question is, what do you understand by the term 'friends'?" she said. "Do you stretch it to include all the people who come to your home?"

"Naturally," cried the Privy Councilor's wife, "and even beyond that. As far as the district extends within which we meet our own kind, God's peace must reign. Otherwise, we would not be sure of the women with whom we sit at the table in all friendliness and of the young girls whose hair we stroke in motherly fashion."

"In that case it really depends more on the women," said Marion Follenius, looking into her coffee cup and licking her lips with her tongue. Mrs. Vallentin sat bolt upright. She scented a new story in which there would be much to forgive.

"Won't you explain yourself more fully?" asked the hostess.

"I really can't do that," said Marion Follenius troubled, "for in so doing I would abuse the hospitality I extended a friend and would gladly offer again."

The three women sat deep in thought.

Who had visited the Follenius household?

But this house was so hospitable and lodged so many who came and went, that any conclusion would have been hasty and arbitrary.

"I could go a little further," said Marion Follenius, who saw that she could not stop here if she wanted to achieve certain results, "but I take for granted that should you guess a name I can count on your eternal silence."

"Naturally, naturally!" cried Mrs. Vallentin, whose eyes fairly spouted fireworks of curiosity from behind her glasses. Her ship of fortune laden with the choicest tidbits was nearing its harbor.

"You may have noticed," Marion Follenius continued, "that it has been my custom to encourage Professor Sieburth to be with us a great deal."

The women nodded affirmatively and with the greatest respect. Marion's reputation was above reproach and anything she did was considered the right thing.

"Well, unfortunately, I had to find out that he was unworthy, absolutely unworthy of my trust. He approached a lady in our set, in a manner—you know this lady even though I, naturally, can't mention her name—which brought her and me as well (since she was my guest) into the gravest danger. I don't mean to imply that it reached the ultimate stage but if it didn't she can only thank the intense watchfulness with which I guarded her. I went so far as—"

She hesitated a moment—what was to follow would irrevocably destroy the reputation of a woman whose name had been spotless; but the occasion demanded it and so she continued, "On an outing of several days' duration which we took together—"

Mrs. Vallentin sighed contentedly. She had heard of that strand excursion and now she knew who was meant.

"—went so far, as I've said, as to try to prevent a night-time rendezvous with my friend almost by force . . . but unfortunately I have evidence that in spite of everything I did, it took place just the same—evidence—well, I really can't go into further detail but you must believe me for I am a pretty shrewd observer . . . and therefore, I ask you, can one tolerate a person any longer of whom one has become convinced that he—I can't help using the nasty expression—that he is not house-broken?"

The three professors' wives were silent. Even the worldly, lively Mrs. Kemmerich could not find a word in reply.

Marion Follenius cast a bashful glance of triumph around the coffee table and when she noticed the depressing effect her tale had created, she went on more boldly. "Then on top of all this, came this dirty affair which has made the town breathless for the past week; one can forgive the one or the other, although it takes a good stomach, but both together characterize a person of such depravity and such—I don't know—I wouldn't want to touch the hand of such a man again. Would you?"

Again there was silence. Each lady looked at the others in an effort to get an intimation which would help her to reach the proper conclusion, for it involved their favorite charge who had enjoyed their good opinion to a greater extent than any other of the younger generation.

It was the Privy Councilor's wife again who rallied to a last defense.

"I admit, dear Mrs. Follenius," she said, "that things look pretty serious for him and I can well understand your bitterness, but shouldn't we make one last effort to save this soul for a better future? I would hate to have a damning verdict arrived at, particularly in our little circle. Even without this we have been given the outrageous name of 'The Three Fates.' . . . I would not care to have that name confirmed—or if it must be, at least let it be in a good sense. The only thing Sieburth lacks is a clever wife, and this wife, I believe, was already discovered sometime past. We were speaking of it before you came and wanted to suggest that you help us to that end."

Marion Follenius smiled even more kindly than was her habit. It seemed as if the reflection of all the goodness about her had made her more radiant.

"I know what you mean," she replied, "and this union was always a cherished idea of mine, but I really can't understand why just you three are so fanatically interested in Sieburth for he always made jokes about you. No one but he coined the name of 'The Three Fates.' But aside from that—good heavens, we all have our little frailties and vanities, but most women have their good and venerable points too, but nothing was safe from his sharp tongue, whether it involved the 'sanctity of the German rabbit's hutch' or 'tout comprendre c'est tout corrompre' or 'the not altogether natural growth of hair'— I beg your pardon, I myself wear false braids—in short, he sneered at everything without exception, without mercy. And in gratitude for all this you want to induce the good Cilly to throw her life in a— in a cesspool?"

That was the final blow.

This horrible word could be neither eradicated nor surpassed. And the gloomy, acquiescent expression on the faces of the three seemed to tell her who had spoken that it would grow ceaselessly, inevitably and even beyond the possibility of contradiction. For there are verdicts that exercise such a grotesque influence that, despite inner convictions, no one dares to set them aside.

The name "The Three Fates" was no exaggeration. What happened here was not far removed from a decree of Fate.

CHAPTER XVIII

CHANGES

And the consequences were not long in coming.

The expressions on the faces of his associates grew colder, their greetings were extended less frequently and were more casual; more and more often his acquaintances slid by without shaking hands with him, letting a curt nod suffice, and only when it was unavoidable did they indulge in an exchange of opinions on the most commonplace topics.

A sullen tension overcame Sieburth. Whenever he put his hand on the doorknob of the Faculty Room, he experienced a convulsive feeling that made him hesitate and start back.

So he was careful to come in as late as possible allowing only enough time to hang up his hat and coat so that he would be spared the necessity of bowing to people and looking around.

The only one who acted as he had used to was Pfeifferling. He never failed to give him his right hand, and sometimes his cry of "Good morning, Colleague Sieburth" resounded over five or six heads who, startled, would then accentuate the greeting they accorded him.

The only one who let it come to an actual break

17

was Hildebrand.   He passed Sieburth with a cool
nod and even avoided doing that whenever possible.
Such behavior was so foreign to the simple, straightforward character of the man that Sieburth could
only assume that there had been an exchange of
marital confidences which of necessity had been responsible for bringing about this silent hostility.

But he had not deserved that from Herma.   He
felt assured that he had behaved honestly and con-
siderately.   No other woman would have gone forth
from such a nocturnal escapade untouched; no one
would have persuaded any other man to give her a
voluntary release.

And instead of the promised gratitude, and re-
doubled trust, came this!

She was the only one whose attitude he resented,
perhaps because she was the only one of whom he
was fond.

No, no, not the only one!   True, he scarcely ever
thought of Marion Follenius—he did not have the
smallest doubt as to what he might expect from her
—but some one else crept oftener and oftener into
his thoughts, and she was Cilly Wendland.   And
many a time when he sat engrossed in his work and a
new idea flashed through his brain, the question of
"What would she think of that?" would occur to
him.

But she was far away and even the possibility of
hearing from her had been eliminated.

For like all the homes at which he formerly had been a welcome guest, the Wendland establishment was closed to him.

The winter social season had begun long ago but not a single invitation found its way to his table. The family boycott which his old circle of friends seemed to have imposed upon him was not lifted by so much as an occasional word or a furtively beckoning sign.

New charity committees were formed and old ones reorganized, popular lecture cycles announced their programs,—the whole ado of the social urge parading as welfare work advertised its undertakings on placards and in the newspapers, but no one invited him to become a member any more. And no one seemed to remember that he had always been a ready and willing participant in the pursuit of the so-called noble and beautiful.

Indeed, all these indications created a gnawing, boring feeling within Sieburth which spoiled many a minute during the day, but the effect was not lasting. They did not humble him nor infuriate him; he passed it by with a shrug of the shoulders until a new affront was offered that spoiled his humor for some few moments.

The lonely evenings were hard to endure for he devoted himself to actual work only after the voices of the ending daily activity were hushed and only night prowlers and drunkards filled the streets with occasional clamor.

As for him, he refrained for the time being from all excesses for he said to himself that in the new position into which Fate had flung him, he could not spare one iota of strength or time which he might need to face future difficulties.

As to the form they would take, he was not quite clear, but he had not a doubt but that they would arise.

It was both strange and comforting that his teaching activities had never prospered as they had just this term.

His special course on the history of modern philosophy was filled to the last seat. And his general course on modern pantheism was better attended than ever before, even by many outsiders.

At the same time he realized that he could no longer postpone his obligation of writing the promised obituary of the great Hegelian.

And as soon as he began its fulfillment, the voices of bitterness and angry thoughts were hushed. So forcibly did the form of the venerable patriarch appear before him and so benignly did the recollection of that unforgettable conference work upon him.

And uneradicated by the turmoil of his recent experience gleamed the words of warning the old man had given him to take through life.

What did he say in speaking of those who led an irregular life? "That works as long as it works, but one fine day quite unexpectedly some foolish little thing, totally unworthy of notice, occurs and on just that thing one breaks one's neck."

How true! It almost seemed as if a prophetic instinct had been at work, a premonition at least that had harked away back into the maze of his early experiences.

"If he were still on this earth," thought Sieburth, "I would go to him now and smilingly talk over with him what troubles and distresses me."

But since he was no longer here, he remembered him reverently, as if he had been his spiritual father. And yet he had always called him "the old idiot."

Every line he wrote was permeated with this reverence. It was not a glorification, surely not that, for again and again he stressed the fact that he was not in accord with the trend of thought expounded; and yet never had a departed had such a memorial erected by an opponent.

It was pure joy to work on it. The lamp seemed to shed an added luster. Whatever there was of conflict outside seemed to pass away into a mist of unreality. The hard and glaring world seemed dissolved into a soft glow.

It took six weeks to write and had turned into what was almost a little book, and it was to appear as such as soon as it had been published by the philosophical monthly which had already reserved space for it.

"Now my poet's dream is at an end," he said when he wrote the concluding sentence, and never was the phrase which Plato attributed to Socrates, that philosophy was poetry—and of the highest order— brought home so clearly to him before.

The Christmas vacation arrived and his teaching duties no longer took him in the morning on the now much hated way to the Faculty Room.

"How would it be," he asked himself, "if instead, I made an effort to meet her? No doubt she still goes to Mass, even if not quite as early as during the summer."

This meeting would bring him small comfort, of that he was sure, but if he spoke to her, she would undoubtedly have to grant him a word of explanation even if only so that the curiosity of passers-by should not be aroused.

And so one December morning between eight and nine he took his position on the Castle Pond Bridge just as he had done before.

On this day his effort went for nothing and the next day too, but during the third on which the wintry snowflakes fell in the half-light, she came along slowly and lost in thought, ambling almost like a sleepwalker.

He recognized her from the distance even though she was veiled and her head was muffled in her fur collar.

"What will come of this?" a voice cried within him.

Then she also recognized him, and her cry was as inaudible as was his, but he felt it vibrate through his entire body. He saw how she tottered and closed her eyes, and how she, seeking support, stretched her left hand toward the bridge balustrade.

And what did he do? He straightway turned around to the opposite side of the railing, leaned on the melting layer of snow and attentively observed the thawing ice below which barely held the weight of the sparrows.

Was it compassion? Was it cowardice? He was not able to define it. Only one thought was uppermost: "Let her alone. You have no further place in her life."

And when he ventured to glance in her direction, she had already disappeared in the crowd.

For the next few days, he was obsessed with a regret that was very like grief but which wore off, giving way to a salutary upheaval of his soul born of the tranquillity of the approaching Christmas.

It began on his solitary walks.

He could not sit at his writing desk forever, and social diversions, tea parties and the like, no longer formed a part of his life.

So he loitered about the country roads.

The surroundings of Königsberg are as devoid of

charm as are those of any city of the Prussian plains. Through each fortress gate a highway flanked by low trees issues forth into the open country with its level fields.

There were no suburbs in those days, only here and there the bright red structure of a steam mill, or a brewery or a repair shop belonging to the railroad towered into the gray sky.

There were sprouting crops and fallow fields as far as the eye could reach; in the ditches the last remnants of the summer's vegetation, muddy, shriveled and torn and half buried in patches of snow which lost themselves in dirty puddles at the bottom.

And triumphing over all of it, the only victor in this forlorn world which was three quarters dead and tormented by frost and rain, blew the late fall wind, simultaneously destroying and reviving, wounding and healing, chilling and imparting fire.

If you came under its sway you ducked, shuddering with discomfort, because of its despotic and bullying force but soon you relished its lash, and facing it in joyous defiance, you felt exhilarated and caressed.

In this mood Sieburth wandered for hours, in fact for whole afternoons. Rarely a wagon came towards him, even less frequently a wanderer like himself; crows, singly or in swarms, were the only living thing far and wide.

And out of all this he developed a new strength of

soul with which he combated and fought off the decree that Fate had imposed upon him.

No longer did he regard his fate as a misfortune
—as ostracism or as a stunting of his growth. On the
contrary, riches were his beyond measure—intuitions
of an undreamed-of profundity—Dionysian revels
replete with exultant abandon, reaching to heights
of delirious madness out of which icy wisdom was
born—flashes of wit that asked no grace, occasional
love without lasting ties.

To whom did he owe any consideration? Who
was leading him by the nose, or watching him?
What he did was right, because it suited him.

Let his colleagues tear open their mouths at their
meetings, at their reserved tables, or the professors'
wives at their coffee parties and their reading circles
—all of their self-important gossip rolled off his
back, unnoticed.

Bluebottle flies can become very annoying; this
did not even have that effect. Poisoned darts can hit
their mark, but what there was of poison in these
utterances fell to the earth without accomplishing
their purpose.

Of course, his climb to the top could be impeded
by it.

The chair of Kant which for some time past had
loomed as a certainty could be offered to some one
else.

But just let them try it!   Just let them have the face to pass him up!

Up to this time no notice that there were negotiations pending with any one from another locality had appeared in the papers, and it was already more than six months since the great Hegelian had died.

The latter had given him to understand that all of his influence would be used to further this end and surely nobody possessed the wretched courage to act contrary to his last wish.

So he could easily afford to await further developments, in the meantime showing them by his growing activity in the teaching field his utter worthiness, far in excess of that of any one whom they might out of sheer perversity call from the capital for the position.

One day—during the week before Christmas—he met Marion.

He walked into the bookshop of Graefe and Unzer to buy a book of some sort for Helena for Christmas when suddenly he found himself standing beside her. A high stack of Christmas books was piled up in front of her and two or three clerks were busy waiting on her.

Even before he saw her or heard a word from her lips, he knew it was she.   So strong was the influence of her personality upon him.

But a feeling which was almost a certainty told him that in her he had before him the least conciliatory of all his enemies and so he wisely refrained from calling attention to himself, when, quite by accident, she dropped the book through which she was glancing and it fell directly at his feet.

He stooped quickly and in handing it to her, their eyes met.

"She is a handsome rascal," he thought.

She turned pale, the corners of her mouth contracted haughtily, and taking the book gingerly as though with tongs, she said addressing him as if he were a clerk, "Oh, thank you so much."

Saucily and with the perfidious smile so familiar to and feared by all his acquaintances, he bowed slightly and said, "It has been an undeniable pleasure to have been of service to you, madam, once more in this life."

A deep red blush suffused her face, her right hand made a twitching move as if to reach for his and a softness that was almost a pleading came into her eyes.

Undoubtedly it had just dawned upon her how much she owed him in the past and how entirely dependent she was upon his gallantry. It would not have taken much for an understanding to be reached but without taking advantage of his victory he went on and busied himself at another counter.

When he left the store, he knew by the carriage which was standing in front of the door that she was still inside.

His triumph tasted bitter as gall to him.

Had he only encouraged the hand that started to-wards him the least little bit, had he only spoken a few conciliatory words after his crushing reference to the past, a conversation would have followed in the course of which her hostility would have succumbed and everything might still have righted itself.

She could have reinstated him under her Christmas tree and have presented him once again to her guests and not one of them would have dared to withhold a cordial greeting.

But he no longer desired it.

The defiant bitterness which had taken root in him engulfed even the smallest regret.

The path into which he had been forced had long since become the one of his choosing.

Only in this way could one rise above one's fate.

CHAPTER XIX

A LONELY CHRISTMAS

CHRISTMAS EVE had arrived.

Previously he had always spent it at the Follenius home and had found the colorful trappings that surrounded the lavish gift tables irksome.

For the first time he was alone and free and could spend these hours of beloved German festivity as it pleased him to spend them.

When twilight came he gathered together the gifts he had bought for his landlady and her daughter and carried them over to them.

Out of the semi-darkness shone a gleaming, heavily laden pine tree which stood on the sofa table and which seemed to fill the entire room with the magnificence of its presence.

"Who is there?" he heard Helena's voice say as she busied herself somewhere behind the tree.

And when he said his name there was a sudden rustling and clattering and she stepped from under the boughs and stammered all kinds of things about not being ready and about Mamma who would be here right away.

With that she slipped out of the side door and, astonished, Sieburth thought how little he knew of the world that lay just beside him and which by rights was really his own.

After a very few minutes Frau Schimmelpfennig came in, taper in hand, and behind her, in her charge, Helena.

She was already in holiday attire. A brown silk dress with green pleated lace at neck and sleeves spanned the high-laced bosom, and a gold buckle nestled in the black braids which softly framed the haggard, rather severe features.

Sieburth expressed holiday sentiments and jokingly laid the gifts before her.

But his joke found no answering chord. He looked into a dismayed face, into eyes which told of departing elation and destroyed hopes, and at the same time a caressing, girlish hand had laid itself consolingly on her shoulder.

She stammered haltingly. "I had thought, Professor—you go out so little these days, isn't that so? —and therefore would perhaps spend Christmas eve with us, could you?"

"I would have had to know that sooner, dear Frau Schimmelpfennig," he lied; "now unfortunately, I've already accepted another invitation."

"Oh, in that case—" And her voice froze. She stood as if turned to stone and the girlish hand on her shoulder patted her unceasingly.

Then he unpacked the gifts for them, the pretty set of skunk furs for her and for Helena, Weber's

"History of the World," the weight of its heavy volumes having nearly crushed his arm. In addition there were all kinds of knickknacks with which to decorate the festive table which would be cherished later on as keepsakes.

But up to this time there was not one bit of happiness in their faces, and their smiles only accompanied toneless, courteous bows of acknowledgment.

With the crushing feeling of having spoiled the holiday spirit of well-meaning people, he left the room. But how absurd, having escaped the fetters of one family bliss, to allow himself to be shackled by another!

His desires inclined to darker channels.

He wished to join the lonesome and cast-out—he who himself was lonesome now and shunned . . .

As he stepped outdoors he was met by a light flurry of snow. The snowflakes flitted past the lamplights like night moths and tickled his burning lips as they touched them.

The streets were dark and empty. Only a few shops had their shutters open and from only a very few taverns were lights reflected and did voices resound.

It was the hour when heretofore they had gathered at the Follenius home for the distributing of gifts.

A feeling of painful and malignant joy drove him to betake himself thither so that he might observe in secret who now as before were coming within its radius.

The front door was wide open. Coaches drove up and unloaded their passengers. Pedestrians— such as he once had been—passed in modestly. He recognized this one and that one. "Enjoy yourselves," he mumbled after them, shrugging his shoulders. But one, the one whom without confessing it to himself he had expected to see among the guests—he did not see.

For that reason he left and went to her house.

Black shutters stared down at him. Nowhere behind them a fleeting glimmer of light. And the reflected lamplight glistened mockingly in rounded panes.

"Maybe they have gone on a journey. Perhaps they had already entered the Follenius door before I arrived," he thought. Be that as it may—they were not at home, and why should they be? They were childless. In Herma's heart that wish of all wishes remained unfulfilled.

He pulled himself together by sheer force. She, too, together with everything else he had once called his own, must sink into oblivion.

Then he continued his wandering about the streets.

Now and again some one going by laden with bundles shouted "Merry Christmas" to him, and each time he answered as jauntily as if this wish had already been fulfilled.

From the archway of a door a soft "pst, pst" was hissed at him.

He stopped. He knew that sound well, but that it could be heard even on Christmas eve was hardly to be believed.

In the dark entrances to the yards where people rarely come and go, lurked these dregs, the most degraded of their sex and in the passageway between the wall and gateway, where no one looked, they plied their filthy trade.

Sieburth would have liked to stop and to give this shadowy form whose outline could scarcely be recognized, a word as a token of charity—and a jingling token too—as a Christmas present, but there was no reply to his greeting. She was too shy or too conscious of guilt to part her lips. She only cowered further into her corner expecting him to follow her.

"Who are you?" he asked.

"Pst" was the answer.

"Where do you live?"

"Pst," she replied again.

"If you tell me something about yourself I'll give you a thaler."

The unheard-of enticement did not fail of its magic. A torrent of words of justification were hissed and spit at him. She was a respectable person and nobody could speak ill of her and she did washing for families.

"Mother" flashed through his brain.

But her husband was an old hog and drank up everything, not coming home sometimes for eight days, and instead of bringing her wages, he even asked her for money, and she had three children at home. They had to be supported and went to school too, and the neighbors called her "little madam"— that's how much they thought of her. She even had a sofa, and to-day a Christmas tree stood on the table in front of it, just as it did at the homes of the best people. And the children expected her to bring them presents, but for that she would have to earn the money first. Yes, if he really was such a fine gentleman and wanted to give her the promised thaler . . .

"What good will a thaler do you?" he said, refraining from a more familiar address in deference to her great respectability. "You can't buy anything with it to-day any more."

She laughed cunningly. She had a neighbor who was one of the pious ones who went from house to house where gifts were being dispensed and cried or sang, depending upon which pleased the listeners most. She had been given stacks of things for her children and did not even have any. She need only go to her and she would get all of it for a thaler and perhaps even something for her husband if the old hog were to come home to-day, which was uncertain.

He reached into his pocket and handed her the coin.

A hard hand, rough as a grater, reached eagerly for it, but when she felt it she was afraid to take hold of it.

"But, young man!" he heard a puzzled voice say.

"Just you take it!" he said. "I'm one of the pious kind too, but you don't have to cry or sing for it."

Then the searching hand grabbed the thaler, the shadowy form drew away without so much as a "Thank you" and in the next moment had disappeared into the darkness of the court.

Laughing, he went on his way. A solicitous home body—even this woman was nothing else. Even in the depths of the most gruesome vice, this sentimentality of family feeling from which he wished to escape, existed.

By the way of streets, the names of which he did not notice, he came to a dive, through the heavily curtained windows of which a strangely confused noise issued, which indicated that there was activity inside even to-day.

"Surely the Christmas hubbub will not have penetrated this far," he thought, stepping into the dirty corridor in which the smell of kerosene cans and tar receptacles mingled with many other equally disagreeable odors.

A low, bare room lighted by a hanging lamp came

into view while a strident bell above the door announced his arrival.

But no one came. And that was small wonder for the noise which came through the glass door of the back room topped it considerably.

Men, women, children's voices, tin trumpets, mouth organs, quacking frogs, fire rattles, snapper bellows, and a great many other things fused into a shrill combination.

He sat down in one of the wooden seats and listened patiently.

"If I wait long enough some one will come," he thought.

But he was mistaken.

Then he adopted a drastic measure. He went back to the entrance door and opened and closed it a number of times so that the hoarse clang of the bell had to be heard in spite of everything.

At last the glass door opened and an overheated, tousled girl's head looked into the room.

What did he want?

He wanted a glass of grog—good and strong and piping hot.

The girl's head disappeared.

Things quieted down behind the glass door. Obviously, they were in consultation. Then it opened again and a paunch-bellied, fat-cheeked man in a brown sweater which hung to his thighs, waddled in with the saccharine smile of an innkeeper on his face.

"Good evening, and a Merry Christmas"—naturally he could have his glass of grog, but wouldn't he prefer to share in the modest family party to which he and his wife gave themselves the honor of inviting their regular patrons? Thoroughly home-like and without conventions—around the lovely Christmas tree—with the sweet children. A little gift had already been provided and if he cared to show some little material appreciation, no one would take offense. But it was not compulsory, for it was Holy Night.

Sieburth was amused by this blending of business and sentiment and, eager for new experiences, he followed the hospitable man into a room filled with people where the Christmas celebration was in progress in a form entirely foreign to him.

Around the tree was a wreathlike circle of flushed blinking faces which stared at him, half in distrust, half in merriment.

"Merry Christmas," shouted a chorus of many voices from which the children's piping tones were not missing.

And "Merry Christmas" he answered, taking a dozen of the hands near by in enthusiastic friendliness.

A dark, puffy woman with the dark tender eyes of an erstwhile barmaid came up to him and made herself known as the mistress of the house. Two little girls hung on to her, the one, perhaps fourteen, brunette, with dark glowing eyes like her own, the other, a lanky sallow blonde gawk, possibly a year younger, but already showing more lust than curiosity in her all-knowing expression.

His little surprise would soon be ready for him. In the meantime would he make himself comfortable, and in almost the same instant the overheated and unkempt girl, who had received him before and who seemed to be acting as waitress, brought him a child's trumpet into which he blew as requested.

During which he observed the world into which he had been drawn.

Small-town citizens good and harmless, carrying the mark of their subordinate positions in their bloated faces distorted by gayety—clerks, doubtless, or assistants to officials, whose relatives lived elsewhere and who were enjoying their freedom in tantalizing lust for the opposite sex—interspersed among them, two Falstaffian figures who were trying to find recompense for the drudgery of the day in continued beer-drinking, all of them prepared to go the limit, but kept simple and foolish by the domestic surroundings.

Then he allowed his gaze to shift to the table of gifts. There, in rows, in picture and in toy form were the suggestive things that are charitably designated as "bachelors' jokes" which owed their origin to the lowest desires and sexual requirements.

Embarrassed, he looked around for the half-grown girls who had to see all this obscenity.

To cap this all there were two little boys present, ten or eleven years old, to judge by appearances—but every one played so innocently and in such a matter-of-fact manner with the mirth-provoking articles that all the harm seemed to be taken out of them.

His present was brought to him in the meantime. Whether it was evident that his taste was several notches above the others or whether there were none of the spicy things left, it differed with certain pleasantness from the lascivious articles that littered the table of the regular guests. It was a pasteboard coin pig which willingly relinquished its coin as soon as you lifted its left hind leg which the hostess herself proudly showed him, while the elder daughter completed the instructions by taking the coins which appeared in the back and replacing them inside through the snout.

"And now, for a change, ladies and gentlemen, let us sing a Christmas song," commanded the voice of the host.

At the same time the rattling and squeaking of a piano so badly out of tune that one might have imagined that its strings had been doused like a rusty throat, with alcoholic stimulants, sounded from one corner of the room.

And see! The noise subsided, people's features

melted into a soulful calm and any one who could find a seat sat peaceably in it. The daughters of the house, as well as the waitress, found room on the laps of the guests but not in sensual antics; instead, guarded and full of a sudden dignity they sat rigid as though in church.

"Begin again," called a voice.

And as the pianist acceded to the wish, the voices chimed in with full force: "Holy Night, Silent Night."

And so on.

Sieburth's glance flitted from one face to another and in each one he discovered the same emotion. Here was childhood, here was innocence, here was the blessedness of paradise—true enough the larynx contracted, the mouth opened like a wide torn abyss and what streamed out was for the most part a horrible false note, but the eyes—one had to look into those eyes! They told long stories of maternal admonitions, and pride in deportment and heart-consuming longing—of grown brothers and sisters and little ones, and of jubilant chimes.

"I never experienced that at Follenius'," he thought.

But, yes! Only his soul had been impervious to it.

"Blessed loneliness," he thought further.

Then the song came to an end and the magic vanished.

The silence lasted only a little while. Then the noise, isolated at first, and timid, then in even bolder self-consciousness started again. The young girls were tickled and they ran off screaming. The waitress went from lap to lap and fought laughingly with one who tried to retain her, and the one who had just played the Christmas song worked the piano keys with his seat.

Sieburth came to the conclusion that there was nothing else to be learned here and looked up the hostess in order to tender the expected thanks in secret.

A quick look into the palm of her hand and she recognized that the coin was a gold one.

Then good wishes and prolific bowing followed, and even the two little girls were called to ask him to come soon again and the brown-sweatered host who escorted him to the door declared with emphasis and conviction that in the future he should consider himself one of the family.

A little confused and somewhat benumbed, he once again began his wandering through the dark streets.

A tower clock struck eleven.

He had used up more of the Christmas eve than he had wanted to spend in this insipid company. But then he scolded himself for his lack of gratitude.

He felt that he would probably never forget the impressions of the last hour.

Perhaps it was only a specter. But in his life what was not a specter?

Further, further! More adventure, much more before this Christmas eve ended that night in which the human heart opens its doors—doors to temple halls or to privies.

Be that as it may, one stepped inside and often found them both together.

He noticed a girlish form laden with packages walking ahead of him. In the motion with which she forged ahead, there seemed to be an uncertainty, a waiting quality as if she, like himself, was not yet finished with the day's adventures.

He caught up with her, and as he addressed her, he noted two large, suspicious eyes which looked squintingly up at him.

She was used to being alone and asked him to leave her.

Hers was a dull hard voice that sounded almost masculine.

No one must celebrate Christmas eve alone, he replied, and one must have a care for any one so unfortunately situated—that was only one's duty to humanity.

"You see that I have celebrated," she replied, pointing to the packages.

"If the celebration is already behind you," he said, "it could hardly have been to your satisfaction, otherwise you wouldn't already be on your way home."

The hard, suspicious eyes which were set in a thin, unyouthful face, looked up at him in surprise.

"You are right in your surmise," she said. "I hate all such things because they are compulsory and are usually insincere and a tissue of lies."

A short-lived joy, bitter as gall, arose in him.

"Then we two belong together," he answered, "for I agree with you. But in that case why didn't you remain alone as I did?"

"Because I have a family and must keep up the association; particularly on occasions such as to-day, or else——" And she made a contemptuous sound which established her stubborn independence beyond a doubt.

He decided to get to the root of the peculiarities of this harsh creature and began to question her carefully.

It did not take many questions to find out what he wanted to know. Hard parents, hard children, restrictions, stubbornness, love affair, banishment, a reconciliation which was not genuine, and as the final result, the joy of youth gambled away.

"Now I do only what is absolutely necessary to preserve appearances that we remain a family, but I live alone and earn my own living and no one has anything to say and if I take a hundred lovers it is

my own affair. But none of them are good enough
for me after the one who has since married some one
else. And when I pass his house, I can stroke his
children's heads, but that, when you come right down
to it, is a shabby pleasure."

The icy chill of a lost life shuddered through him.

"And what nice gifts did you receive?" he asked,
pointing to the packages, trying to evoke a softer
sentiment thereby; but she only laughed a short
shrill laugh.

"A warm petticoat," she said, "as warm as my
feelings, and a silver lace scarf which will make me
ten years younger, so it was promised. And a colored plate of sweets, many sweets. If you like, I'll
divide with you. You will surely spoil your stomach
on them."

He thanked her and said that he would gladly do
even that but that he would have to know what he
might give her in return.

She gave a sharp look that penetrated searchingly
into his face.

"You are a clever and a shrewd man, otherwise
you wouldn't have understood how to pump me.
Send me a book that you like on the chance that I,
too, may spoil my stomach."

"But in order to do that I would have to know
where you live."

"That is very simple," she replied. "We are just
passing the house and if you like you can come up

with me. There's no one I need to consider and we can't very well do the dividing here in the street."

He thought, "So I'm to have a little happiness after all," and followed her up two dark, steep steps through a smoky kitchen where a stove still glowed with a coal fire, and into a room which lay before him in mellow gloaming and received its failing light from two windows hung with yellow draperies and a shaded night lamp. It smelled of lavender and of medicine and a little like Christmas too.

And after she lit the lamp he saw on the table a tree about two feet high, black and untrimmed just as it came from the forest, and next to it a plate of toasted zwieback.

This was a truly forlorn aspect and he was not surprised that she had brought a stranger along in order to escape from this impression.

He allowed his gaze to travel farther along, and next to a red-covered bed he noticed bookshelves stretching along for a considerable distance and above them the heads of Schiller and Goethe.

"I am a public-school teacher," she said, noticing his questioning look and unbuttoning her coat.

"And in the face of that you need exercise no consideration?" he asked astonished. "A visit such as mine could suffice to break your neck."

"Nobody is watching to-day," she said calmly, "and at other times, I don't do it. That conversation about a hundred lovers was nonsense, of course.

What doesn't one say in order to convince oneself of one's complete independence?"

She had put the lamp next to the black tree so that its boughs cast curling shadows over her.

A long gold chain framed the flat chest in two gleaming semicircles, the haggard neck protruded from a white mannish collar and from the narrow pointed face those suspicious eyes were fixed upon him like gripping braces.

"She is not made for love," he thought.

Then his eyes lit on her quantity of chestnut-brown hair combed straight back into a massive knot which hung deep into the nape of her neck.

"Isn't that a burden?" he asked, and let his hand glide over its smooth surface.

"What isn't a burden?" she asked, shrugging her shoulders. "But don't you want to sit down a moment?" and she pointed to a chaise-longue which took the place of a sofa; behind it was a drapery of three or four festoons made of pale brown rep which was there instead of the usual wall cushions.

He did as requested and as she pulled a cane chair forward for herself, he said, "Come next to me, so that you will be comfortable too."

"You are right," she replied. "On this evening one does well to creep close together." And she sat so close to him that their shoulders touched.

He did not exactly know just what to do about

her, and out of an impulse of sympathy, he took her hands in his, laid them on his knee and caressed them gently. Sighing wearily she let her head droop to the drapery and lay so, motionless for a while with closed eyes.

"Loneliness," he thought, and stroked her hand incessantly.

And then when, absent-mindedly caressing her, he lifted his arm toward her neck, she sprang up suddenly, her eyes glittered with hostility and in a piercing voice she cried, "What do you want of me? What are you doing here? Do you think perhaps that you can seduce me? Do you think I'll throw myself away? Get out right away or I'll call for help!"

He knew the chaos of a woman's soul too well to marvel at this display of emotion. Silently he rose and reached for his hat. He had not even removed his overcoat.

She stood in a cowering defensive position leaning against the table and staring at him.

"Unless you show me the way downstairs, you'll hardly get rid of me," he said.

At which she gave a start and ran around the room looking for the key.

"You laid it on the stove," he said, remembering a clinking sound as he had crossed the kitchen.

She cast a wild, pained look at him and she went past him out of the door with dragging steps.

He saw how she fumbled with the matches as she tried to light a candle.

"If I may be permitted to advise you," he said, "you'd better not light up. Homecomers would recognize you immediately on the stairs."

She threw the matches away from her, opened the hall door and stamped on ahead of him in the dark.

In front of the house door he lifted his ·hat and said, "I hope that you will never have to spend another Christmas eve like this," and when, after taking three steps, he turned around, he noticed by the lamplight how she stood motionless and with burning eyes in the black doorway looking after him as if to call him back.

He roamed the streets for perhaps another hour, but outside of several groups of homecomers in high spirits who called "Merry Christmas" to him, nothing else happened.

Crowds were gathering around the Sackheim, presumably so as not to miss the midnight Mass, and he thought, "If you stand close to the door, you may see her."

But he threw the thought from him almost immediately; however, it was none the less like the thrust of a knife through his breast.

Now the time had come to go home. To spend the night in the street was also no joy, but a fear of the dark, lonely room as he had never known it before, still made him hesitate.

"I, too, like that poor scarecrow, would like to have some one to take home with me," he said to himself.

And yet at the same time, he breathed more freely in the joy-dealing thought that to-day no stranger was clinging to him.

Before he unlocked the driveway gate—for he wanted as he always did, in order not to disturb the mother and daughter, to use the back door—he had to take himself well in hand, so little desire did he have to be alone in his four walls.

And as he stood in the corridor which led directly to his bedroom, it seemed to him that he saw the reflection of a light through the keyhole and as he listened he distinctly heard whispering and rustling inside.

Stepping inside, he found the bedroom dark, but through the half-open door which led into the library towered the lighted structure of an illuminated Christmas tree, and going further, he found Helena standing on a chair stretching herself to quickly light the last of the candles. Her mother leaned close to her, supporting the chair with the one hand and the tree with the other so that neither should fall.

When they discovered him there was a concerted scream. Helena sprang down hastily and ran out of the door and her mother seemed inclined to follow her, but he was already out in the hall and pulled her back.

"First we're going to have an explanation," he cried, "as to how you came upon the idea of a giving of Christmas gifts in the middle of the night. That certainly has never been the case before."

The mother was silent and bit her teeth together, but Helena who was usually so shy did not seem averse to talking and after some hesitation and stammering the truth came to the surface. He had said he was going to a party but had kept on his everyday clothes and from that they had gathered that he would probably be alone. And so that Holy Night should not end too altogether sadly for him, they had put the tree in his room and had looked diligently out of the window in order not to miss his homecoming. By rights he should not have found them there, but the time between first seeing him and the unlocking of the door, had been miscalculated, so he must excuse the fact of their still being there.

Something like gratitude arose in him. He allowed them to lead him to his desk which was cleared in honor of the festivity and spread with a white damask cloth and listened quietly while Helena, who in her fervor became more confidential, made clear to him what awaited him in the way of gifts.

She had knitted a pair of wristlets for the morning hours when the stove was not yet warm, and the sofa cushion intended for his birthday had finally been finished. Her mother, however—but she must tell that herself.

And she turned toward her who stood behind and pulled her to her side.

But still the mother did not speak and the tears coursed down her cheeks.

Laughing, he cheered her up and stroked her arms in an effort to console her.

She choked down her emotion and began to apologize for her gift which lay on the tablecloth in the form of a white linen package.

He could just as well have ordered the shirts in the store and she had often reminded him that his would hardly stand further laundering but as his head was so full of other things, he had always postponed it, and for that reason—

He took her hands in his own and thought—when before Christmas we men go into a shop and jumble together anything that happens to be on display, what do we really know of giving?

And as mother and daughter modestly wanted to withdraw, he asked them to stay awhile so that the holiday they had prepared for him might be complete.

Mrs. Schimmelpfennig obediently sat down. Helena remained standing behind her chair and looked at him, questioningly, waiting for developments.

"These two," he thought, "now constitute my home."

But he did not know of anything to talk to them about.

Then his glance passed from the tired, cowering form of the mother who, with half-dried tears, stared dully ahead of her, to the daughter. And suddenly it seemed to him that his eyes were opened. Instead of the undeveloped half-child that he had seen beside him, as insignificant and uninteresting, for so long, he saw standing before him a young woman blossoming into smiling splendor. Pale blond curls framed the untroubled, beaming forehead behind which waves of calm, joyous and harmless thoughts played their springtime pranks . . . in her eyes, large, blue and zealous, lurked the triumph of furtive happiness in having made him happy. The mouth with its sweetly arched lips was half open as if it wanted to say confidential things but did not dare. The cheeks which were still untouched by adverse fate and secret guilt were still unlined and sank in soft curves toward the almost plump neck which lost itself in a rosy furrow in the high collar.

He looked and looked—and was amazed.

"But that is truly a gift of the gods," he thought. "Where have I had my eyes until now?"

Through her his life could be given a new joy-giving impetus which would more than compensate him for what he had lost, and he resolved to become her teacher and fashioner in his leisure hours.

He expanded with the knowledge of this unhoped-for possession which brought light and peace and promised to grant him the gift of pure and noble sentiment.

"On her account I will even endure her mother's sad eyes, as part of the bargain," he thought.

But as he directed his glance to the motionless figure sitting there, he was almost frightened for the eyes were far from sad—burning, eager, suspicious and searching, they ate into him as if to overpower him and call him to account.

Something distorting and tarnishing that destroyed the benignity of this hour lay in those eyes.

"What do you want of me?" asked his answering look.

But he could have given himself the answer without any trouble. She who knew his leanings had misinterpreted his thoughtless, ungoverned staring and amazement, had read lust into it and had perhaps even felt neglected.

And then she had already risen.

"Go to your room, my child," she said, "the Professor doesn't need us any longer."

That sounded angry, reproachful. It actually sounded like jealousy.

Helena stepped towards him, embarrassed, and

waited for him to give her his hand. He felt hers for a moment warm and twitching between his fingers, then she was gone.

"I suppose you will put out the lights yourself," said the mother.

And he said he would.

Then there followed a forced thank you, clasp of two hands that were quickly withdrawn, and he was alone.

Reclining in his easy-chair, he let the candles burn down smoking and sputtering and pored over the thought of how much happiness and how much havoc a single glance can provoke and he felt that he was lonelier than if he had had no Christmas celebration.

CHAPTER XX

THE MAD PROFESSOR

BEFORE one realizes it the hands of the year's clock have glided around unheard and unnoticed. The eternally new game of budding and awakening, the wanton tossing of May blossoms, the humid summer magic, the melancholy tomfoolery of the autumn glow—all that passes as though it had not been; and again, as the things of most importance, the apparently enduring things which would for all time consign to darkness and stupor the heart and the brain—the frosty fogs now brew, the snowflakes fall and the stars shine mercilessly in the winter night. Merely another year, and yet more than enough to readjust a man's viewpoint; to change a light-hearted into a thick-blooded individual; to convert a dreamer into a matter-of-fact person; to turn the man of restraint into a libertine.

A further change seemed to be taking place in Sieburth; but one who had already pried around in the secret chambers of his being would have acknowledged that there were no actually new developments, that, as seed and tendency, everything had already been there which now had merely found room and a fertile soil in which to grow and become visible.

But who, indeed, saw him in his entirety? It remained his principle to separate his life into two parts, the apparent and the hidden, and to lead both; and even though he seldom considered it necessary to don wig and chin beard on his night excursions but, on the contrary, frequented dives without hiding his identity, and though he boldly sat at tavern tables till morning with any of his pupils he chanced to meet, it was only most infrequently that a rumor of it reached his spying colleagues. Besides, it happened that among them were a number who were drinkers themselves and out of consideration for them his shortcomings had to be overlooked.

Those nightly escapades, two or three times a week, became an actual necessity to him, particularly since quite by accident several companions were thrown in his way with whom it was, indeed, socially a blunder to associate, but who behaved in a sufficiently obstreperous manner to create diversion for him.

He had come across them in a dive in the old section of the town where he had stopped one night after a mad chase.

He sat quietly at a neighboring table and listened while, enveloped in the vapors of the beer and the fumes of their tobacco, they—all three of them—

discoursed on the sublimest questions of humanity with cries and emphatic banging of fists upon the table and much spitting.

Their arguments were of droll bluntness and savored not infrequently of the pig-pen, but like Whitsunday flames, there floated above them the holy spirit of Dissipation, who raised those forgiven for his sake from the level of the commonplace to heights where the noxious alcohol was at once deliverer, illuminator and redeemer.

At an opportune moment he arose and with seemly respect asked permission to take part in the discussion which he had followed for some time.

They looked up at him in surly astonishment.

"We will soon see with whom we are dealing," said the oldest of them, a hoary giant with thick stringy hair and side-whiskers and bespectacled eyes and knobby, inquisitive nose. "Unless you are a builder of the universe, you had better make yourself scarce."

"Unfortunately, as to its construction, some one has gone before me, but if, in the demolishing, I can be of service, it seems to me I have come to the right place."

Laughingly, they moved closer together and the waitress brought his grog glass after him.

"Must I introduce myself?" he asked.

"As far as we are concerned, you may remain anonymous," his neighbor on the right retorted.

A bloated beer tanker on the edge of the thirties, with frayed linen, the fat beardless face disfigured by scars: "Me, the girls call 'Rotschimmel,' 'Schimmel' in this case meaning 'mold,' and my whole body is moldy, and soon will be consumed by drink and syphilis; you see, there is not much to be proud of."

And the third of the combination, a thin man of fifty, with bearded, hook-nosed profile and unsteady glittering eyes, speaking through his teeth, laughingly added, "There must be a Fair in hell. He who can take part in it is accepted."

And with that he was admitted into their circle.

It was not long before he knew the names and characters of his new companions.

That aging powerful person who with massive upper body and untrimmed head commanded the opposite side of the table, had an established reputation. Until a short time ago, he had been a teacher at a school of high repute, idolized by his pupils and upheld with difficulty by his colleagues until drink finally led to his being retired. Chmelnitzky was his name and the stories connected with him could be counted by the dozen.

The second (Totenhöfer was his actual name), after having twice vainly sought admission to the bar, decided to become a perennial student, and an inherited farm furnished him the means. He had been thrown out of his fraternity, and so he pursued its members with a bloody hatred. The pale red hair, which grew low on his forehead, had gotten him his nickname. When his small sharp button eyes sparkled, when his hacked-up lips curved merrily, it was a pleasure to listen to him, provided the smutty story which had thus announced its arrival proved witty.

The fate of the third was the most variegated. He was a theologian, Möwes by name, and had enjoyed a fine ministerial position, on the Eastern borderland, from which by reason of annoying predicaments, in which light-minded Lithuanian womenfolk played a considerable part, he had been very quietly compelled to take his departure. Now he had become an insurance agent, conducting business deals in city and province, and placed little value on being reminded of his former holy state.

From now on Sieburth spent many an evening and late night with these three and had no reason to complain that his time was wasted. They soon overcame the timidity with which they were at first affected when they found with whom they were associated, and with East-Prussian candor they scolded him in a truly intimate manner. They even applied to him the familiar "du" appellation, which, in spite of the difference in age between them, had been adopted; and he gladly submitted to it.

Although in regard to philosophic thought they were laymen, each in his own way tried to give the impression of understanding. Sieburth had in them an audience in whose presence he needed to put no restraint upon himself and the rebellion which seethed in him, born of the disorder of his loneliness which sought vainly some amelioration and relief; he found in these wrecks, whom, in spite of intellectual distance, he nevertheless considered to be related to him and in some shadowy way like himself, an outlet and release.

In his lectures he had to adhere to the usual methods and prudently swallow what might interfere with his beaten path; he scarcely ever could allow himself the least digression as a heart-balm, while here, on the other hand, what was most heretical was just the thing, here what was most paradoxical was received with the greatest approbation and often when he was successful with a word, the formation of which he had always refrained from, he asked himself, "Is it really I who am speaking or some one who takes pleasure in presenting a distortion of himself."

But once said, it stood, and what, in the moment of its conception, seemed to him a jest or a monstrosity, maintained its right to existence.

Besides, in the end there was always some truth behind it; something which thought out to the end would do away with the traditional, and show a brazen front to the professional "State and Mock-Philosophy."

This phrase of Schopenhauer's he was fond of

There were nights which the silver light of new ideas brightened with joy and others during which dark flame of madness singed him and the others. But behind both, as the one symbol, stood the great Nescience which rules the world and humanity.

Whenever the former minister tried to collect the residue of his early stream of religious fervor in the hollow of his hands and tried to present it to the others as a so-called "Meaning of Existence," he only evoked mirth and ridicule, as soon as Sieburth with a playful turn spilled it for him. But always and again there were heated debates about "World Purpose" and the "cosmic order," and from these the universal senselessness in which Creation drifts about deliriously, emerged a triumphant victor. All the heroes of the spirit were called on as witnesses, and Plato and Aristotle, those great corrupters of human thought, sank down along with Leibniz and Kant; while the line of those who formerly were stamped as false teachers, having their beginning with Democritus and Protagoras and shining to advantage through the modern philosophy of science, overrode the former gloriously. The subject of "to be or not to be" was also eagerly touched upon.

On a late evening at the end of the winter, Sieburth, who owing to difficult work had avoided the round table for a number of weeks, made his appearance again.

The three sat wrapped in clouds of smoke as

always, and as usual overheated from alcohol and gas fumes. He was welcomed with a "hallo."

Why had he stayed away so long; had he been busy catching fleas for his sweetheart, or was he constantly battling with mental specters?

Sieburth laughed, well pleased. Here again were the dear sounds, which brought a lightening and an exhilaration. Since he excused himself because of his writing, they were determined to know with what subject he was employed at the moment.

He, who was averse to discussing what was in the making, replied with an evasive joke, "I am harassing my brain to prove that *'nothing'* is the only thing that really exists."

They accepted this as a fact and demanded to know more. So he found himself, partially against his will, involved in an analysis, which became more serious than he had intended.

"You are only inquisitive," he said, "because you, like every life-craving creature, are in abject fear of the naked, chilly *'Nothingness.'* And yet this Nothingness is the world principle, and existence is only its degeneration."

That, of course, they regarded as contradictory and they wanted to have the statement explained and verified.

"If you understood, you would not talk of contradiction. The great Hegel established the fact that existence and *'Nothingness'* are identical. A thousand five hundred years ago Augustine said the same. In these thin, ethereal regions, besides, there is no such thing as paradox, but if you want to know about something much more astounding, just pay attention."

He pulled a piece of paper out of his wallet, which he had there for chance use at a lecture, and continued, "A pupil of the great master, whose name is Werder and who was Professor at the University of Berlin, or still is, delivered himself as follows: 'The *nothing* is more than the existing, namely the knowledge about one's "existing"—about its fullness, about its self-fulfillment, about its untrammeled action, about its formation by the self.' Now I hope you are clear on this point, what a colossal thing this *nothing* is."

Following this, there was unbounded laughter which only ceased when Sieburth started to develop his theory about that which he chose to call "the nuisance of being."

"Namely, if there is such a thing as 'being,'" he lectured, "it is in the first instance nothing but 'consciousness.' Everything else revealed itself long ago to the sharp thinker as an illusion and humbug. But before this 'consciousness' every one formerly took a reverential attitude and accepted it as a given quantity. . . . *Cogito ergo sum;* isn't that so? But now it is firmly established psychologically and biologically that consciousness is nothing but a surface phenomenon, an accidental reflection of the great Unknown which is its foundation. Unconsciousness is non-existent, however, as we noted and presupposed, and so consciousness is surely non-existent, and for the 'being,' there, therefore, remains no place whether in identity or non-identity. The old sophist Gorgias is consequently right when he says, 'Nothing exists,' and if there were something that did exist, it could not be recognized, and if it could be recognized it could not be imparted, and for that reason I, too, forego further statements, gentlemen."

The three, bewildered, were silent, until "Rotschimmel" rallied to the issue, "This shabby residue in my beer glass is then 'nothing'?"

"Naturally."

"Just as you, yourself, are nothing."

"Didn't I just convince you of that?"

"I will then douse the nothing with nothing, as I empty the dregs over you," which he did.

The others protested; but without paying any attention to such a clumsy argument, Sieburth pulled his handkerchief out of his pocket, and while drying head and neck, he continued, "Let us take for granted that there really is 'being' and 'not being.' If so, then there is for man, in the midst of eternities of 'not being' a single second of 'being'; and that is insufficient for him. Hoping, therefore, to lengthen this moment, he swallows for this purpose the most difficult nonsense, such as divinities, traditions, paradises, and resurrections. He binds himself together with his own kind in governmental clusters, which seem to guarantee him or his progeny permanence, although they are really destined to destroy each other; and he establishes over all as the highest, as the eternal Goddess—Stupidity."

"Stop, stop!" cried the erstwhile minister. "You were going to speak of 'being' and now you speak of humanity. Didn't you get too far into the narrows?"

"I speak of the 'being' which I acknowledge for myself and my kind, and with that the limitation establishes itself of its own accord."

"And with what you call stupidity," the former teacher, who to-day was passably sober, interjected, "you evidently mean inherited wisdom, which humanity has been constructing for thousands of years and by which one lives. Why do you rail at it?"

"If 'being' and 'not being' can be identical," replied Sieburth, "why not a thousand times more plausibly wisdom and ignorance? But I will speak more clearly. Faust says, 'In the beginning was the deed.' That is all wrong. In the beginning was the need—to meet it all sorts of ties were created which showed themselves effective in holding together existing associations, and these ties became petrified into laws. Out of the expedient developed the divinely ordained, and what God commands admits of no contradiction, and this endures for hundreds, yes, for thousands of years. That sense becomes nonsense and blessings become a curse does not deter the high and mighty. Inherited wisdom or inherited stupidity, it's all the same, sits on the throne and society lives by it, but gradually something develops from it calling itself 'personality,' and this begins to question the claim of the ruling authorities. Now follows the turning-point. In that moment in which the individual concentrates on himself and recognizes in the God-given mandate only an expedient measure, disintegration is at hand."

The others could not see it that way.

"Well, but why?"—"Is not that the beginning of real cultural progress?"—"Is there no room in human nature for a sensible insight into life?"

So the questions came tumbling one after another.

"Just let me continue," Sieburth said, cutting them short. "The expedient may be very beautiful, but can ask no reverence, and, also, can be exchanged for any other expedient thing. Perhaps one might even prefer the aimless, since it is so convenient and gratifying. You want examples, yes,—well then: Fear of God? Sancta simplicitas. . . . Parental blessings? Rot. . . . Love? Young girls' twaddle. . . . Faithful friendship? Romantic humbug. . . . Marriage? Deprivation of freedom. . . . Adultery? Restoration of identity. . . . Giving birth to children? A misfortune. . . . Honor in business?

Lunatic asylum. . . . Dishonest business methods?
Sporting advantage. . . . Yes, what else? . . . Patriotism! In peace time, molestation of the purse;
in war, something still worse. All that is, no doubt,
very cleverly and very correctly thought out, and to
most of it we, too, assent."

Stormy protest interrupted him and even the seedy
candidate declared he wished to have nothing to do
with such besmirching of sacred things.

Sieburth allowed the bawling and spitting to pass
unnoticed and continued, "I, in your place, would
not be so enraged. Under other names and not
brought to such a fine point, it all sounds harmless
and is long known to you. For example: Do we
need to discuss our attitude toward the Deity at
all? . . . Furthermore, has not the older generation
played its rôle to the finish by the time the new one
is full-fledged? . . . And further, has not for the
polygamous man,—and as such, I take it, we all
acknowledge ourselves,—has not for him love, the
great fateful passion, been absolutely abolished?
. . . It has long been a simple commonplace that
matrimony hampers the untrammeled development
of the individual, if not annihilating it altogether—
and we know too that marital infidelities bring forth
the best, sometimes the only impulses in the unavoidable dreariness of middle life . . . and friendship,
after the first imbecilities of youth, changes into a
palship of common interests, or at best into a tavern

comradeship. . . . What else was there? Oh, yes, the good honest merchant surely seems old-fashioned to you, for to fool the one who holds a contract of ours is approvingly called 'smart.' . . . The instincts of patriotism may, indeed, be said to be the most lasting, but even they, too, will be shattered when through internationalism or through corruption or even through party hatred the faith in the value of the Government edifice is destroyed. We have many times witnessed such processes in history. The downfall of Greece, latter-day Rome, the ancien régime and what not. . . . It seems to me, it is now our turn. The great Goddess of whom I spoke before with reverence has turned her face from us. We have become too wise, my friends."

Silence ensued. Each of the three seemed to feel that behind these exaggerations lay a truth from which there was no escape.

"If we understand you rightly," said the former schoolmaster, "the way which Kultur is taking can only lead humanity to destruction?"

"Kultur, Kultur," scoffed Sieburth, "every blue-bottle fly declares it has Kultur. It is only a question of what we understand by it. As long as it only serves the purpose of association, it is nothing but a form of animalism—whether ant-hill, gazelle herd, or despotism—it is all the same. Only when the individual reaches maturity begins the way upward which terminates invariably with a plunge into the abyss."

"Oh, come now, we are not children whom one can frighten," remonstrated Chmelnitzky. "You must prove your assertions."

"Facts are proofs," replied Sieburth. "That it is a step forward to become free of the lash of the church, none of you will deny, least of all our one-time preacher, yet without it no people have existed or endured for any length of time. And, further, you will acquiesce that the creation of equal living conditions belongs to a worth-while existence. But what up to now has become of any Democracy? Food for the pigs who knew how to live off her. And if you still believe in the ascent of man, I ask you, what can you think of an institution that goes to pieces on the rocks of the very theory of the highest form of existence which it has created? If it wants to continue to live, it can only do so through ignorance and misery."

In the first moment none of the three comrades could compose themselves for a reply.

At last the former preacher said, "In the Proverbs of Solomon it says, 'He that hath no rule over his own spirit is like a city that is broken down and without walls.' When I look around the world and see the thriving of civilized peoples, it brands you as a liar."

But the seedy candidate was this time entirely on his side.

"That is right," he shouted, and accompanied his remarks by the clattering of the cover of his beer glass. "They can have all the Kultur as far as I am concerned; Jean Jacques and primitive conditions are my watchword. Ah, I already scent the air of Paradise in which the roast pigeons are flying about ready for the palate and the Eves are to be had without serpents. Your open towns mean nothing to me. Here the motto is open mouth, open pants; to be prepared, is the issue."

"You are mistaken, my worthy friend," said Sieburth, "if you expect to find an Apostle of Nature in me. Old Mother Nature is in reality a low creature, bloodthirsty and a vampire, murderess out of niggardliness and murderess from wantonness, temptress to every transgression and hypocritical when restitution should be made, wheedling those who cross her, and at the same time awaiting the moment when she can seize and destroy, flirting with everything mediocre and sponging on him who exceeds those bounds, an impostor already in creating us, an impostor through fear and through hope, an impostor in every opportunity she grants us, an impostor even in death, in which she in seeming transfiguration turns us into poisonous carrion, an impostor as far as thought can reach, and therefore it is our holy duty to cheat her in turn. Amen."

He had talked himself into such a rage that his whole body shook, his voice broke and the bell-like tone turned to a hoarse squeak.

"Well, well, calm yourself," said Chmelnitzky, putting his stained paw across the table and taking the womanish hands which were twisted in one another. "You, yourself, are really nothing but a bit of nature. Don't you know what Goethe says in his hymn, 'We are surrounded by her, encircled by her, powerless to depart from her'?"

"He further says, 'Even the most unnatural is nature,'" quoted Sieburth, glaring at him, "and the positive sciences uphold him. But that does not hinder me from putting myself against her with clenched fist, and renouncing her like the son who renounces father and mother, although knowing all the time their blood to run in his veins forever, no matter how he hates them."

The three comrades who had always found him cool and collected even in his paroxysms, thought because of this disturbed state of his nerves to hold the trumps in their hands.

"Why do you hate so terribly?" asked the former preacher with a supercilious smile. "You hate nature, you hate God and civilized humanity. The whole creation seems to be the object of your hatred, and yet withal you are alert and merry, love women and love the tavern. Even if, alas, you drink no beer, grog and red wine answer the same purpose.

Your lecture room is full to capacity. You are to be the successor to Kant at some future time. I really don't think that all this hatred is very philosophical."

Sieburth was taken aback. That thrust struck home. But then he laughingly shrugged his shoulders.

"Thought leads its own life, just as the child in the mother's womb, which the pregnant woman only observes but cannot influence; at any rate, the whole fault rests in your confounded beer vapors. On the lecture platform, I would formulate these matters quite differently. In reference to nature for example, I would say, 'Gentlemen, according to our great teacher Kant, man stands outside of nature, indeed above nature; for he wrote thus, "What lifts man above himself is his personality and his freedom and independence of the mechanism of nature as a whole." ' No one could find fault with that, and doesn't it amount to the same thing?"

With this turn he saved the situation and regained his intellectual superiority.

But the heated companions, excited like himself, had no thought of giving him respite.

"How do you figure out cheating Nature?" asked Chmelnitzky. "She is cleverer and more powerful than you, and whoever thinks to have subjugated her by building a tunnel through a mountain and by converting a primeval forest into a rice field, will find pretty soon that he has not even grazed the skin; and, especially, to cheat her would be difficult, my friend."

Sieburth measured him challengingly.

"If it is not hard for any of you three, why should it be for me?"

That was again a new puzzle and one that annoyed and nonplused them.

"He is surely thinking of birth control and similar trash," sneered the candidate.

"I will tell you of what I am thinking," he replied, looking morosely from one to another. "I am thinking of self-destruction."

Following this they were silent and their faces assumed a thoughtful expression.

"If we want to proceed so mythologically," he continued, "as to assign a purpose to every act of Nature, then we can also presuppose that she has plans for each one of her creatures, assigning to each a certain span of life and the like. And to jest with that I call cheating, and you three pursue this as well as I. Look about you, Death stands behind you all.—To your health!"

And while he drank he noted with satisfaction that with their involuntary turning around a shudder ran through each of them. The besotted teacher gulped in painful gasps, the erstwhile preacher cut a face conveying many regrets over matters he had perhaps till now considered excellent, and the ex-jurist clenched his fist behind his beer glass.

"Don't worry, it's all the same in the end, and if you before quoted me Goethe's hymn, then I can serve you another quotation from an even greater one than he."

"Is there one?" asked the schoolmaster, almost frightened.

"Yes, there is, and he is called Buddha, of whose hymn is written, 'It echoes in the Heavens when the brilliant beams of his smile pierce through the clouds.' The text is quite short, and is as follows: 'Everything is perishable, everything is miserable, everything is immaterial, everything is void.' To be entirely saturated with this, does away with so-called 'Nature' as well as with ourselves, and our revenge on her becomes complete."

His eyes again sought theirs with an expression of triumph.

The preacher murmured something of fruitless pessimism and one's duty to battle against it.

Laughingly, Sieburth rose.

"My great optimism is not yet established and until then," he said, shaking hands in good-by, "I play the dilettante as a pessimist."

With that he went toward the door.

And as he passed the tables of the adjoining room there was a whispering behind him.

"Look, look, there goes the Mad Professor!"

CHAPTER XXI

AFFAIRS WITH WOMEN

If Sieburth in roaming from one tavern to another hid his identity only rarely, he was, by contrast, more discreet than formerly in his tender affairs.

His roving expeditions took place in the night hours when the gas lanterns illuminated only dimly, and those whom he took for his own at such times had good reason not to make public such amorous adventures.

Most of these casual companions of his did not even discover his name. He took them to his home in a roundabout way, and if they, in spite of this precaution, discovered the street and the number, the darkness of the court and the fact that his name plate was missing on the back door, assured him the comparative security that later on they would not be clear as to the exact place of the occurrence.

Only to a few with whom he considered a continued association worth while and on whose silence he could depend did he divulge his name and station. When he grew tired of them they accepted dismissal in good part, and even if a tear was in evidence, now and then, there was never a catastrophe. A present to assuage the pain of parting would do its part towards consolation, and if accidentally a meeting should occur at some future time, the greeting would be according to the propitiousness of the hour, either a knowing wink or a friendly little chat which would not infrequently lead to a slight relapse into former relations.

Variegated and richly animated was the picture world that unrolled before him in this fashion; but beside these ladies of colorful destinies there were many insipid and average individuals who found refuge in his lap.

Yes, when he passed judgment upon himself, he had to admit that the latter species predominated. But what did it matter? They all helped the tired brain, and when the distress of loneliness overcame him, they threw the mantle of forgetfulness over it.

It was a firmly established resolution of his not to let his experience with women of accidental contact interfere with his attitude toward the opposite sex. And even if he did not fall in obeisant devotion at their shrine, yet he was careful not to let a disparaging feeling gain ground.

It seemed to him that he was a partner in a secret association which united the priestesses of this silent erotic cult. They all led a double life, as he did. At home in the bosom of the family, in the constraint of legitimate occupation, they were demure, respectable, and, at the most, endowed with roguish cheerfulness, which the unsuspicious middle class designates as coquettish and sanctions grudgingly; here in darkness and in secrecy opened the flood gates of pent-up emotions.

There was, indeed, no display of bacchanalian freedom to be observed in them; jubilant uproariousness was not their fashion. Only now and then did one, better versed in affairs of the heart than the rest, show herself thoroughly at home in the situation in tittering and gushing delight. And it was this sort who threw horror into the two souls at the other side of the separating wall.

Most of them took what they desired, that which occurred by their sanction, with tightly compressed lips, helplessly and submissively as Fate's decree. Their real nature came to the surface only when they awakened from the troubled transport of passion. Then they revealed their innermost feelings, told stories, of which, they claimed, no one had the remotest knowledge, not even their former lovers, and sunned themselves in the importance of their own misdemeanors.

Sieburth extracted from them all that their budding youth could give, and marveled at the hazardous game youth was playing. They misrepresented, lied, throwing all discretion to the winds, they danced on the edge of the knife, and trembling with the fear surrounding every secret step, they behaved to all appearances as though they were not of the world.

Then there were others, who had reached a defiant freedom, who aimed for independence and yet were bound hard and fast by many conventions.

Others there were, the finished, the experienced ones, who indulged in a little digression from the beaten path of virtue with full knowledge, and gladly returned to the restraints of duty after their escapade. In this class belonged this or that gay young married woman, who indulged herself in all innocence while her spouse was on a trip or doing night duty.

And all this happened in a city which justly could pride itself on its stringent moral restrictions and which pointed with envious horror at the sinful Babel, for as such the capital of the country—thank God, so far away—was described to frightened souls.

So Sieburth gradually arrived at the conclusion that the accepted fact of womanly virtue, which holds sway throughout the civilized world, was only a transparent disguise, beneath which, if not by acts then surely by desire, the naked instincts of primitive life still persisted; and that woman's behavior, prior to the entrance of a child into her life, differs from that of man only through the selfish laws which male domination imposes upon her; so that it might almost be considered a meritorious deed to help in breaking down these laws whenever opportunity and desire allow.

Sometimes, of course, like a faint echo of times

long past, the thought occurred to him, "You once had very different experiences; women filled your life for whom all this meant nothing."

But it sank again, together with the image of the one, which in such moments appeared before him uneasily and admonishingly.

Never again, since that early winter morning, had he met her, nor did he wish to. She had to remain obliterated from his life, along with everything which once from heavenly heights had surrounded him with peace and happiness.

Instead, wherever opportunity offered, he attempted to raise his present mode of life to a higher level. He, the far too discerning observer, read into the individuals who peopled his home perfections, which afforded him a sort of seeming satisfaction, and made him feel that he had not entirely wasted his interest.

When he found himself ultimately disillusioned, he laughed at his own folly, but soon after set out again in pursuit of phantom lights.

One evening just before the beginning of spring, he met a Sister of Mercy, slenderly built, erect and well rounded. Her sidelong glances assured him that his attentions would be welcome. He found his efforts rewarded beyond his expectations.

This was no average nurse who assuages her marital disappointment by working for the good of her fellow man. This was a woman of the higher pro-

tected station and of undoubted nobility of soul who
left the home of her fathers because the dull selfish
life threatened to destroy her better self and who
found in self-sacrifice an inexhaustible happiness.

Unfortunately, one must content oneself without
love and that was hard, particularly when intense
longings disturbed the nightly rest.

Would she not call on him one day?

Why not, if he were a man of honor, and that
he was,—that one could read in his dreamy eyes.
He would surely not deceive trustful high-mindedness and not drag virginal purity into the depths.

So a meeting was planned, at which she did not
appear in her uniform, but instead in an elegant silk
gown, which she had quickly put on at a friend's
home, in order not to arouse undue curiosity, coming
into a strange house. She carried a little suitcase
in her left hand. In this was the sister's garb which
she would have to don in his rooms, as it would be
too late to return to the friend.

High-mindedness and virginity did not prevent
her from sitting on the edge of the bed, in a lace-
edged chemise, and the mooted question now was
whether it tallied with the rules of chastity to re-
move the silk stockings which still antedated from
the parental and lordly home.

In what followed there was no longer any question
of restraint, but she remained true to the inherited
"noblesse," in not permitting the familiar "du."

That was not fitting for a girl of her birth! And what had happened to-day must be forever forgotten; above all, marriage with a man of the middle class would be entirely out of the question.

He amused himself at her expense, but she was worth seeing again; and as a surety that she would not disappear forever, she asked him to keep the little suitcase, containing the silk dress and accessories until—well, until the next time.

On the next occasion, toward the close of the visit, she put on the silk dress for a change and packed the uniform into the suitcase, for to-day she was not returning to the hospital but going on a visit to her father's castle.

He accompanied her a little distance and found himself followed by a man, who would not inspire much confidence, and who on being questioned by Sieburth angrily, as to his business, responded with gruff regrets that he must request him and his lady friend to follow him to the Police Station. There it was revealed that in the hospital where she was nursing, articles of clothing were constantly disappearing and that the silk dress she was wearing at last furnished proof as to where the guilt could be attached.

It was his good luck that he could prove conclusively who he was and how little he knew of his companion. It was even more fortunate for him that he was spared the necessity of appearing as a witness at the trial which followed; otherwise there would have been more material for anger against him among his colleagues.

Nevertheless, the desire to find higher values in all these experiences did not vanish from his soul and if the hands of the giver remained empty, he felt compelled to fill them himself, and had to give a motive to each happening, placing it above the wretchedness of its commonplace circumstances and elevating it to the enjoyment of visioned recognitions and actions.

As he was returning in the early dawn of a May morning from a not unintellectual and not unfruitful session, he saw on a bench in the budding green of the speckled flower beds of the railway station's park grounds, the rounded form of a fair-haired girl, huddled together in uneasy sleep.

He awakened her.

Shivering in the cold, she jumped up and began to cry.

He asked what ailed her.

She was the daughter of an innkeeper, she said, and had come to the city to seek a position, but the relatives with whom she expected to find temporary quarters had moved, no one knew where, and she did not know what to do.

Why had she not gone to lodgings, he asked.

Her money did not allow of it; but that was not the worst. Her fear of the bad men in the city of which she had been warned, of robbers and seducers, through whom one could come to one's death, *that* was the worst.

He looked her over carefully, a blooming young thing, with a red-cheeked doll face and braids wound round the head. The grass-green beribboned hat which lay beside her looked as though it could trace its origin to a second-hand shop. Clumsy shoes hung on her feet, and the hands, coarsened by hard labor, crept forth from brown wristlets; in fact, she was the typical "country-innocent." Every word she spoke had the ring of truth.

Carefully he scrutinized the surroundings. There was not a soul far or wide, and the morning light was still sufficiently uncertain for one to risk a walk by her side. Moreover, across the street, in front of the station building, were several cabs with sleepy nodding coachmen and horses standing in readiness.

Would she like to go with him, he asked. She could sleep on his sofa and would be neither robbed nor seduced.

In grateful appreciation two pale blue eyes gazed up at him in astonishment.

Yes, he was a fine gentleman, one could see that at once, and if he wanted to take her, she would gladly go.

With the tranquil satisfaction of performing a gentle deed, he secured one of the carriages and brought her home.

She was no longer shy, and when he had led her into his study, her eyes fastened themselves on the supper laid in readiness for him.

She hardly required an invitation, but went for it with silent enthusiasm.

In the meantime he reflected how he could account for her presence to Mrs. Schimmelpfennig and how he could locate as soon as possible the relatives who had moved. He would apply to the police head-quarters and to the home directory; no matter; for if one says A one must also say B.

Almost immediately she had put away all the food, had emptied the water bottle and was looking about furtively for more; and as he brought the secret stores of chocolate and candied fruit out of his cupboard, with which he regaled his customary guests, she proceeded with a sigh of contentment to make herself happy with them too.

At last she seemed satisfied, and he thought he could now go to bed. He left her his top pillow, and a warm cover lay there too, so there seemed nothing in the way of a refreshing morning's sleep for both of them.

Smiling over this unaccustomed kind deed, he crept into bed and as he listened the rustling from the living room which he heard at regular intervals ceased gradually and he dropped off to sleep.

In the midst of a dream it seemed to him as though the connecting door opened softly and a white glimmering form slipped in, bent down and looked searchingly under the bed, busied herself around the night table, and was only satisfied when a clattering something, which would not be missing near the resting place of a civilized being, was at last in her hands.

Yes, yes, he thought, these innocent girls, they too must . . .

And made an effort to fall asleep again.

The bell-like tone, however, which began to sound and grow in volume, became louder and louder and more toneless and would not allow him to rest, and when he sat up after a while, he saw her sitting beside him in her chemise, looking up at him with faithful pleading eyes, while about him was a flood, which was spreading into the crevices of the flooring.

"This is really too much," he cried.

Then she raised herself full length, shook herself a little, and probably with the laudable intention of making amends, she sprang in all innocence and dampness into bed with him.

But he quickly pushed her out.

"Hurry up and get out of here," he bawled at her.

And with a double sense of guilt she disappeared, closing the door behind her.

In his vexation, he could not sleep much more but rested for an hour or two and when close to eight o'clock, jumping over the deluge, he entered his study to actively start on getting his charge under way, he found the nest empty, just as empty as the boxes which had held the goodies, which she had either quickly eaten or stuffed into her pockets.

This grotesque experience bade fair to prevent him from any future plans of offering a night's shelter whether of an idealistic nature or otherwise.

So, for the immediate future, his landlady was the only feminine association he enjoyed.

He had not been in Helena's vicinity since that Christmas night. He avoided sitting in the living room with the women and even though often drawn to the dear child in all purity and without amorous intention, of course, he carefully refrained from all efforts to attract her again.

For the mother watched; he felt that because of the painful doggedness with which she attended him. A pact of silence had arisen between them, which was only broken as necessity required. A matter-of-fact game of question and answer, cool or bantering, as occasion demanded.

Swelling to a continually fuller richness the spring unfolded itself; hot days, white nights, lonely both and consumed with a desire for something indefinable and unrealizable which became more and more keen, the more soul and senses plagued themselves with dull privation.

It almost seemed as though this mood was not un-recognized by his landlady. She, who formerly performed her obligations quickly and without loss of time, now paused more often at his desk asking about this or that, which was scarcely worth talking about, and always longer and more fixedly those sadly veiled eyes peered into his face; and his eyes also began to find pleasure in resting on her.

For she was still full of charm; the strongly formed profile, the Indian-like low-growing hair, which sank in black glossy waves down over her ears, the pale yellowish neck which even in fading retained its velvety contour, the much-promising high bust, which told secrets of belated and laboriously suppressed longings for love, even though in apparent contrast to the haggard limbs; all this made restrained desires seem pardonable.

"Here is one who worships you like a god," he said to himself. "She would be at your disposal, without restriction, according to your whim and desire; why don't you do it?"

To hold in your arms a human being, who belongs to you with every fiber of heart and soul, after all those easy-going persons, who only wanted the pleasures of the moment and forgot them as soon as they stepped forth into the street—this would be the solution of discord within himself, this would surely be deliverance.

But always when the thought came, he turned it far from him. To give in to it would mean to put himself and his life in chains for all time, for the most obtuse could foresee that he could never again get loose or have another quiet moment.

The summer was becoming hotter and hotter. The walls became hot from the overheated roof and even the hours of the night brought no relief.

One could hardly breathe, and sleep was entirely out of the question.

More than ever Sieburth tried to drown his restlessness in work.

He even neglected his companions, realizing that their company only accentuated his appetite for adventure.

One night came which was more tormenting than any.

The lamp was even more heating than the sunlight. A breath of air as from an oven came now and again through the open windows.

The letters swam before him. The pen dropped from his hand. Leaping images darting about him ushered in the morning hours with dreams.

Marion's form rose Rubensesque before him; Cilly's fuzzy blondness caressed him like a swaying blossom-laden bush; and then came Herma, victorious over both, with the sweet tenderness of her body pressed closely to him, and with the sunrise of her eyes beaming into his.

Lost all this, lost the wealth of a life crowded with love!

But one love remained; she longed for and awaited him only two walls removed. There on the corner of the desk lay the key which gave him access to the apartment at any time where he would be welcomed with stifled exultation, of that he was certain.

It became light; the sun dyed the chimneys red. He sat, the key clenched in his hand, pausing and reflecting.

Then suddenly the longing for a fondling embrace became so strong in him that every consideration was swept aside.

He jumped up, stepped out into the hall and unlocked the door leading to the apartment on the opposite side of the hall.

The front room lay with drawn curtains in stuffy semi-darkness.

The door of the alcove, where her bed stood, was partly closed. He opened it as quietly as possible, for in the room beyond slept Helena.

Out of its interior a shaft of light, the breadth of a hand, fell across the night table and over the headboard of the bed toward the wall, where it remained like a bright golden pillar in the midst of semi-darkness.

As if leaning on this pillar lay the gleaming pale, yellowish countenance of the woman with the loosened black hair about it, older, wearier and more worn than it had ever seemed to him before.

Strange that she does not awake, he thought, as he sought for an excuse he could offer for his presence, if she did.

In the meantime he sat on a chair which stood next to the bed, sunk in deep and uncertain thought. Then as his glance roamed from her and across the top of the night table, he saw placed against the foot of the candle stick something which he had never seen before and the significance of which he could not immediately fathom—two semicircular rolls about the size of two hands, gray-brown, loosely filled, as though spun of wire or wool.

Inquisitively, he touched them and held them in his hand. They were composed of horsehair. They permitted of pressing and would jump back again into shape, as though springs were concealed somewhere within.

Then slowly it dawned upon him just what purpose they served. He comprehended at the same time the source of the fullness which contributed to the fading woman her last vestige of youth.

For one moment the softening thought came to him, "It is for you she simulates the bloom of youth," but it faded, faded forever at the sight of a picture that like a vision of unbelievable beauty entranced eye and soul.

As he turned his head to the door in the back of the room, from where the golden yellow light emanated, and said to himself, "You should have locked that door long ago," he saw, resting on a red-flowered robe spread over the floor, bespun with a network of light, the nude body of Helena. On account of the heat she had doubtless left her bed for the cooler floor and thrown the last bit of clothing from her.

This was no longer a maturing girl, not flesh and blood such as youth and charm produce; it was a luminous vision, evolved of chastest phantasy, a fairy dream of folk-lore, a just created, still child-like Eve, confined in an altar niche by an artist of ancient times.

Seized with reverence, involuntarily he was about to fold his hands, but could not, for they still held the horsehair rolls.

With a small shudder, he replaced them on the night table. Then throwing a last lingering look of farewell into the adjoining room, he glided out of the door as quietly as he had entered.

He failed to notice that the woman to whom he had come, rose up gradually and looked with tearful grief on his retreating form.

CHAPTER XXII

IN THE ENEMY'S CAMP

THE summer term was once again nearing its close.

Not only did the benches in the lecture rooms become empty, but gaps also began to appear in the Faculty Room. One lecturer had closed earlier, another omitted sessions, and many a one utilized the academic quarter to pump fresh air into his lungs amid the flower beds of the Königsgarten.

One morning when the room was almost empty, Pfeifferling came towards Sieburth with both hands outstretched. The old blow-hard had, indeed, never joined those who had made a point of avoiding him, but such an attack of enthusiasm had not been evident even in him for a long time.

"Dear one, why does one see you so seldom?"

"We see each other daily," thought Sieburth.

"Why do you neglect me; why neglect a house in which a dear old lady asks for you repeatedly, and colleagues who visit complain that you—yes, you, I emphasize, you—pass them in the corridors with scarcely a greeting? I won't allow you to become a hermit; no, I won't."

"That warning is somewhat belated," thought Sieburth.

"For that reason, I take you summarily by the

scruff of the neck and declare to you the following: Pfeifferling's house desires you; the Pfeifferling house is crying out for you; Pfeifferling's house is preparing to build portals of honor for its truant protégé."

Sieburth bowed. "I am at your disposal, Herr Privy Councilor."

"Then listen, my friend, to-morrow evening I am having a few friends at my house, who are also yours, or would very much like to be, for up to the present no opportunity was given them to approach you. One of them even belongs to the Faculty, and the importance of having friends—real friends—in the Faculty in that crowd of hypocrites," he said, hardly lowering his voice, "can't be underestimated."

Sieburth looked around among the remaining ones, but they stood about in groups and had apparently not heard anything.

Pfeifferling, noticing the precaution, laughed his crashing laugh.

"Ho, ho, what they will do to me! I'll tell them a good many more things to their faces before I'm through. Ho! Well, then, to-morrow at eight for supper; very simple, just enough to satisfy one's hunger, but as far as the intellectual is concerned, oho!" And with that he trudged to his lecture, and Sieburth reflected that for a year and a half he had not dined at a family table.

The next evening when he went on his way to the Pfeifferling house, he experienced a species of stage fright which seemed new and humiliating to him, for he had still felt himself equal to every occasion. But although he laughed at himself, his apprehensions would not be assuaged.

As he entered the rooms, from which at a previous visit he had fled in horror, an enticing homelike air seemed to reach him, causing his breast to expand and filling him with an absurd feeling of joy.

There was a rounded, fading, feminine hand stretched toward him heartily, and behind the hand a matron's face shaded by a tucked lace frill, a face from which two kindly pale eyes smiled into his.

"What a long time since I've experienced this!" he thought, bowing over the warm clasping hand, feeling prepared to condone anything disagreeable which might occur.

It did not take long before exactly that happened.

As his host in welcoming him drummed heavily upon his shoulders, he saw in the semi-darkness three dignified men whom he scarcely knew personally, but whom he had always regarded as his natural opponents; three champions of reaction, hated and, as far as possible, avoided by all to whom the freedom of intellectual thought was a precious possession.

Two of them were theologians, Professor Bindewald, exponent of the Old Testament, and beside him, Professor Löhmann, the exponent of homiletic theology, both known as religious enthusiasts, both active in religious meetings as leaders.

The one was a spare gawky stick, with a long curved neck, the other a broad-chested and goitrous ram, with gray tufts of hair over a low forehead. The third, a quiet, tired little man, who seemed behind concave glasses to be constantly asking forgiveness with half-faded eyes. He was a teacher of domestic economy and known as a morose and cranky junker and withal a name which was usually found only in regiments. One might have taken all three of them for emissaries of Satan had they not been on most intimate terms with the good Lord himself.

And still a fourth something arose out of the dark background, where it had hidden itself modestly, young, pale and peevish, but with the flashing eyes of St. John, in a hollow-cheeked triangular face, one of the instructors, Licentiate Erl, D.D., who lectured on the Epistles to the Corinthians and the like.

"Heavens, where have I landed?" thought Sieburth as four hands, the one spider-fingered and hard as bone, the second domineeringly forceful, and already taking possession, the third flabby and apathetic, the fourth, full of shy cordiality, stretched out to him.

"How shall I get through this evening?" he

thought, cursing his acceptance which had brought him into a situation where each word coming or going could be converted into a slap in the face.

For the time being, to be sure, everything was amicable.

The hostess had assigned him to one of the seats next to herself although he was next to the youngest and already acquainted in the home, and conversed with him in a well-intentioned motherly fashion.

Two long years, she said, had passed since he had sat there; but now he must come soon again and often. Older people too knew how to be agreeable; yes, especially they, for with them there was no jealousy or change of mood.

He thanked her with heartfelt words, and something not unlike emotion awakened in him.

The lamplight gleamed snow-white on the long oval of the table; the meat-filled omelets threw out a savory odor, and even the thin white wine, sour as it was even to look at, gurgling in the glasses comfortingly, threw out a sense of well-being.

On the other side of the hostess, an argument had arisen between Pfeifferling and the purveyors of ecclesiastical knowledge about the now vanquished rationalism in preaching and its ensuing consequences on the true faith.

The specter of a "religion of reason" stood giant-high behind the speakers and threatened to engulf the evening.

The professorial Baron, who also was the possessor of a manor, contributed his opinion. "The husband-men of those times," he said, in his sickly and grating voice, "did not fare badly at all, for if you spoke down at them from the pulpit, entertaining them with a sermon on the best methods of stable feed-ing, they not only went home spiritually elevated but also materially enriched, and thanked God, their Lord, that they were also cared for in this quarter."

The pious men wrinkled their foreheads. They instinctively felt a divergence towards liberalism.

"We, on the other hand, want to thank God," said the alert homilist, "that he sent us Schleiermacher, who directed us to the source of all religious feeling and put an end to all this nonsense."

Sieburth had, as was known to all, written a book-let on the philosophy of Schleiermacher. Several compliments were naturally extended, which he ac-cepted modestly as a sign of good-will.

As said before, all went as well as one could wish.

Then followed as the next subject of conversation the system of having pericopes and the question as to whether to assign for reading at Sunday services, according to the time of the year and regulations of the church, a certain portion of the Bible on which to base the sermon. Spener had declared openly companions in misery, excluded from the general social life, simply because we adhere to the principle, 'the sovereignty of the State.' Should one not, Colleague Bindewald, like your national Hebrew deity, intervene with fire and brimstone, when you consider how few of us there are?"

"They already count me as one of their number," thought Sieburth.

The Old Testament teacher replied, "Liberalism is a power, dear colleague, which we have for the most part underestimated as we are often wont to underestimate the power of the devil. When you reflect what these people in the smug consciousness of their majority are enabled to perform in the way of moral condemnation, only then do you realize the devilish satire that lies in the very name of their party."

"He is right there," thought Sieburth, the ever-ready anger arising in him.

Now the hostess, too, joined in the conversation.

"It seems to me, gentlemen," she said, "that this is the fault less of your colleagues than of their wives. Take, for instance, the incidents that take place at the coffee parties of 'The Three Fates'! Didn't you give them that name, dear Professor Sieburth? It's attributed to you at any rate; what filters over to us from there is,—well, beyond belief. There one is praised to the skies or destroyed, put into the limelight, or boycotted, according to their whim."

"And add to this Jewish intolerance," the preacher added darkly as though he had made tolerance and sufferance his rule of life.

"Not forgetting democratic conceit," added the high-born teacher of domestic economy.

"In short," summed up the host, twisting his white napkin, "you suddenly find yourself on a lonely isle without knowing why."

Was it accidental or was it imaginary that the glances of all seemed to glide to Sieburth? At any rate, he avoided raising his eyes in order not to meet any of these looks, and the anger in his soul turned to dull plaintive rage.

Then with quickened heartbeats he listened attentively, for out of the void the name of Hildebrand suddenly came to his ear.

"Yes, yes, it seems that even Hildebrand can't stand it with them any longer," said the hostess. "That rumor that he will accept a recall to the interior as early as this fall will not cease."

For the first time the young instructor took up the word.

"They say," he related, hoarse with excitement at his boldness, "that his wife cannot stand the cold climate."

"That surprises me," crowed the Baron, "for, if what one hears is true, they have made it hellishly hot for her over there."

What was that?

of us scared and pussy-footing, as though we had a guilty conscience."

"You are wrong, dear friend," the other theologian said. "Forceful action by all means, where it belongs; but here it can only do harm. Any one who is not an actual Red can subscribe to the text as it now stands. I don't know the political views of our friend Sieburth, but I'll wager if I were to hand him this sheet—" He pulled a folded paper out of his pocket. "Would you look at it, colleague?" he said.

"Gladly," replied Sieburth, with politeness, and bent beneath the globe of the lamp, suppressing a smile, for it was clear to him already where this was leading.

A glance at the paper sufficed to reveal the conventional election-time catch-phrases naïvely strung together.

The State should look after trade and commerce, protect the artisan, prevent the exploitation of the poor and weak, and act as well-meaning helper to the sick or injured workingman and the like. But in order that the Government should be able to do this, one had to support strongly these good intentions of the Government, and above all, see to it that the rights of the crown should not be insidiously curtailed by its evil-minded opponents.

The name of Bismarck, whose much-discussed

plans were at the bottom of all this, was carefully avoided.

"Well, colleague," the preacher asked impatiently, "couldn't you subscribe to this whole-heartedly?"

"That's a great idea," cried Pfeifferling, playing the rôle of one who has been suddenly enlightened on some point. "We four,—little Erl hasn't anything to do with it yet,—are considered black reactionaries. We would only frighten away the Philistines; but Sieburth is a blank page. At best he was counted to those on the other side. If he joins our forces we have a witness who is unsuspected. Then we gain ground right in the opponents' camp. How they would foam at the mouth! Eh, Sieburth, wouldn't that be great?"

The two professors of theology exchanged disapproving glances. The methods of the speaker appeared to them too direct not to call a blank refusal down on them.

"You bamboozlers," thought Sieburth, whom nothing escaped, "you foxy barkers."

Yet one of Pfeifferling's words had struck him right in the heart. They would foam at the mouth; they would feel the kick in the pants which they would herewith receive.

What had he said to himself before, "No matter who you are, or what you want—"

Yet he would not act without reflection, nor show himself too willing; that would depreciate the extent of his sacrifice and would degrade him.

"I thank you, gentlemen," he said, "for this mark of confidence which you give me. If I might follow my sympathies, I would not hesitate for a moment to espouse your cause, but you can understand that it means taking a position which must influence my whole life; and you would indeed think little of me if I were not carefully to study every line and every word before saying yes."

The impetuosity of the gentlemen was thus checked, without causing dissatisfaction with his hesitancy, and when they separated near midnight, he could feel assured that for to-day at least, he had come forth from the skirmish intact.

As he walked down the moonlit street alone, Herma's name went through his head and what had been said of her at the table.

A feeling of fear suddenly gripped him, and before he could overcome it, hurried steps tramped behind him in an effort to catch up with him.

Then close beside him a hat was lifted and the timid voice of the instructor, which had only been heard several times during the evening, asked with awkward coughing whether a short conversation might be granted him though he was young and unimportant.

"You see, Professor, you are reported to be independent, undaunted and cool. I, on the other hand, am somewhat undecided and am constantly struggling with myself."

"Every time I see her she has grown thinner and more transparent," thought Sieburth.

"It would surely be a blessing for me, if I were to gain a certain corroboration from you for my future line of thought."

"It is surely his duty to take her away," he thought further, "even if through this she is entirely lost to me."

"I know I can repose confidence in you, and out of this confidence I must admit I absolutely am at variance with some of the dogmas set forth by the church; yes, I even believe my ideas somewhat resemble yours. How do you, for instance, regard 'original sin'?"

Sieburth roused himself from his reverie. "What sort of word is that?"

"Don't scoff," the young theologian pleaded, in a rather whining tone, "for that question cannot be without significance for you too. I'll disregard Luther, who in contrast to the Arminians agreed entirely with St. Augustine . . . 'peccatum originalis,' you know. . . . But Kant surely concerns you. Although he does not entirely coincide with these, he, too, emphasizes occasionally the essential evil in man's nature, which since the protoplasts is said to be unalterably infested with it. Is not that most discouraging for the human race?"

"What do you mean by protoplasts?" asked Sieburth almost gruffly. "I know protoplasm as the principal constituent of animal and plant cells, but your protoplasts I don't know."

"But that is only another name for Adam and Eve," said the young scholar in an injured tone, "the first created; indeed, it is their scientific designation."

"Well, well, if that is their scientific designation, I must plead ignorance as my excuse; and as far as your previous question is concerned, everything in the world of science is discouraging to mankind. And the freethinkers play the deuce with it as well as the pious ones. Only those who have a well-paying berth are prepared to make concessions. But permit me now to ask you a question in turn. When we spoke of the wife of Hildebrand, the historian, to-day at the table, the Baron said that they had made it 'hellishly hot for her over there.' What could he have meant by that?"

"As to that I can't give you any information, for I have only been here two terms and what is behind that must have happened before my time, but if you wish I can make inquiries."

"That would be very agreeable to me," replied Sieburth. "I could do it myself, of course, but as

I was, as you heard, a friend of the house, I would rather refrain. For the same reason I would enjoin you to withhold my name from any inquiries."

"Certainly, certainly," promised the other, glowing with zeal.

"And as to the problem of 'original sin,'" replied Sieburth, "which always interested me too, my depreciatory remark was, of course, only a joke; we'll talk about it at length in the future. Good night, dear colleague."

CHAPTER XXIII

LEAVE-TAKING

Unrest took possession of him.

"Making it hot." What could that mean, "making it hot"?

Suspicion settled here and there, but it remained impossible to find a solution.

The whole week passed without his coming in contact with the instructor.

He stood in front of the black bulletin board from which one could gather during what periods he might be met in the Assembly Room, and located his schedule, but he was not there.

At last Sieburth saw him in one of the corridors on his way to the lecture room.

"Dr. Erl, Dr. Erl."

A shy glance backward; almost a frightened look met him and he was gone.

That it was accidental seemed improbable, and he could not be in a hurry either. It was apparent that he wanted to avoid the meeting, because a discussion would prove embarrassing.

The restlessness grew.

In the show window of a florist's shop Sieburth saw a bunch of those pale, frail La France roses similar to those he had brought Herma two years ago. Without accounting to himself for the action, he went in, had an extravagant bunch of them arranged and gave Herma's address.

"No card to be enclosed?" asked the young lady.

"It's not necessary, and should there be any inquiry as to the appearance of the sender, no information is to be given."

The young lady smiled understandingly. She met with that same wish every day and it was adhered to, according to regulations.

Only when he was alone again did he realize what trouble he could cause by so doing even without taking into account the husband who had an indisputable right to know the source of the gift.

So he had inadvertently drawn her into the maelstrom of his anxiety, though unable to lighten her burden, or even to be near her.

The only consolation was that she might attribute a perfectly harmless spirit to the gift, and perhaps even imagine that a present-day friend had sent it.

And with that, he lulled his conscience to rest.

It was on the evening of the second day after the thoughtless gift—the late twilight already caused the letters to merge on the sheet, when Frau Schimmelpfennig came excitedly into the room, saying that there was a lady outside, in mourning, who wished to speak to him urgently.

What did she look like, he asked.

One could not tell for she was veiled.

Was she tall, stout, or what?

"No, very thin, and so frail that you could blow her over."

His heart bounded.

"Ask her to come in."

Tottering, he laid his head against the crossbars of the window. He was actually dizzy.

And she entered.

She was a shadow, a slender gliding shadow, that stood in the twilight, like an upright shaft in front of the gleaming white door.

"Madam!—Herma—dear madam!"

Her hand sought his.

And that was her voice, by God, it was her voice, almost unaltered, a little shaky, a little hoarse, perhaps. The echo of her heartbeat sounded in it, just as it had been manifested in his case by the incomplete framing of even her name.

"I thank you for the roses. I recognized the giver at once. I would not have come but for them. I often wanted to come, but one is so cowardly."

"If you had only come, had only come," the soul cried within him, but it dared not cross his lips.

She threw back the veil and looked around her.

In the meantime, he searched her face eagerly. The two suns, rising larger still, more brilliant than formerly, seemed not of this world. A redness lay on the cheek-bones that seemed almost painted on. There were deep shadows below, and around the corners of the mouth lurked sharp wrinkles.

"She is sick," an inner voice called to him.

"Sit down, dear one, please, please sit down."

"No, no, not yet. I must first look. I imagined everything so differently, but, of course, one can't see much."

He reached toward the lamp.

"Not yet; no light, please, no. So this is the writing desk." She stroked the oilcloth top. "And what kind of an etching is that on the wall?"

"Guido Reni's 'Aurora.'"

"Oh, yes, and the marble bust between the bookcases?"

"The funds have not allowed of marble. It is a Plato in plaster. I must honor him because he is my enemy."

"Do you honor all your enemies so nobly?"

"If I did I should have to open a big museum— but what nonsense am I talking? Herma! Herma!"

He dropped into his desk chair and covered his face with his hands.

She, too, sat down behind him, and when he turned around to look at her, he found her cowered in the corner of the sofa as on that night in Rauschen, clutching the arm with her right hand, her eyes glowing into space.

"My husband has gone to Heidelberg," she began, "to arrange for his recall."

"It is really true then that you are leaving?"

"We must for various reasons; and when your roses came, I said to myself, 'If you do not act immediately, you will never see him again; never again'; for, you know, I will not live to see another spring."

"For God's sake, what are you saying?"

"No, no, that is to be; that is Fate. My lungs were always weak, and then came this murderous climate, and all kinds of other murderous things added to it, and so I'll have to take the consequences. Now the doctors want me to go to the mountains, but I would like to spend the last winter with my husband. He needs me so badly, and I have caused him so much sorrow which I would like to expiate, as well as I can, before I leave him."

He felt as though his heart was being hacked in pieces at these words, and like a lurking demon there sat in some corner of his soul the feeling, "Mea culpa, mea maxima culpa."

She continued, "It has not gone well with you and me in the meantime. The wives of your colleagues did not neglect to report all the ugly things that people said of you, for they knew they hurt me deeply by so doing."

He started up.

"What does one know then of you and me?"

"One always knows everything, how, from what source? In our case, I can only imagine that you, my poor friend, in the heaviness of your heart, confided the happenings to some one and that this person betrayed us."

"Herma, darling, darling, how could you, how would you attribute such a caddishness to me?"

"Then it was not through you. Oh, I am so glad, even if the result is the same. I'm so glad, for whether one wants to or not, something like a reproach mixes in notwithstanding."

"And you carried this suspicion about with you for two years?"

"A year and a half; yes, just about, since the time that my husband received the anonymous letters."

"Anonymous, what about?"

"Well, about my visit that night. I was supposed to have been with you till well towards morning, and to have come home wet to the skin, and if I cough now, it is all caused by that, and many similar things."

He let the images of that night pass before him. "Nowhere was there a soul in evidence. I scanned the whole section; there wasn't a light in a window, not a shadow in the roadway. Everything was dead and empty."

She laughed softly. "Whether this be a little more or less mysterious does not matter now."

"And your husband?"

"My poor husband, I told him everything then."

"You did!"

"I could not let him go on suffering, and he suffered enough even then. So the cat-and-mouse game began for us. You know we were spoiled from the beginning, being received like a royal couple, but now came the little social slights, and the needle pricks in every conversation, insinuations as to this and that,—but why should I complain, you know all that."

"Making it hot for her," he thought, so that was it. And aloud he said, "From my own experience I don't know it, for I was kept at such a distance that I, during all that time, socially at least, have spoken to no one."

For a while she sat motionless.

"Did that happen on my account?" she then stammered.

"Oh, not at all," he quickly assured her. "That rumor never became so audacious. There was another matter with which the morality of the community concerned itself, a piece of foolishness, nothing more."

"Undoubtedly that newspaper insertion," she laughed in surprise.

"Did you hear about that?"

"Oh, it was sent to me, perhaps ten times over."

"And so it became clear to you many times over that you had wasted your affection on one altogether unworthy of it."

She pondered. "Good Lord," she said, "what do we women know of life and of you men? We conceive an image patterned after some ideal in books and then we are surprised that you are unlike it."

"And if, on that one occasion that December morning, do you remember, I had spoken to you, you would have ignored me. Wouldn't you?"

She did not raise her eyes this time either. "So much culminated at that time," she answered softly, "the letters and,—oh, it hurt so,—and that meeting hurt the most, and only gradually, when I no longer ever saw you—but enough of it. I am here with you and can stay as long as I like, or rather, as long as the spirit of the hour demands,—I must make the most of it, for there will never be another."

"Then this is really good-by?"

"Why good-by? As long as we live we can be as one, irrespective of where we may be. I was religious while I still wanted to live; now that I want to die—"

"You want that?" he asked, in pained protest.

"I want to, because I must, and it is best so for there is no other solution. Since I am so clear on that point, my religion is no longer a comfort. I find it elsewhere. 'Not being does not hurt,' I always tell myself. That is consolation—don't you find it so?"

Much could have been said about this, but it

seemed perilous to him to break into the peace of that soul even with an affirmative.

Outside the gas lamps were being lit and their reflection was thrown ghostlike on the rows of books. Over her form also a shaft of light glided, making her cheeks glow golden and imparting a seraphic brilliance over the deadened shadows of the eyes.

When he did not answer, she continued, "I only wish I did not have these great worries about you both. My husband will perhaps learn to get along without me. He was always fortunate formerly and will be again when I am gone, but what will I do about you?"

"You are worried about my future, dear?" he said, being scarcely able to master his emotion.

"How could it be different?" she asked in reply. "I have only you two in the world."

At this he sank on his knees before her and buried his head in her lap.

She stroked his bristly hair, and he heard the crackling beneath her touch as the sparks flew.

Now and again there was a faint cough from her throat, quite faint like the chirping of a sleeping bird.

"This is the sign of another presence, the third with us," he thought shuddering, burying his head deeper in the tightening folds of her dress.

"Get up," he heard her whisper close to his ear, "so that I can hold your hands; there is so much warmth radiating from you, and I'm always cold."

And so he sat opposite her again and took her hands which then lay dry and hot in his.

"You are surprised they are not cool," she said; "that is because of the fever. The fever is the nicest part, for one always feels as though one could fly from this earth. I have to hide all this from my husband. He worries so. Even the doctors tell him nothing. I have trained them so well."

He sought for a word of encouragement. "I have helped so many unworthy ones," he thought, "and just here I am so awkward and stupid." Just to say something, he praised the benefit of the mountains, which worked wonders. "There all this will disappear," he continued aloud, "above all the feeling that you are no longer of this earth."

"Oh, no!" she said triumphantly, "that feeling I won't relinquish. That's what's keeping me alive. Do you think that without that I could have come here? Somehow I seemed to fly in at this window. I wanted to visit you like a departed spirit, wanted to bring you a kind of sanctification, and instead I take holiness with me."

"You, from here?" he cried, gulping down the scorn which rose in him.

"Isn't all this sanctified," she asked, looking about, "there where you reflect, there where you write, where immortal ideas are ever about you?"

He could contain himself no longer and sprang

up and with laughter, pointing around him, he screamed at her, "Do you know where you have landed?   In a mire, in a dive, where only trash go in and out, each spot is pestilential; where you're sitting whores have performed and next to it, and all over.   Get up, so that you won't be contaminated. Wipe yourself so that the atmosphere of wantonness will not cling to your skin,—and you want to sanctify yourself. Ha! Ha! Ha!"

He ran around the room, he kicked at the furniture as though to destroy it, and the rage continued to grow.

Standing before her, he continued, "But you must not believe that I repent; don't think that I accuse myself, I only laugh at the worldly farce out of which you and I grow—two human beings as unlike as if from different planets, and they should love one another, must love?   Could there be a sadder joke of Fate, you poor being?   Before you came all seemed as it should be and now,—Herma, what is wrong?   Herma, for Heaven's sake, Herma."

She leaned back into a corner of the sofa, as if overcome by faintness.

But as he in fear tried to help her, she sat up and looked up at him with an expression as though far removed from mundane things.

"Why did I not come sooner?" she whispered.

"Yes, why did you not come sooner?" he ejaculated, gritting his teeth.

"If I were well, and felt assured that I were not jeopardizing your future, I would come to you altogether, for you need me now more than he."

"Herma!" A sob of release and expiation was expressed in that exclamation.

"But as things are, I must leave you alone, first in this hostile town, and then, soon alone in this hostile world. That will be one great sorrow to me."

"Forgive, dear one, forgive my outbreak of before, forgive . . ."

"On the contrary, it is a good thing, for at least I can be something to you, and why do you fight your own impulses? If it is true that we all live by a law of predestination, it cannot be a crime to obey these laws. What has happened is the natural outcome and perhaps you gathered new strength out of what appeared to be wrong."

"Where does she get that prophetic insight?" he thought, astonished, and that feeling of predestined belonging together which had once overpowered him at their first meeting grew strong in him again.

She rose.

"Don't you think it is time for me—" she asked.

Now the door of her soul was closed again. No, no, it was not; only the moment demanded its rights.

"When you are gone from here—" he said falteringly.

"What then?"

He was silent. "Enough of confessions," he

thought.   He was afraid of what his future held, so much had she softened him.

"When I am gone from here," she said, anxious for him, "what then, oh, God, what then?"

"Will you never write to me?" he asked.

"Yes, I will write to you once."

"When?"

"When the time for it has come."

He asked no further.

She pulled the veil down over her face. "I put on mourning," she said, "so as to cause less comment.   This visit, I believe, will not encourage any gossip."

"When does your husband return?"

"To-morrow."

Now it was time to say good-by.   They stood opposite each other, but neither could master enough self-control to give the parting clasp.

There was still so much to say.   A whole life was to spread before them before the conclusion.

"Do you know how I feel?" she asked.   "As though I knelt at Gethsemane."

"Why, dear?"

And then suddenly she threw her arms around him and crushed herself to him.   "You, you, you," pleaded she, "you have meditated upon all things. Is there no possibility then of meeting in the life beyond?"

A wild frenzy at the nonsense the preachers had

taught for thousands of years, thereby consigning humanity to mortal weakness and tearing from this harassed soul, threatened by death, the needed consolation, assailed him, but he checked it.

"Only mysticism can help here," he thought, and softly he spoke to her, saying, "Didn't you yourself say, dear, that 'not being' does not hurt?"

"But 'being' hurts all the more," she complained. "I fully realize that only now."

He took her in his arms, so that in standing, she rested tightly in his embrace, and said, "See, darling, we know so little of life here, how much less do we know of the beyond? But one thing we can imagine, what has been will be forever, because it has always been, whether we are aware of it or not. There can be nothing transitory to the one who carries the feeling of perpetual being in his nature, and as you said before, as long as we both live, we might feel as one no matter where the other may be, so I say to you, that there is only real merging when we no longer live; when there is a return to the one great sun in which all life has its origin and its goal."

"But will one recognize this unison?" she asked, trembling in his arms.

"Is it not enough to feel this as long as one has cognition?"

"Yes," she breathed, and looked up at him with sincere faith.

Then she freed herself of his embrace.

He kissed her through the veil on forehead and cheek, went for a light and escorted her into the dark hall and down the steep stairs.

After he had extinguished the light and set it down on a step, he and she united in a silent embrace finding rest therein once again, and this unity was no deception nor delusion.

Then the house door slammed and all this belonged to the past.

CHAPTER XXIV

A LEAP IN THE DARK

THE outcry of disappointed longing became gradually dulled.

What remained was rage; that burrowing, lashing rage, which now often overcame him who formerly, with the coolness of the deliberate man of sense, had measured and mastered the happenings of the world about him.

He needed only to imagine how they of the other side—"the other side," he, too, was already saying—had vented their poisonous rancor on the defenseless loved one, who was at their mercy, and cried unconsciously for vengeance. Vengeance; yes, but how? What weapon had he, with comparatively no influence; he who stood alone, without so much as a single ally at his command!

And yet, the new friends had not entered into his life in vain. No matter what strangers they were to his world of thought; even though they were to him the tools of Acheron, they were at his service to be utilized as soon as he decided to join forces with them.

Then why hesitate any longer in becoming one of them. And one day the proclamation which he had taken home to look over was sent back to Professor Pfeifferling signed.

A perfect torrent of exultation was the answer.

The reference to "the prodigal over whom there was more joy in heaven than over the thousand just ones," was not lacking, and there was joy over the consternation this act would provoke in the camp of the Liberals. If one whom they expected to use as a matador suddenly turned his back on them without any notice, it must be evident to the most dull-witted adherent that their cause was a lost one.

In conclusion followed several sentences which gave abundant food for thought: "And do you think, dear friend, that your gratifying step will remain unobserved by higher authorities? You will never advance to the position you merit with the sanction of the Faculty, of that you may be assured, but you shall secure it, against their will. Just let me and the Ministry of Education look to that."

A prickly feeling of discomfort came over him. Here were hidden traps, which might snap without warning. He had never been overambitious. Every shady method of catering for the grace of those in power was foreign to him, but if one withheld, through trickery, what he had rightfully earned through devotion to duty, then even this means was justified, or any other as far as he was concerned, to foil the enemy.

Two years had passed since the death of the great

Hegelian, and the second chair of philosophy, which actually was the first, was still vacant, and as far as one knew, neither he nor any one else from the interior of Germany had been called to occupy it. They hesitated, they eliminated, they tried to overlook him, and yet seemed unwilling to drop him altogether.

The vacation began and teachers and pupils fled from the stuffy town.

But Sieburth relinquished, as in the previous year, the recreation, with which his iron nature could still dispense. It was enough of a relief to him not to meet the hated beings, the sight of whom was gall and wormwood to him, for almost three months. Since the "Three Stages of Ethics" was completed, he occupied himself with a new topic which he called, "The Natural History of Fundamental Problems of Philosophy." In this it was his purpose to offer, from the standpoint of a strictly positive relativist, an inventory of all that had been traditionally thought, and to throw out all the disproved, unworthy trash which the dogmaticians had piled up.

The preliminary notes of this treatise were piled up mountain-high when a craving to disburden his soul and clear the honor of the sophists came to him. They, who since Plato, for fully two thousand years, had strayed through the souls of these narrow pedants, as the moral pestilence of their era, had long since appeared to him as the fathers of all freethinking, unspoiled by theological speculations. What the English historian Grote had attempted with insufficient material, and what had only recently been advanced by Ernst Laas of Strassburg in a new and as yet uncertain light, he wanted to present with strictest exactitude and with established partisanship.

The preliminary studies of these treatises lay there and all this was to serve as preparatory before the "Natural History" was to be completed.

For all this no trips and no relaxations were needed. No matter how merciless the rays of the sun beat down, no matter how oppressive the air was to the senses, yet they could not hamper his brain, nor deter his will.

What perplexed and disturbed him were the demands his new political friends made on him.

The nearer election day, which was settled on for late October, came, the more active became the preparations.

To be sure he declined to take part in the sessions, for he had reason to believe that his experience with the champions of the opposite cause, which he still remembered with consternation, would repeat itself with only a slight shade of difference. But even though he kept the professional wire pullers at a distance, this did not prevent him from being stormed with requests to write flaming articles in favor of the holy cause, and to be active not only in town, but in neighboring election districts as a speaker. Even though he did not deviate from his decision, it was a great effort to decline in a courteous manner.

At last, after a two months' casting about, the election proclamation appeared, more colorless, and more calculated to catch the unwary individual, than the previous project had been.

The candidate was a man of no importance, little known, immune from attack, but also devoid of strong characteristics on which to build; he was independent by virtue of being an attorney, but that was perhaps the only praise one could give him. All the more pitiful appeared the crowd who rallied about and who had raised him to this distinction, and who now lined up in motley throngs as constituents.

The names of University teachers were lost among those of innkeepers, distillers and contractors. Officials in every capacity, who ate the bread of the Government and who could not fail in their duty of being the heralds and banner carriers. All ranks were in evidence down to the lowest railroad official and police sergeant. A purveyor to the royalty distinguished himself in an outstanding demonstration for the cause of freedom.

"A shabby crowd," thought Sieburth, crushing the newspaper which announced to the world also his enslavement.

Those "on the other side" were better situated.

The very name of their candidate offered subject

matter and told stories of manhood and the spirit of a martyr.

As a member of the Faculty of Medicine and Director of the Polyclinic of Internal Diseases, he had, during the time of conflict about twenty years back, thrown himself into the breach to battle against the infamous press ordinances which had consigned everything journalistic not meeting with their approval to extinction, and as punishment had immediately lost his position.

To support him would have meant to serve real academic freedom and to smooth the path to his own advance in an honorable manner. Instead of which—

Luckily he had not as yet come forward politically, and no one could prove a change of view, for one could not attach much importance to that visit as a guest at the meeting of the liberal party.

In the beginning of October Pfeifferling returning from the mountains again assumed his duties and Sieburth was invited to supper.

Tanned, with peeling skin and red swollen nose, the merry old abomination came towards him.

After the first greeting he already began, "That won't do, colleague, you dare not bury your head in the sand up to your neck. No, that doesn't go. When there are meetings in reference to the election, you must be enthroned at the committee table and make a fine contrast to the little insignificant fellows. If the gentlemen who are high officials hold back somewhat, it may even seem gratifying, but every Tom, Dick or Harry may not, nevertheless, defame our edifice."

"Very well, I'll come," Sieburth assented reluctantly, "that is, if I don't have to speak."

"I want to plead with you earnestly, if not so courteously, about just that very thing; what is that supposed to mean, not have to speak? That the lukewarm are spit out, one reads already in Holy Writ. The discussion must rise out of the very depths of the citizens' dungheap into which the so-called general and direct voting privilege has thrown us, and must be put on a decent level, now and then, and when it reaches this pass, it is your turn, honored sir. You can't howl with the wolves and be taken for a lamb; nothing will help you, at any rate; the gentlemen of the administration are watching and a good mark in the conduct roll can hurt no one, particularly when one has all sorts of black marks chalked up against one like certain people whose names I won't mention."

That was plain enough, and Sieburth felt a flush rise to his face.

"You are making a mistake, my dear Privy Councilor," he said, "if you believe that the opinion of the gentlemen of the Ministry of Education enters into question here. If I joined you it was for other reasons and if I am not comfortable, there is nothing in the way of my separating from you again."

The old gentleman saw that he had gone too far and quickly steered into other channels.

"Well, well, well," he laughed, "I look after scraps myself, but if I really have hurt you, you will get a kiss of reconciliation and that will be worse, so soften your Achillean anger. Speak, you'll have to, if occasion demands. Let your new friends see to that, and now come to my wife, or the food will get cold over your temper."

With that he opened the door of the adjoining room, and saw the table gleaming with the damask and silver in the lamplight.

Sieburth stepped in, thinking meanwhile, "I hope this supper is not too dearly bought."

CHAPTER XXV

PILLARS OF THE STATE

I⊤ was on a humidly warm, early fall evening that an unruly crowd gathered in front of the locked doors of the Citizens' Club house.

The candidate of the Government parties had announced through his supporters that he was prepared to-day to state his views and plans at this place. In addition to his slated speech there would be a discussion to which those holding contrary opinions were invited, and in which they might take part.

Next to small middle-class men, in carefully brushed holiday coats, and members of the lowest official class, who wore war emblems, while the certificate of civic maintenance seemed to peep from their buttonholes, crowded workingmen, whose jackets hastily adjusted over their blue working blouses, covered these but scantily.

Only very few of higher station were intermingled. A few slashed, youthful faces gazed haughtily at their neighbors, who barely existed for them, and several old men with long shaggy Kaiser William beards and spit-curls embodied the glory of old Prussian discipline.

A tall, well-developed young man with pale

gashes and an early matured expression in a healthy determined face stood, paying close attention, in this variegated crowd. No one had come with him, and he attached himself to no one.

Then one of the young fellows, decorated with many slashes, called the attention of others to him.

"Look," he said, fairly loudly, "there stands Kühne."

"So he is in this vicinity again too," remarked another, and a third advised paying no further attention to him.

But he, who had heard everything, was not inclined to let them off so easily.

With a smile, which was not at all embarrassed, but rather condescending, he lifted his hat, and speaking over the shoulders of bystanders in the friendly bantering tone prevalent among old pals, he called, "Well, how goes everything nowadays?"

So they could not do anything but greet him likewise. Yes, checked by his superiority, they even stretched their hands out to him, which he took and shook heartily.

"What are you doing here again?" one of them asked him.

"I have my barrister's degree and want to add the doctor's to it here; so it seems the natural thing to attend this election rumpus, and I see you do the same."

"But after your previous behavior you seem to

have come to the wrong quarter," said one in a poor
attempt at heckling.

But he refused to turn into these channels.

"Not at all, I am interested, particularly since I
read the name of one of my professors on the election committee, a name the presence of which is
more surprising than my being here."

"Whose is that?" asked one from the other side.

"It's immaterial, since you probably never attended his classes."

With that the conversation came to an end and no
one resumed it.

Soon after the doors of the hall were opened.
The crowd stormed forward, and the erstwhile fraternity brothers were separated, the urge to notice
each other any further not having acted strongly
enough to keep them together.

The benches were quickly filled.

Fritz Kühne was lucky enough to secure a seat in
one of the first rows.

In front of him was the platform, draped with
painted cloths and slightly raised, from which the
speakers were to hold forth. As yet it was empty,
as was also the long green table, which was behind
the desk and evidently intended for the members of
the Election Committee. A smaller table, with a
few chairs around it, was leaned against the left wing.

There was a wild stampede for seats throughout
the hall.

With jumping and climbing, stumbling and pushing, scolding, pleading, pulling, threatening, every one tried a different expedient to secure a place from which to see and hear; from which to become either inspired or enraged.

Fritz's two neighbors were a study. The one on the right, a kind of mechanic, gray-haired with a worldly-wise contemplative look, sought to start a political conversation with him. He complained of the annoying "Progressives" who soured Bismarck's existence, for he stated, "This great man, who founded the Reich, knows exactly what is needed."

The one on the left, a broad expansive figure with full-moon cheeks, and rust-red sergeant's mustache, talked only to himself. "I served my Kaiser faithfully," he growled to himself, "and if he entrusts all this to Bismarck, I do it too." This sentence he repeated many times. Evidently that was the sum and substance of his political understanding.

On the first bench sat a group of young artisans who were quiet for the present and, only through furtive nudges, gave their companions an inkling of how much amusement they were getting out of it all. In the meantime some stragglers, who threw their weight like breaking waves against the solid wall of those in possession, had ranged themselves behind Fritz's back. Among them the time for patriotic outbursts was not yet ripe.

At last there appeared on both sides of the

wooded, hilly landscape, which looked peacefully
down from the stage on the seething mob below,
several men who looked perplexed, acting as though
they had forgotten how to stand and walk. Their
trousers seemed too short and they tried vainly to
adjust their drawn-up sleeves with crooked, awkward gestures of their arms.

The one who seemed to feel himself master of
the situation came to their rescue, escorted them to
the long table and looked to their seating which,
after many bows, was successfully accomplished.

The noise in the hall had subsided, only now and
then a brazen "Bravo" sounded in the pregnant stillness. The small table was also filled. Stiffly and
with much clatter a police lieutenant approached it,
followed by two sergeants, who, awaiting his signal,
sat down as he had done.

New arrivals came from behind the scenes, who,
to judge by their dress and demeanor, belonged to
the upper classes.

Fritz recognized Professor Pfeifferling whose
white short-cut beard was familiar to him; and suddenly Sieburth stood there too, a little more haggard
of form, a little thinner of cheek than he remembered him. The smile about the mouth seemed more
watchful, more bitter, and only the supernatural eyes
flickered as always from their oval shadowy hollows.

Fritz felt his heart pounding just as it had when
he stood before his door for the first time.

He had been in town two weeks, and had not brought himself to call on his former teacher for, although he realized that he owed him gratitude for much of what had developed in him and grown to knowledge, he also resented in many a dark hour the advice by which he had perhaps taken a false step. Even the image of that dear girl, always interwoven with recollections of him—"Woman and Thought," that was it—even this was not potent enough to draw him to that house.

When he saw Sieburth's name attached to the election proclamation of the Conservative party, he was more at sea than ever.

Here was something of a jeer lurking in ambush which humiliated his good faith and made him doubt the stability of the universe, for if this apostasy was possible, what remained on earth to which one could pin one's faith; in what conclusions, in what serious line of thought could one put confidence?

What took place during the beginning of the proceedings was utterly lost to Fritz's mind, which was in a daze. Everything was a confused murmur of words to him, so strongly did the sight of his once-worshiped teacher affect him.

A gong sounded. From the end of the table a man spoke introductory words which presaged the appearance of the speaker. Another, greeted by applause, stepped behind the desk, which was in the place usually occupied by the prompter's box. He

spoke with forceful tones, using wide, spreading gestures, and of all sorts of topics, of taxes, the pay-
ment of which did not hurt, of the tobacco monopoly
through which the poor would be supported, of accident insurance and rights of the crown, and the ex-
ploiting of the poor and weak such as Liberalism
demands.

"All humbug," thought Fritz, looking steadfastly
in the direction of Sieburth, who sat with downcast
eyes and fixed smile, busying himself by rolling a
scrap of paper into a ball.

Only when the opponents of the speaker voiced
their dissent by loud hallos did he look up hastily,
seeking to find the source of the commotion. He
paid no attention to the bravos, but every contradiction seemed of importance to him and worthy of
notice. He got out a stub of a pencil, and made
notes on his left cuff.

"He will speak later," thought Fritz, and awaited
the great moment with fear.

He could not determine the length of the candidate's speech; it seemed an eternity.

But at last he stepped back, wet with perspiration
from the effort, grasping the hands of his political
friends, while below in the hall applause and disap-
proval mingled for some minutes.

The man at the end of the table sounded the gong
and declared the discussion opened.

"Who wishes to speak?" he asked, looking down into the hall.

"I,—I,—here,—here," it sounded from all corners.

Arms were raised, names were called, and not understood. In angry confusion, all pushed forward.

For a few moments it seemed as though the merged masses would be transformed into a chaotic mob.

Fritz saw that the police lieutenant became restless, but in the meantime the presiding officer had managed to recover the mastery. He had discovered a familiar face among those who desired to speak, and called upon him by a forceful ringing of the gong.

Now gradually the noise lessened, and the new speaker was able to make himself heard.

An attorney, for that was what he was, and therefore capable of extemporaneous speech.

He began in a friendly and agreeable manner, apparently unwilling to stir up trouble, to substantiate his opposition.

"Our colleague has spoken of Bismarck's plans at great length, hardly calling the originator by name, however. That is strange and yet it isn't, for the man who is holding the position of major-domo in this young Hohenzollern Empire."

"What kind of a major?" came a shout from

below, but the speaker refrained from wasting time and opportunity in historic references. "This man has awakened the suspicions of all independently thinking people with his ideas for the public welfare."

"Well, we all think independently," shouted a voice accompanied by vociferous applause.

"I don't doubt that," he replied, "but the question is how long you will be able to enjoy this freedom of thought, for the Imperial Chancellor is planning for the destruction of the people's rights."

"Oh, impudence! Down from the platform!" sounded in Fritz's ears. The man with the sergeant's mustache had jumped up and cried, "That fellow must be put in jail," but the young artisans turned around and threatened him with clenched fists.

The gong of the presiding officer restored order.

In face of the provoked dissatisfaction the speaker found it expedient to proceed cautiously and continued, "I beg you, gentlemen, not to misunderstand me," he said. "I absolutely do not want you to believe that I question the good intentions of the Chancellor."

"Aha, well then, see how gracious!"

"Only I fear he has used wrong measures, and to add weight to my opinion, I will quote the words of a man who is wiser than I am, and whose judgment counts for more. A few days ago at a meeting in Berlin, the representative Lasker said—"

"Oh, another such Jew," a voice interjected, but the cry met with little favor, for at that time anti-Semitism was still in its swaddling clothes.

"He said the following," he resumed: "'When a man has outgrown his people, when he has risen above all the powers of cultural development, his final ambition is in his own person to overcome all difficulties. All the Cæsars perished through it. Only the suppression of freedom survived,' he said, but I cry, German citizens, defend your Kultur. Heed not the betraying Fata Morgana. Down with Bismarck's Cæsarian ambition."

A tremendous tumult arose. Like mad creatures, friends and enemies rose one against the other. The speaker, however, friendly and agreeable to the masses, as before, bowed towards the committee table and carefully climbed down the steps, which had no railing. A few flaming words more or less meant little to a good attorney. They were not spoken in bad part. He only served faithfully the cause which he espoused.

In Fritz's soul reigned supreme exaltation; that was how he himself felt, that was what Professor Sieburth had taught him to feel.

In that same moment, penetrating the sound of the gong, could be heard the announcement by the presiding officer that Professor Sieburth had the floor.

Behind Fritz were shouts, "Sit down, remain seated." Confused, he looked around and realized only then that the cries were directed at him.

Ashamed, he sat down again and saw with half an eye that there was something of a scuffle at the committee table, and that Sieburth, still keeping to his seat, was resisting coercive prodding and instigation.

This lasted four to five seconds, then he shruggingly assented and with drawn-in underlip went to the speaker's desk.

Then one heard the voice, the husky, faint voice with the gurgling bell-like resonance, which Fritz had not forgotten in the two years.

"Louder, louder," came cries from the wall at the back.

Then the hoarseness disappeared, and a high, forced, but far more audible tone rose from the straining throat.

What will he, what can he say, who formerly saw in Bismarck only the great destroyer?

And he said the following:

"What drives you gentlemen to such angry opposition as we just now saw displayed here, is not the man whose giant form is surrounded by strife; neither is it the domestic situation created by him: it is only the ghost of an era that is past which still stalks among us."

Churchlike quiet ensued. Probably each one felt

that with this speaker a new idea had been presented in the program in which they sought to find themselves.

"I would like to ask you," he continued, "does not the year '48 and the later conflict still seethe in your bones? As defender of the Government or revolutionist, as one or the other, you participated, and whoever was too young imbibed these sentiments with his mother's milk. And now here comes one who says, 'All that has lost its value; now there are other questions at issue; now there are new things to build.' In principle we all would agree with this; but the one sees it as a Democrat, the other as a Conservative, and neither knows that both no longer exist, that they are fused into one, and that the embodiment of that one is Bismarck."

Until now quiet had reigned; now the first contention arose.

"And what about the struggle against Rome?" one cried.

"And the anti-Socialist legislation?"

The first question did not disturb the calmness, for one was in a Protestant country, but the other provoked all the louder applause.

Sieburth did not allow himself to be disturbed by either.

"Gentlemen," he said, calmly, and moved as if to raise his transparent hand toward the light as he had always done in class. "Each period has its battles and must have, otherwise it stagnates; but look at your election programs, ours and those of the other side—by what petty things are they ruled?"

At the committee table were signs of uneasiness.

"Taxes and more taxes, tobacco monopoly and other petty things. At the most, such measures as contain protection for the workingman foreshadow higher goals. What does that mean, that in spite of all these artificial grounds for provocation, there are no serious causes for quarrel between citizens at the moment? And why not? Because by far the most of what democracy once wanted has been achieved by the reactionary Bismarck."

The opponents in the hall were surprised and murmured as Sieburth continued, "Well, gentlemen, have we not that for which you so ardently strove, the reunited German Empire? Have we not in this all the freedom which the active citizen requires— freedom of property, freedom of industry, freedom in the choice of a vocation, freedom to lead your life according to each individual taste, and even the Police Lieutenant there"—he pointed during general merriment to the table of the surveillant officer— "what more can he want of us but that we in all fairness understand one another?"

In Fritz's brain assent and contradiction were in turbulent commotion.

Only a little more and he would have been en- snared by the assured superiority of his former teacher, but he then again asked himself, "For that the change in my whole life, and for that the estrangement from all my merry companions? For that the dark loneliness, in the midst of the sparkling joy of youth; for that the tormenting distress of exclusion from association with the happy who sunned themselves in the radiance of the Fatherland?"

He still could not comprehend the change in Sieburth's convictions. He knew of old in what labyrinths his intellect was accustomed to travel and still waited for a sudden twist to carry him back to his former point of departure.

Sieburth continued, "As far as the new socialistic political plans of the Chancellor are concerned, I understand the objection of the Liberals fully. The freedom they espouse is a ticklish matter; it is a matter of 'Don't touch me, even if it benefits me,' and to perish in wretchedness and misery,—mark my words, —when it entails suffering for others, still seems a blessing, compared with that blessing which is showered upon me from above by the hand of a hated one in power."

An assenting laugh answered him. The scorn which hit the opponents of the Chancellor at their most vulnerable spot, even the simplest minds comprehended.

And Sieburth continued, "No one but Bismarck prepared the bed for the gentlemen of the Left from which they now send their mattress wisdom out into the world. Let them bring up their wooden cannons. [Bravo.] They don't frighten him nor those who are trying to understand his ideas. Even though they behave ever so belligerently, they are devilishly afraid of their own daring, and the blows they deal out are not those of a hero, at most those of an electric eel [great amusement], but even if we are adherents of Prince Bismarck, we do not necessarily sing his praises. We do not, therefore, build rice porridge walls for the destitute; nor do we guarantee a sinecure for every aging workman. To make the sun stand still forever, which the gentlemen from the other side would like to make a universal law—progressives they call themselves for that reason [much merriment]—seems to us rather undesirable, and to run about like ghosts as they do, equally so. [Quite right.] For that reason it is the duty of every one who wants actual progress, not to refuse to follow in the ranks of the man who is leading us to a new solidarity. [Bravo.] At least, it seems so to me, and will, perhaps, appear that way to all who place their patriotic feeling above the stupid idolatry of self."

If heretofore the cutting sharpness of the sentences hurled out in the shrill voice had held the opponents in a state of numbness, now that he had ended, together with frenzied applause, a storm of bitter opposition broke loose. The fists of many who jumped up were raised toward the stage, and toward the background groups formed themselves in which blows were offered to bring home conviction.

Fritz, too, started up. Hall, stage, people and lights, everything turned in circles before his eyes, and only one thought possessed him: "I'll not be made a fool of."

Gesticulating wildly, he called out his name to the platform. At the same time he discovered empty seats in front of him. Over two, three, four benches he leaped and suddenly stood in front of the steps which led up to the stage.

The police lieutenant had risen and held his helmet in his hand. If he put it on, it meant the adjournment of the meeting.

The presiding officer, who rang the bell convulsively, looked helplessly around for a speaker whose appearance as before would cause the tumult to cease, and seeing Fritz's tall form in front of the step, and thinking it not unlikely that he could pacify the crowd, he beckoned quickly to him to come up.

So it happened that the former Cheruscan, Fritz Kühne, found himself on the very spot where his teacher had just stood.

Only then he asked himself, "What is it I want here?"

But the noise had already subsided, for the tall young man up there presaged fresh excitement.

A member of the committee had stepped behind him and asked his name.

And immediately came the announcement of his name from the presiding officer there, "Attorney-at-Law Kühne has the floor."

And now all was quiet.

There was no turning back.

And already he heard his own voice saying, "If I may be permitted in spite of my youth to speak a few words, I am doing so because it so happens that I was a pupil of the gentleman who spoke before and because I know his original views most minutely."

Up to now all was well, but what now?

"Go on, go on," came cries from the hall.

Well, then, go on in God's name.

"So for that reason, gentlemen, I must say that everything that we have just heard cannot be meant very seriously for—for—for—"

"What then, go on," they screamed.

"For what I learned from him then was the exact opposite of what he has affirmed here."

"Oho!   Very interesting, more, more!"

"I have not meant to voice any reproach against him by this declaration."

"Really!"   "That isn't meant to be a reproach?" "Such an exposure should not be considered a reproach?"

The sounding of the gong again curbed the growing indignation.

"I believe on the contrary that—that—"

A pause.

"Well, what then, out with it!"

"That the mood of the moment—or perhaps—"

"Oh, what! Nonsense! Down from the platform! F-i-n-i-s-h!" A general cry cut off his words.

How he descended, in what manner he left the hall, remained a mystery to him. As he mingled unrecognized with the home-going crowd, his coat collar turned up, an inner voice called to him, "You miserable accuser," and another voice answered, "A renegade deserves nothing better. You had to do it."

CHAPTER XXVI

POISONED WEAPONS

FORTUNATELY the newspapers took no notice of the occurrence previously described. Apparently, in the general confusion, the appearance of the young man made no serious impression. Interruptions had quickly quashed his accusations or put them into the class of the ludicrous.

Unsought people who wished to assume an important rôle were to be found at all such gatherings whenever freedom of speech overstepped its bounds. One tolerated them and let them run. They were not even worth remembering.

But even though Sieburth tried to laugh off the affair, the worry over it would not subside.

Only once in his life had he taken a human being into his confidence and shown him the inmost recesses of his convictions, and that this one deviation was now being avenged made the revenge all the harder to bear, because his former pupil had no insight into the circumstances which had happened in the meantime, and had nothing on which to base his judgment except these outward indications of a characterless disloyalty.

Be that as it may, the matter had to be lived down and that became less difficult as no further consequences appeared to develop.

The election day came nearer.

Speeches, newspaper articles, tavern brawls, heightened the excitement immeasurably.

Up to the present the fight had been carried on with comparatively clean methods. Personal accusations and slanders were not brought out openly, even though they were made use of secretly.

Then it happened that out of the maelstrom of the Government party an announcement was thrown out into the world which left nothing to be desired or feared as to the depths of its depravity.

"A perjurer."

"Who is a perjurer?"

"The candidate of the United Liberals is a perjurer."

A circular which was distributed in the street without any police interference read something like that.

Why was this man who had grown gray in honor, and who had through the hateful machinations of the Government lost his position, suddenly become a perjurer?

Because he had manfully fought against certain infamous press ordinances, which had been put aside as unconstitutional; but this act was considered disloyal to his king to whom he had sworn fidelity.

That was his entire offense.

But on the streets the shouts continued. "A perjurer! The Liberal candidate is a perjurer!"

The leaders of the Government party turned shamed faces aside; even more, they denied all guilty knowledge. Only one of the newspapers of their side had the daring to defend this revilement.

In the Liberal camp justified indignation was brewing, but even among them were freebooters who were not averse to a little self-defilement.

An opposing circular appeared.

Expecting an immediate confiscation, the authors wisely kept their identity shrouded in mystery, not even having it printed at all, just drawn off the plate. Nevertheless, they succeeded in circulating it. It was clandestinely pressed into the hands of the people who streamed to the next election meeting. It lay on the tables of some taverns. It even found its way to some private houses in sealed envelopes delivered by letter carriers.

The contest as to which would carry off the palm of being most vulgar was decided in favor of the latest publication the moment it appeared.

There was not much in the way of evil that could be said of the candidate of the Government party; he had not embezzled funds of minors; neither had he accepted bribes at the hands of representatives of the opposing sides of lawsuits; at best he was a mis-

erable creature, who would have liked to take part
in fiscal affairs, and whose buttonhole was aching for
a government decoration.

There was nothing to be accomplished with such
inoffensiveness, the authors knew that well, and so
they directed their venomous outbursts particularly
against members of the electoral committee, whose
names were mentioned in the proclamation.

"A shabby crowd," Sieburth had said, but how
shabby he only fully realized when this circular
came into his hands. Everything of rubbish that
gossip could dig up was gathered together and
utilized.

As happens among small people, one had been
sentenced for assault, the second for patronage, the
third on account of disturbing the peace. Here it
was emphasized; furthermore, one was called a gam-
bler (the cheating implication was left to the imag-
ination), and many were branded as hopeless drunkards.

But Sieburth discovered more—discovered that
his own disgrace far outtrumped that of any of his
associates. Of him it read after the following
manner:

"As far as Professor Sieburth is concerned, we see
embodied in him a horrible example of a deserter
of his colors. Two years ago he took part in the
voting sessions of the Liberal party; two years ago
his democratic leanings were so decided that he

avoided the student celebration in the Kaiser's honor, and now he graces the table of the reactionaries. Is not that eloquent enough? But to make his disgusting desertion plain even to the blindest: During the last meeting launched by these gentlemen, a former pupil of his asserted that his erstwhile teacher had completely changed his views, as you change a shirt. We extend our best wishes to the Professor. May he succeed to the chair of Kant, which he is so ambitiously seeking, and which as a reward for his stanchness should not be long withheld even against the wishes of the faculty."

That was a blow, harder than any administered to him during his whole life. And yet it was only to be laughed at; all this was transitory and would evaporate when the heat of the election was dispelled.

Therefore, one must carry one's head higher than ever before and laugh,—just laugh.

He had the first opportunity to try out this resolution when, a few days later, he was invited to Pfeifferling's.

"Well, you have been pretty much pulled to pieces," said the old Privy Councilor, after his greeting.

"I have been washed in the gutter, and dried in the chimney," he replied, apparently in high spirits, "and whomever I don't please can leave me alone."

"That's right," praised the old one. "I believed that all my life, and in the end they came crawling."

And then they both laughed merrily.

But the wife of the Privy Councilor showed uneasiness in her demeanor and when she looked at her protégé, her eyes were anxiously questioning in their expression.

In the end the men decided that Sieburth should attend the next meeting, the last, just as he had done when all the trouble took place, and should he be attacked in any manner, he who had never been at a loss in fencing bouts, should send the trouble-seeker home with a bloody head.

But when the meeting came in due course, everything seemed forgotten. No combatant appeared, and the men of the committee, those who had been assailed as well as those who had been spared, acted, to say the least, as if they knew of nothing.

Two days later the election took place.

Result, thirteen thousand against two thousand; not mentioning the two hundred votes of the Social Democrats.

The thirteen thousand belonged to the opponents. A defeat the equal of this had never been known. For that reason robbers and murderers! One and all, even in the camp of the victorious, all were ashamed of the past events.

Now the fighters could return to peace, only one of them could not—he was hit too badly. For this he lacked the iron brow, and even laughter was of no avail.

But now to be equal to this situation, the new and worse one.

That the colleagues would not overlook his latest escapade, was certain, and if they had up to the present hesitated in definitely excluding him from occupying the chair of Kant, the recent happening would have furnished them with a plausible excuse. Words, such as were impudently broadcast in that circular, are not forgotten, even if you condemn them ten times over.

But surely one did not even condemn them, for they stated no more than every one was ready to believe, and what was always threatening to result when an objectionable candidate had influential friends in Berlin.

The term began, and the Assembly Room was filled once more.

If Sieburth thought that the cool curt intercourse, which had existed now unaltered for two years, would become still more frigid, he was greatly mistaken. Here and there even a certain suspicious assiduity became apparent, which showed that he was no longer regarded as unimportant.

Yes, since he had formed affiliations, he had become dangerous. More dangerous by all means than he had been as a hermit whose hatred was lost in infinite space.

But behind the sour-sweet friendliness lurked the enduring resolution not to let him rise again. And this knowledge he carried about with him day in and day out.

And even more crushing was the other knowledge, that he had gotten into an environment to which he stood in scornful opposition.

Different alliances crowded in on him, each more grotesque than the one before. War organizations invited him to speak at their festivities. The Provincial Union for Home Missions wished for just such a man as he, a non-theologian, to be active in its next appeal, and the League of Loyal State Officials, a name coined from the murky stream of the superfluous, invited him to membership. All kinds and conditions of office seekers, bigots and time servers, saw in him their helper and their friend.

When he on one occasion complained of this appraisal at Pfeifferling's, he only reaped derisive laughter.

"I'll admit they are fellows who are as objectionable as purgatives," said the old man, "but don't think for a moment that those who are ever ready to mount the barricades are any better. The principal thing is to belong somewhere. The wanderer who goes about alone on the village street is bayed at by the dogs."

But that was just the worst feature,—that "belonging." To free himself of that feeling and be himself again, was now the most urgent demand. It were better to cast reputation and position in jeopardy on the other side too than to continue to drag the chains into which thoughtless resentment had cast him.

And again began that life, which meant the nightly chase of women and late revelry, only conducted more carelessly, and succumbing altogether and more blindly to the urge of the moment.

Of women he soon found what he needed, and chance, the god of the seekers, was kind and gave lavishly of his bounty.

Two girls, black-eyed, frowzy-haired, regular fiery witches, flirted with him one evening as he passed the Town Theater close to the stage door, which led to the dressing rooms of the actors.

He asked them their reasons for standing there, and whether they were on the lookout for an adventure.

"Pah, there are no adventures to be had in this poor hole of a town."

Would they like to experience one, he asked.

"Gladly," they responded, "but only together." Hating and loving, and whatever else there was, they always indulged in jointly.

That was the beginning out of which many mad hours developed. They were chorus girls swept hither from the interior of the empire, partly of Slavic blood and of such an uncontrollable temperament that any restriction was an abomination to them. They romped around in his rooms like two newly caught wild-cats, and only quieted down when he pinched and choked them. This was a species of fun in which he had never before indulged and for which he dispensed with any other diversion of this kind for the time being.

Every evening of this sort of thing would have been too much; once or twice a week was quite enough. And so it happened that what might in polite language be called a "symposium" came into its own.

The three comrades were delighted. For a long time they had seen him but seldom and then only casually; now, he was more amenable, and would drink with them till morning.

But his line of thought, it seemed, had taken on a new face.

He who previously had found pleasure in negation, had become a panegyrist of life.

He brought topics on the tapis, which granted justification, even necessity, to the individual and to the social structure of every age. The historical became the organic and, when it was not, it was because the jest of concatenation had perverted it.

"The jest of concatenation" became a catchword in his mouth. What he meant by it was not clear. The others accepted it as a formula for something dark and incomprehensible, the explanation of which was for the present not forthcoming.

Yet he praised again and again that gracious gift

of God which was given man on his entrance into
the world. Happiness and suffering, fullness and
sparseness, glaring fever of personality and soft-
footed self-sacrifice, all radiated an equally harmo-
nious impression, and created the same glorification
of vital energy.

For a while his friends allowed this game, which
they regarded as half crazy, to go on.

One evening, however, as they sat more restless
than usual in the smoke-filled room, they resented it.

"You seem to have become one of the most saccharine of optimists," sneered the schoolmaster, who
was pretty much under the influence of drink.

The freethinking preacher added to this, "I
would not be surprised if you supplied the pious ones
of the land with a new theodicy."

"At any rate it sounded entirely different before
dinner," appended the law-candidate.

"It looks anyway as though you took a return
ticket for every theory you advance."

Sieburth twitched. Whether this was meant as an
insinuation or not, he felt himself painfully hit.
Till now no one had made reference to the vexations
which the election had brought him. As it seemed
hardly possible that they knew nothing, it had presumably been consideration which had prevented
mention of it, although this was usually not their
habit. He, himself, had not yet found the intellectual courage to put his finger on the wound.

So he answered casually even now, "I told you that my great optimism was not yet complete, perhaps now it is reaching fulfillment. Ideas exist for the purpose of being outgrown and as it happens every thought only exists by virtue of our dearth of thought, or it would soon go to pieces by its antithesis, so permit me this pleasure."

"The pleasure is all on our side," replied the preacher Möwes. "If we only knew how you expect to bring the present and the past under one hat, for there must be transitions or one would be crushed by one's own inconsistencies. I know that through my own experiences."

"Fear of contradiction only affects the weak-minded," replied Sieburth laughingly. "Moreover, there is one philosophy which is just to both parties: the philosophy of 'and still,' I would call it. By rights we should all have died long ago of the utter hopelessness of things; but you see in spite of nature, in spite of science, in spite of folly, in spite of the individual and universal death, we are here with our activities. Is not that enough to set up a robust optimism?"

The opponents were silenced. He once more had the victory on his side, and continued, "The old skeptics had thought that all out and reached this one result which is of value in the course of life; callousness, my friends, *apathia*, exemption from suffering, they called it, or better still, *psyches gale-*

notes, becalmed soul, and my becalmed soul says,
'To your health' to the storm in your beer glass."

With that he sucked up the red wine which stood
in the glass before him.

Weary and yet wide awake, he appeared, and the
horizontal furrows of his forehead almost met the
close-cropped scalp.

"And what about your theodicy?" asked Möwes
obstinately, who still would not acknowledge himself beaten. "You wanted to serve both parties
equally in the bigness of your heart so God, too,
must be justified accordingly."

"The only justification God can offer for what he
has done is that he is not present."

"Very well, let us say instead of God, 'Religion,'"
the other corrected himself.

"Religion, what is religion? The Christian religion when it dispenses its noblest? The overtax-
ing of sympathy; well, exercise your sympathy,
when the shark in shallow water flounders itself to
death. And we have in our ranks at the present time
ever so many of these estimable fellow sharks who
happen to be in difficulties. No, my friends, I know
something better than that. The religion of the
clenched fist; that is the right one. 'Securi adversus
homines, securi adversus deos,' as Tacitus says of the
Germans; with that you come pretty close to it, and
that will recur, and in that every one will be secure."

"Secure—in chaos," said Chmelnitzky.

"Secure—in death," added the preacher in answer.

"Very well then, in death," cried Sieburth. "What is there to it? One who has no prescription for life should quietly withdraw without looking back and without hope,—to be buried and forgotten. Blotted from the 'tablets of humanity'; for the 'deadest death is the most salutary,' a great connoisseur of life said, and this death of deaths, my friends, is the death I want to die some day."

His tavern associates looked at him in silent terror. The scorn they had vented on him had taken too horrible a turn to be continued.

"We wanted to talk of life and landed again on the subject of death," said Chmelnitzky.

"That seems to be our fate," added the minister, "and for that reason, I believe your new theory of the affirmation of life can't amount to much."

"I must always in such an instance think of the young girl who wore no drawers and whose skirts were blown up by the wind," laughed the candidate. " 'I am not looking at all,' said her embarrassed lover and did not look away at all."

"Right," commended Sieburth, "we are all such bashful lovers of death and from that arises life's negation which flourishes most opulently when it poses as the desire to live; so then quite unabashed, 'Long live death,' my friends."

With that, he raised his wineglass, but before he

could determine the attitude his companions would take toward this toast, a tall young man with dark expressive eyes and bearing several deep scars on drawn cheeks, came closer to the table and stood in front of Sieburth.

Disgruntled, he looked and recognized—Fritz Kühne.

"That is funny," he said, shaking in silent laughter. "You, no doubt, want to drink with us, young man."

When there was no answer, he became aware that the face of his former pupil was deathly pale and that his trembling lips battled with unspoken words.

Becoming serious, he arose and said, "What is it, what do you wish?"

"I must ask for forgiveness," stammered he, "for annoying you here. I was told that you were often to be found in this place."

"Well, and—"

"I cannot rid myself of the feeling that I was the means of bringing upon you severe mortification."

"I don't seem to remember, my dear sir."

"I did—at that election."

"Aha, how do you figure that out?—very interesting."

"Professor, if only I had reflected before on the unpleasantness which could arise from it; I am not ungrateful, nor am I an informer, really not, even though I did reproach myself with that term, I only—only—"

"Well, what did you only—"

"Because I no longer understood you—because I was—beside myself."

"Then you could have come to me. Didn't you find the way to my house at other times?"

"Yes, truly, I could have done that, and since then I tell myself that daily, and because I am sincerely sorry about the occurrence and don't want to carry that regret about with me any longer, I looked you up here, and—and—"

"But you did not trust yourself to come to me."

"No," crunched Fritz Kühne.

"This candor does you credit. Well, sit down; yes, yes, you are to sit down; we are being observed. We have both given enough public demonstrations for people's amusement."

He beckoned to the waitress who quickly brought a chair.

In the meantime he introduced the newcomer to his friends who had listened to the whispered conversation in astonishment.

"I am glad you came, I am glad for all our sakes. For what happened to me during that election hubbub has sat with us like a skeleton at our table. No one would touch upon it but now we will get rid of it."

And then he explained to the three that this was the former pupil whose intervention was perfidiously referred to in that ominous circular—they just nodded, knowing all about it.

"Yes, my friends, do I need to justify myself to you? It is the duty of a real man to turn his wrong actions into right, presupposing, of course, that I was in the wrong, and that will always remain a matter of doubt. Apropos, since we have arrived at the subject of 'Right,' that fellow who rules all of us outwardly and many of us even inwardly, has given a twist to this conception, which up to the present only one, Hobbes, with his 'Might is right,' had foreshadowed. Right becomes force and force becomes right. So he has worked havoc for twenty years and we look on and wonder and become enraged. Some cry 'Hallelujah,' and others scream 'Crucify,' and some cry both. What is your opinion, young man?"

"I, too, screamed both, but not simultaneously," replied Fritz Kühne.

"That is no stunt, dear fellow," laughed Sieburth, and the others laughed with him.

Fritz Kühne flushed red for he felt he had said something decidedly stupid. "I only mean," he tried to explain, "that one can't expect more of a person than that he should be honest with himself."

"What is honesty?" cried Sieburth. "The good Jonathan Swift said, 'Honesty is a pair of shoes

In spite of this, Fritz Kühne looked forward to the approaching hour with fear. How different it had been that other time when he with supple superiority had mastered the dangerous situation and later too, in the midst of all the dissoluteness, how he laughingly had wielded the scepter; and what a contrast to-day!

"Well, my friends," he raised the steaming tumbler out of which one usually drank grog, "our new member of the order, he who once left his fraternity because he was overfond of liberty and would not drink a toast to Bismarck (greatly misguided young man). If freedom takes the liberty of falling into the dirt, why should not the honest finder do with it what he likes? He gave us the German Empire and the German Parliament. Parliament, ha, ha, ha, Parliament. Do you know of what that reminds me? In Scotland the peasants— they are sly dogs!—when a cow cries for its calf that has been taken away, and acts obstinate and does not allow itself to be milked, they place a stuffed replica before it, and then it quickly submits. Thus our German cattle let him milk them not even noticing that their latest offspring is a delusion—and shouldn't we toast the fellow who can perform such a miracle? Why, of course! And to that harness you will now have to adjust yourself, young brother. That shall be your punishment, young brother. Or

do you also want to bolt this corps of avengers now?
Well then, bolt, bolt."

"I ask permission to speak," said Fritz Kühne.

"You have it, young brother."

"Herr Professor Sieburth was mistaken when he
thought drinking this toast would be a punishment
to me. Meanwhile I have become two years older
and, thanks to him, especially to him, I have become
correspondingly more mature. I have learned to see,
in the person I oppose, his value as a man and so
can easily drink to him."

The glasses clinked together dully, as thick water
glasses do, and the menacing drink gurgled down
their throats.

. . . .

It was towards four o'clock in the morning when
a quaint pair landed in front of the house where
Professor Sieburth lived and which had never before seen its most distinguished inmate in a similar
condition.

Staggering, stammering, muttering, and carefully
led by Fritz Kühne, he seemed willing to sit down
on the threshold.

The words he uttered were hardly understand-
able. "*Psyches galenotes*, do you know what that
means? The becalmed soul—is the meaning. Now
I have it, and the apathy, that is the great exemption
from suffering, if you must know it. *Psyches
galenotes* means the becalmed soul, it means,"—and

CHAPTER XXVII

HIS SAVIOR APPROACHES

WHILE Professor Sieburth constituted his life more and more along the lines of amusement, he had no idea that a young girl separated from him only by a wall was wearing away in anxious worry about him.

For almost two years now Helena Schimmelpfennig had lived next door to him, and yet he never met her except by mere chance.

The change in his attitude toward that household had begun on that Christmas eve, and the relations had become more distant and had led to an ever-widening estrangement.

He no longer went into the living room to pass an hour quietly smoking, and no one came to him from over there, unless their care of him required it, and when he knocked on the neighboring door, it would be only the mother's head which appeared in the crack of the door.

He would occasionally see the outline of Helena's form for a fraction of a second, and her brief thanks would reach him in answer to his greeting, but then the mother interposed, and she would immediately disappear.

He rarely met her on the street. Grown suddenly tall, flamingly blonde, the cheeks as though dipped in red, she would come in his direction, the eyes not knowing where to hide, the feet not knowing how to get by quickly enough; in fact, the whole girl would be so nonplused as to almost melt away in utter fear and confusion.

Once he had detained her and laughingly asked whether she was afraid of him, but she only stood there trembling, stammered a no, and ran away.

So he made no further effort to address her, but let her go her way, as one to whom there is no approach.

Had he known that outside of her studies, only one thought possessed her, her thought of him, his well-being, his work, his nobility, and—his sins, he would have made an effort to reëstablish cordial relations with her.

She was now nearing her nineteenth birthday, had been attending the upper classes of school for two years, and the teacher's examination loomed before her.

She knew her German poets, she could tell the story of every heroic deed, sacrifice, self-abnegation, worldly renunciation, courage in meeting death; in fact, most of the time-worn historic forms of grandeur of soul were as familiar to her as saying "Good day" or "Good evening."

But she also knew the snares with which the malice of the world beset particularly the best, the benefactors of the human race, and dragged them to perdition.

Socrates had drunk the poison potion, Christ was crucified, Huss died by fire, and if the present-day Apostles did not meet a similar fate, it was only because such punishments no longer existed.

But the executioners were on the watch even now and though they had not the power to torture and to mete out the death punishment to those whom they disliked, they could still deprive them of their reputation and ruin their career.

This would happen to Professor Sieburth too. Even now he was already in great danger. That circular had penetrated even to her. The vegetable dealer had given it to her mother to read. Socially he was already blacklisted, and now he was to perish politically as well.

But that was not all. The greatest vantage point was to be found in the life he led, and in the guarding of which secret he became more and more careless.

After that terrible night when the student, Fritz Kühne, had suddenly come to his assistance, he had brought the house into commotion several times over the manner of his homecoming; yes, and even what took place inside of his rooms was being noted.

And how could it be otherwise since those two tittering, squealing, screaming voices came pertly through the dividing wall, since behind it there was trilling and yodling and clucking, chirping and whistling, so that even the other tenants of the house were disturbed and disquieted.

And sure enough, one day the wife of the post-office clerk, who lived on the second floor, said to the mother, "What is the matter with your Professor? He has the jolly company of ladies now constantly."

The mother trembled with fear and anger.

"I'll have to give up the apartment: I'll have to give him notice. My good reputation and that of my daughter demand it," was her thought.

Helena knew that she would not do it anyway, for her mother loved him too well for that. She loved him so much that she wouldn't permit even her, her own daughter, in his presence.

She no longer sent her out of the room when his evening callers arrived. She was too grown up and wise for that now. Sometimes when she looked at her sideways, there was even an expression of secret triumph on her flabby and worn features.

Yes, Helena had grown big and clever. She had known for a long time what governed her mother's soul, what often made her hard and unjust, what gave her tone a guarded watchfulness; it was nothing more than jealousy.

And she had become just as guarded and watchful. She avoided mentioning the Professor's name and when this had to be, she infused so much of indifference, yes, even contempt into it, that her mother was quite satisfied.

But her mother's suspicions did not slumber in spite of it and if Helena had made the slightest attempt to minister to the Professor there would have been an open break.

Her anxiety about him meanwhile grew to the point of agony. She saw him exposed, defamed, deprived of his position and even perhaps accused and thrown into prison.

One afternoon, as she was walking along König-strasse with a friend, he came from the library and greeted her. She had hardly recovered from her confusion when her friend asked, "Who was that?"

She was so struck by the strangely eager tone of these whispered words that instead of answering she asked, "Why?"

"That man followed me the other evening. If a policeman had been in the vicinity, I would have called him for protection."

Helena hated her so at that moment that she was on the point of leaving her, but she gathered herself together and replied, "I don't know him well. I was once introduced to him, but have forgotten his name. If you are interested, I could inquire."

But in spite of all the bad and suspicious-sounding things she heard about him, it never entered her mind to honor or worship him any the less. What he did he was impelled to do because he was so

lonely and so world-hungry—world-hungry, her
mother used to say, when she still spoke openly
about him and when she had tried to explain his actions to her, stupid young thing, that she was then—
and because no ministering angel had come to guide
him back to the right path.

At least he would have to be warned, would have
to be shown in what dangerous proximity he stood
to the chasm.

How would it be to write him, write everything
which threatened to break her heart—in a disguised
handwriting, of course—and sign below, "An anonymous friend."

But shame upon her, one does not do such a thing.
Anonymous letters—only ordinary intriguing plot-
ters resort to such means to poison the minds of
the recipients.

Where was there a savior prepared to put his head
into the lion's mouth?

Yes, there was one: Fritz Kühne was again in
the neighborhood, but she did not know his address
and therefore the plan went for nothing.

But one day, as she was coming from class, deep
in thought, she saw him coming directly towards her,
grown much older than the two years would warrant,
manly, and full of quiet care in bearing and dress.

She did not even await his greeting.

"Mr. Kühne, oh, Mr. Kühne, how fortunate it
is that we meet!"

He lifted his hat and surprised joy shone in his look and smile.

"I was anxious to speak to you, I was really going to write to you. I had thought you might at some time or other call on the Professor and then drop in to see us, too, but you did not let us hear from you—not at all."

But then it occurred to her that her behavior might permit of misinterpretation, and shame almost overcame her—but she had to be brave now.

"That is, you must not believe—"

"No, no, I understand," he interrupted her. "The manner in which we met again that time furnishes enough food for consultation, and if I could have followed my inclination, I would have come long ago."

"Why didn't you do it?"

"Ah, Miss Helena, so much has happened between him and myself that—that—well, in short, I can't just simply go and call on him."

"And yet you must go to him, just you, for he always thought so much of you. You must tell him—"

Now she hesitated after all.

"What?" he asked.

"Do you remember when you brought that newspaper to him?"

"How could I have forgotten it?"

"You must act the same way now."

She could go no further.

They stood together in the center of the crowded sidewalk. Passers-by bumped into them and looked disapprovingly at them.

"Come over there," he said, pointing to the other side of the street. "It is emptier and we can walk a little way together undisturbed."

And as they went on their way, unmolested, he continued, "I know what you want of me, and I share your anxiety. What I lived through with him that night showed me conclusively how much he has changed. But I am fully ten years younger than he. I have not the privilege of reproaching him and even if I found the right angle of approach—as I said before, what took place between us has robbed me of the right to enter his life again unbidden. He must find a way to right the situation himself. Unless—"

He paused, and turning to the side, he looked fully and questioningly at her.

"Unless—what?" she stammered in confusion.

"Some one would have to come who would have a tempering influence on him, who—who— I can't express it, Miss Helena. At any rate I'm not the person suited for it, but as I observed that night, I can only say, things do not stand well with him."

A silence followed.

"And so the last hope has failed," she thought.

And then he asked about other things; how everything had been with her, how her mother was.

She gave short, preoccupied replies and soon said good-by.

Now she was again thrown altogether on her own resources, and once more the thought of writing to him suggested itself.

What one considers right, one must do openly and uprightly and must assume responsibility for even if one perishes through it. She made one rough draft after another, but every attempt to put into words what she felt so ardently failed by reason of the great respect she felt, which caused her hands to become numb.

Yes, if she could stand face to face with him, then the Holy Ghost would descend on her, then she could express the pleading and warning which looked impertinent or curious on paper; yes, and even if she were dumb, the very fact of having been driven to him would exert that tempering influence of which Fritz Kühne had spoken.

One evening when the two girls again filled the house with the sin of their presence and their shouting and trilling, and the mother sat, twitching at every sound and eating in the grief she felt, the resolution which must lead him back to self-communion became fixed in her mind.

What those two could do, she could do too. She had known the way for years,—up the dark stairway from the court to the door with the bell on the left,—even though she had not made use of it for a long time, for the mother no longer permitted her in his rooms, even during class hours, when his return seemed entirely out of the question.

Let him do with her as he would. With joy she would sacrifice herself. She would even gladly have died, if by so doing she could know he was saved.

The mother usually brought his supper to him at half past seven. Shortly after the three-quarters she called for the dishes, at the same time uncovering his bed, and after that did not go back again.

This was the time that Helena went two or three times a week to the Circle where she, together with some half-dozen companions in misery, went to be tutored in the prescribed knowledge necessary for laudable final results.

Her mother, who otherwise watched so assiduously, allowed her to depart these winter evenings, for she knew no danger threatened in that direction, and when she came home between ten and eleven there was not even a question as to what had happened.

These two or three hours were her own, and if at some time she were not to appear promptly at the Circle, there would be no reproaches.

If the possessors of the two voices spent one evening there, they usually remained away the next. The way was open then for her.

To-morrow then,—she would see him the very next day. She slept little that night. She ruminated over the speech she would make, and noted the passages particularly from which she expected telling results. She would appear to him like a priestess. The sublimity of her mission would be like a halo around her head, so that it would triumph over any feeling of lust or passion.

And even taking for granted that he would misunderstand her coming— But the vision halted before this possibility. No matter how one reflected there seemed no illuminating ray to dispel that darkness.

But she was thrilled by a vague and mysterious feeling of temptation.

The following day was filled with studies and housework. Then the evening drew on, and the great hour came nearer and nearer.

She hardly felt any fear. Everything was so fully settled, so fatefully ordained, but a glow arose which inflamed her body feverishly, making it feel prickly and tremulous.

Her mother did not notice that she redressed her hair, and put on her Sunday dress, when at other times, in the darkness, she wore her oldest; neither did she notice that her supper remained untouched; only when in going she left her brief-case behind, her mother noticed it and called her back, but there was no thought of suspicion.

The doorway leading to the court stood darkly open. It never was locked. There was nothing to tempt thieves within those bare walls of the rear of the house; the door leading to the back stairs was also only lightly closed at least until ten o'clock and if no one attended to it, often until morning.

Few went in and out during the evening; one would have to shout or whistle to be noticed.

And so towards half past eight Sieburth, who sat at his desk busy with progressive abstractions, utilizing these hours which were too early to be devoted to the tavern, was disturbed by the sudden clanging of the bell over his bedroom door.

He took the lamp and went to open the door.

There she stood, she who was at all times near to him, but worlds apart, going her innocent way. There she stood white as the lime on the wall, staring at him with big resolute eyes.

"Child, you, what are you doing here, what brings you; did something happen?"

She did not answer; she only stood and looked at him, and her nostrils quivered with short barely controlled breathing.

"Come in. Tell me, what is it?"

Then she obediently crossed the threshold, went through the bedroom and after he had placed the lamp on the desk, again stood motionless and staring.

"Did something happen to your mother? Did some other terrible thing happen? Tell me, do

the first to enter these four walls, who is not un-worthy of her."

And as he closed his eyes for half a second, it seemed to him as though Herma sat there in her stead and in his ears sounded her words, "Not to be does not hurt."

He stretched out his hands and softly stroked Helena's gloved right hand and vowed to himself, "I will keep her as I did that other."

She, however, was ashamed of the wrinkled and cracked leather and quickly took off the glove. Then she slowly turned the palm upward and when he stroked her again, it came quite of its own accord that her fingers clasped his.

"If I understand you correctly, child," he said, "you would like to know something from me as to the future direction your life should take."

"Yes," she said, eagerly, "that is it, oh, yes."

"But to decide that, I'd really have to be acquainted with you. I don't know you at all."

That was true, he did not know her. He had no conception of those qualities which were beautiful and most deep in her, and should not either.

"If—if—you would go to the trouble to really become acquainted with me," she said, hesitatingly.

"Does your mother know anything of your being here?"

She shook her head horrified.

"Then you could come again sometimes, couldn't you?"

"Oh, yes," she said, and mentioned the Circle, which she often attended evenings and which she could dispense with now and then.

But then suddenly she recalled the two voices which she had entirely forgotten together with all the other telltale sounds, which had penetrated to her ears.

"No, I can't," she said abruptly, starting up.

"What is the matter?" he said dismayed.

"I must go, and can't come again either; never again, oh, no, never again."

"But that is all so contradictory," he said reflectively; "there must be much behind all this which you must now tell me."

"No, I will not."

"Oh, yes, you will," he insisted, and then immediately he took hold of her upper arm and pushed her back to her place on the sofa. And this time he used force, against which there could be no resistance.

She began to cry out of sheer helplessness.

"I will wait until you have finished crying," he said, absolutely unmoved.

And because it was entirely useless, the tears ceased.

"Well?"

"How can I come again?" she wailed. "One always has to be afraid there will be other company."

A low whistle denoted his quick understanding.

"What do you know of any company I may have?"

"One hears plenty through the wall," she burst out. Now it was said, very differently from the manner in which she meant to say it, but it was out.

He rose, crossed the room twice, and then stood in front of her.

"I did not know that," he said, "and I'm sorry, sorrier than you can imagine at this moment."

Then he walked about again silently, and again stopped in front of her.

"How long have you noticed this?"

She shrugged her shoulders.

"Well?"

When he asked so tersely, no evasion and no concealment seemed possible.

"Oh, already for years," she stammered.

"Your mother too?"

"My mother even more so."

"Why didn't she caution me—caution me on your account?"

"One does not presume that far towards you."

"But you dared to do it."

Then, and only then, it became clear to her how unmaidenly and devoid of all shame her behavior had been and the tears began to flow again, but this time ceaselessly and she could not be quieted.

"If the wall is so indiscreet you'll have to restrain

yourself, and we must only whisper; otherwise your mother will notice even to-day who is here."

The fright made her limbs shudder with chills.

"Oh, my God, I had not thought of that," she whispered.

"Listen to me, my child," he said, lowering his voice also. "Your coming is a great gift sent by a kind Fate. How much it may mean to me, I can't judge to-day and it will not be inconsequential to you either, provided, of course, that you have confidence in me, so I ask you, will you come again if I promise that no one but you will cross this threshold?"

She did not answer, but he read all he desired in the gratefully sparkling smile.

"I want to make a confession to you," he continued. "It is two years since that Christmas when you stood here close the illuminated tree, and I wished myself what has happened for the first time to-day."

As she heard him speak, an agreeable numbness possessed her. She knew that since that Christmas night much had altered. Through what and why, she had never asked herself. But his wish swept all estrangement aside.

His wish and hers.

"How will it be this Christmas?" she asked.

"I will sit in my rooms and you in yours, as it was last year."

She shook her head violently. "No, this time it must be different. I'll make it possible. Yes, I will."

"And when will you come again?"

No, she had heard correctly, he had used the familiar form of address you would employ in speaking to your promised wife or sweetheart.

"Am I not already the same as a sweetheart?" she thought, for it was self-evident that she could not be his promised wife, for that she was too immature and unworthy.

If he had taken her in his arms, she would have been very happy, but he scarcely touched her hand as he asked, "Why don't you answer, my child?"

"I don't know, I don't k̲ anything; but why do you use the familiar p̲   co̲

She could not imagi̲   ars si̲ she found the courage to ask this questic̲ to ti̲ since everything seemed unreal and as in a dr̲am, this didn't matter either.

"Don't you wish it?" he asked in reply.

"Yes, oh, yes, always and always."

"But now you must go," he added.

"Yes, I must go," she echoed. She would have liked to stay much longer but to have admitted that would have created a horrible impression.

So she gladly permitted him to put on her coat, pulled her hat over the braids, and went on tiptoe to the door.

Only when she had reached the dark court did she remember that no time had been set for the next visit.

But she did not grieve over that.

"If he wants me, he will find a way to let me know," she thought, and it had been so lovely that another time was not urgent. One could live on the rapture of that one visit for the rest of one's life.

And she did not go to the Circle, but ran about for a little while in the unfrequented streets, to let the frosty air cool her glowing cheeks, but they glowed all the more.

The mother did not notice anything, not the remotest thing; she only said, "You are very early."

And Helena thought, "Then the next time I can stay with him longer."

The next day she was not altogether satisfied with her uncertainty, and the following day she became impatient, but to go to him uninvited as she had the first time was now impossible. That would be bold and forward. So she waited two more evenings, really went once to the Circle and became more and more unhappy.

"He surely had enough with once," she thought, "and does not want me—any more. I am really much too stupid."

But then through a fortunate coincidence, it happened (perhaps she had been a little instrumental), that they met on Rossgärtner Square, just as they had at the time when that horrid friend was walking with her.

She was somewhat frightened, but not to the same extent as she had been on former occasions.

He doffed his hat profoundly and without pausing the least bit, he said, almost to himself, "This evening."

Well, then to-night!

And she went. She did not need to ring much, the door opened by itself, and he stood behind it in the dark and admitted her. She did not say a word, nor did he, everything was a matter of course as if previously planned. She laid the brief-case on top of his books, then she took off her coat and unpinned her hat from her hair, thinking all the while to herself, "I am quite at home here."

"Now the gloves too," he said.

And when her hands were bare, he took them between his, warming them, and looked kindly into her face.

Then he asked, "If I had not asked you, you probably would not have come again?"

"Perhaps I would have," she replied, and felt with shame that she was looking at him quite coquettishly, and coquetry was considered something very reprehensible by the correct young ladies of the Circle.

"To-day, we must find a better place, for now we'll have to get to work."

"Work?" she asked, surprised and almost fright-ened. She had not thought of such a thing.

"Certainly," he said. "I dare not steal away your study hours, for if you should fail in your examina-tions it would be my fault."

He was right in this respect. She had been so carried away by this hope of seeing him again that she had not given such a possibility a thought.

He placed a chair for her in front of the round table, at which he usually took his meals, and sat opposite her. A wide space which precluded all familiarity lay between them.

And then she emptied her brief-case, and showed him to-day's assignments. In history the current subject was the Crusades; in geography, Central America; besides that there was an English exercise, and all kinds of precepts of pedagogy.

At the word "pedagogy" a smile hovered about his mouth which conveyed to her how unfitted he thought her to cope with this subject. But she de-fended herself against this insinuation. "In three months I may, perhaps, have to teach and I'll have to know the principles according to which to train my pupils."

"According to which you'll have to train your pupils. Certainly, certainly," he agreed, and as-sumed an earnest look.

And when it came to hearing her, and the dates of the Crusades were recited, the most amusing thing happened—she knew everything far better than he did. He had only a very hazy impression about the siege of Damascus in 1148 and he absolutely had no recollection of the Norman king, Roger of Sicily.

But he was not a bit ashamed and laughed heartily and she, if possible, laughed even more. Nothing merrier could have been imagined.

Then suddenly he pointed to the dividing wall and both were quiet.

In the enumeration of the States of Central America, he did not attempt to know their boundaries and capitals but merely looked at the textbook just as her mother did.

He knew absolutely nothing about the rules of English syntax but read the text as fluently as German.

"The next time you will find me better informed," he said, on parting; "even your teachers prepare themselves as a rule, and it will be very good for me to learn all of that over again."

Yes, he gave himself much trouble with her and she thanked him with eyes that had a tendency to tears.

In fact, the tears came much too often; she always asked herself why, for she had never been so happy before in her life.

The December weeks passed.

All at once she was the best in her class, to the

astonishment of all who listened when she gave vent to her store of knowledge.

Now and then she went to the Circle, but it was scarcely necessary for she already knew what was taken up there. She did it principally as a matter of shrewdness, for if she stayed away altogether, her mother might accidentally hear of it.

And suddenly, it was Christmas eve.

It was tacitly agreed, that he should appear with his gifts as usual at twilight, to take possession of his own presents from his neighbors. Since two years back, there had been no thought of a common celebration.

Instead mother and daughter would go to church between six and eight o'clock when services for the poor were conducted. Helena had been singing in the church choir for the last year and a half.

The darkness approached, and the tree stood trimmed as usual but her mother would not leave the room. Evidently she was afraid of missing the moment of the Professor's entrance.

Then he came.

He carried his packages under his arm, as always, but in Helena's soul it sang, "he, he," and "mine, mine." And her secret was suspended, like the Star of Bethlehem over the Earth.

And he brought her much too much, overwhelmingly much. There were books and there was a picture and a pen-wiper, because some time ago she had come to him with stained fingers. How they had laughed together while washing them.

What she had made for him was hardly worthy of mention; two tidies for the arms of the sofa, no more. There had been no time for embroidery.

And as she handed him the poor little rags, stammering timidly, she noticed that her mother did not take her eyes off his face, regarding him with suspicious and envious impatience.

She scarcely took any notice of the gifts with which he presented her, and they were generous and beautiful. A night clock of alabaster and bronze sparkling from within, and similar things, but all this meant nothing to her. Only one thing was of importance to her: the terms upon which he and her daughter appeared to associate.

God be thanked that this agony was of short duration.

He went, and the tree which stood already trimmed, did not receive a glance.

But she had another. No one knew about that. It was carefully hidden away among the rubbish in the garret. It was not big. One could take it on one's arm and carry it to him.

But you had to be daring, and if you were the plan would succeed.

The time to go to church came; the bestowal of

gifts was not to take place until after their return.

The mother silently put on her coat. She did the same.

The walk also passed in silence. Oh, it was quite disagreeable, but any conversation appropriate to Christmas eve would have been hypocritical, so she was resigned.

They parted in front of the church door. Helena ran up the stairs. The mother remained below with the congregation, which was not numerous. Even the religious had no inclination to sit in the empty church, which was dark and cold.

In front of the organ, the choir were ranged around their leader in groups, men and women, young and old. They greeted one another, took the music sheets and the candles, which, fastened on iron stands, gave only the most meager light.

The leader rapidly gave some final directions so that they would fall in properly. Helena, whose sense of harmony was most exact, was placed in the front row because some ladies of importance, who usually had this position, were missing. But she fought the honor valiantly.

"I have a bad cold," she said, "and I'm afraid I'll disgrace you."

So he left her in her usual place, close to the tenors who were always most zealous.

The Christmas tree was lit, the leader gave them

the key—C. E. G. C.—and they were ready to begin.

"From Heaven high, from where I hail—"
Now she had to be quick.

"I beg pardon, Mr. Lemke," she said, chokingly, to the master of the high C, whose regular occupation it was to measure muslin and cloth, "I'm getting a coughing spell," and with that she slid into the dark background.

Running all the way she reached home and went up to the attic.

There it stood, there it stood, the sweet little tree of which Mamma had no inkling.

Should she light it here or with him?

No, she would light it here, which she did.

And so it happened that Sieburth, leaning on both elbows, staring in front of him uncertain what to do with the loneliness of this evening, heard a dragging and a rustling in front of his door which slowly opened and admitted a luminous cone which, brushing against the frame of the door, entered the room, showing behind it a laughing triumphant face.

"Helena, you!"

He jumped up quickly to lock the door behind her and when he turned around, the tree already stood on top of the writing desk, and she who had brought it hung jubilantly around his neck saying, "You, you, you!"

She too had finally come to employ the familiar pronoun.

He had not given her permission; he had not pleaded for it.

Neither had he begged for the kiss, which, like the wing of a fluttering bird, barely touched his lips.

"She gives all she has," he thought, and took her tenderly in his arms.

"I will keep her holy," he vowed to-day too.

And she was gone!

CHAPTER XXVIII

IDYL

SIEBURTH could not himself account for what had taken place within him since Helena's first visit.

After he had swept the two chorus girls out of his life, he breathed a sigh of relief. That sense of order, long neglected, demanded its rights.

At last he again felt at peace with his innermost self.

Each day, out of work and weariness, recollections and anticipations, he made a new holiday.

He gave no thought to that which might happen, that which probably was bound to come.

She came—she was there—and everything else sank into oblivion.

Sometimes four or five days would elapse before he would see her.

He did not have an actual longing for her. The feeling of knowing that she was so near him, that in order to see her he need only step outside when the opposite door opened, gave him the sensation of being surrounded by her even if she did not come to him for a long time.

He no longer desired any other society.

He even neglected his old boon companions.

Everything about which they had joked and argued seemed stale and absurd.

The irregular verbs supplied more important knowledge than all the pride of ignorance.

A surreptitious sense of triumph governed his mood and he appeared to those who observed him in the Assembly Room to be standing on heights so joyous that he did not seem ever to have been a tolerated outcast.

On the point as to whether or not he loved her, he was quite clear. She glided through his life as a game, as light, as an innocent luxury. Child she might be to him, but never sweetheart.

And he did not lust after her—not that he was blind to the gentle curves of her developing womanliness nor to the unconscious temptations that went out from her to him. Often enough a thrill occasioned by the fragrance of her proximity passed through him, but her absolute frankness destroyed even the smallest vestige of desire.

Accustomed to sensual pleasures, he sought appeasement where his soul neither lost nor gained anything and from where no bridge of phantasy stretched to the heights which now smilingly filled his life.

Her outburst of joy on Christmas eve had affected him violently. This unrestrained giving of self was too good a thing to be passed over without having been touched by it.

But what subsequently happened calmed him
again.

At first she did not come at all. She did not come
for fully a week, and when on New Year's eve she
appeared at last, she seemed as strange and distant
as if his own behavior had been responsible for making her subdued and cold.

It was still early in the evening and the twilight
had scarcely merged with the night.

Silently she put a little flower pot down before
him and swallowed and looked to one side.

"What is it, child?"

"I must go right away again."

"Have I done anything to offend you?"

"I must go at once."

She stuck to this even when he took off her coat
and loosened the cap in her hair.

"Why haven't you been here for such a long
time?"

"First of all, because on account of the holidays
there was no Circle, and anyway,—I can't come any
more."

"Why not?"

"I won't tell you."

"Helena," he remonstrated, "friends have a duty
toward one another; besides which you know you
can't have any secrets from me, so resign yourself
and confess what is wrong with you."

"I only came because probably to-morrow—New Year's day—I won't see you."

"Why not? Since a long time back we've been accustomed to my bringing you my New Year's Wishes each New Year's morning and I expect to do so to-morrow too."

"But I won't be there. I can't stand this business with Mamma any longer—this watching and spying . . . particularly since I know that it's justified and that I am downright bad."

"But that is still no reason for you to be unfair to me too."

"I won't be good any more. I won't be bad any more—I won't be anything at all—I will—I—"

She got no further. She turned to the window and swallowed.

"If I didn't know, my child," he said, "that just at this moment you are distressed, I wouldn't urge the question . . . but why do you want to destroy our dear happy times together? Has something about it annoyed you? Or are you bored?"

"I've become irksome to *you!* I bore *you!* Yes, indeed I do. I behaved so stupidly that Christmas eve that you must despise me. . . . Yes, I'm sure you must. That sort of thing can never be righted and so I prefer not to come at all any more."

"You talk in riddles, my child. I don't know what you mean."

Suddenly she turned on him, entrapped liar that he was!

"You know perfectly well. You are only acting as if you didn't. I was forward. I used the familiar pronoun in addressing you."

"I hope that in the future you'll always do so."

The shock drove her back to the window and it didn't even make her feel glad.

"No, no, no. How could I dare to do that, dear Professor? Don't ask it of me. It isn't proper for me to do it. I haven't deserved it."

"Come away from the window, child. One could readily recognize your silhouette."

"Mother is upstairs," she whispered. And because it was still so early to-day and her mother might for some reason or other come in, he hurried to the hall door and locked it, which never happened at any other time. Then she willingly allowed herself to be led in. To-day, naturally enough, there was no work to be done, so she was again able to sit down in the corner of the sofa. He remained standing before her and stroked her hair.

"Will you say it now?" he asked.

She looked up at him in blissful devotion.

"Yes," she breathed, and hid her head against the tail of his coat.

He thought: "How blessed I am in being granted such a moment!"

Then he sat down beside her, took her hand in his

and talked over with her how to adjust their lives
during the New Year.

"Mamma hasn't as yet the slightest intimation,"
she told him. "On two occasions when I came home
she even said to me, 'To-day there was company
with him again' and she does that purposely—in
order to disgust me with you."

He corrected her, insisting on the informal address.

"I can't," she pleaded. But when he insisted
upon it, she leaned her head against his shoulder
and whispered it.

"I dare not kiss her," he thought, "or else it will
take the usual course."

He put his arms only about her shoulders and
so they sat for a long time and discussed the
future.

In the beginning of March she would have to take
her examinations and toward Easter she would have
finished, and if he would give her his help until then,
she would have nothing to fear. Even now she was
in advance of all the others. She did not know
where all of the knowledge came from. And all
the thoughts! He surely had implanted them in
her.

And while she told him all of these things, he
thought naïvely, "God in Heaven, do not let me be
unworthy of this child."

Then as he became conscious of his silent prayer

and laughed out loud, she asked, timidly, "Did I say something silly?"

"No, no, I am the guilty one," he said, and stroked her cheeks.

She could not stay long to-day. She had told her mother she was just going to drop in on a friend so she would have to be home to supper.

Again they wished each other every possible happiness.

"And may the coming year bring you the Big Achievement for which we are all waiting," she added.

She did not dare to call this "Big Achievement" by name and he thought, "I have never been further removed from it than I am at this moment."

.   .   .   .

The holiday season passed and with it the elation it had brought with it.

Work reigned during the hours she gave him and no suggestion of tenderness crept in.

It was simply impossible for her to accustom herself to using the familiar pronoun in addressing him. If the little word slipped out inadvertently, which rarely happened, she had a shock, and her eyes pleaded for forgiveness, and when he insisted upon correcting her when she employed the polite form, she involuntarily leaned towards him as if the familiar form could only be used with a caress, but almost in the same instant, she started back again.

He never tried to turn this impulse to his advantage and this interlude was quickly choked off by her eagerness in her studies.

It was principally in mathematics and languages that she needed his assistance, and "pedagogy" held sway as something lofty and hardly to be touched upon over and above all other subjects. In this actual practice had already been required of her and she had always been very timid when she had appeared before a class.

She complained most about the difficulties the religious instruction gave her, but when he asked for the reason, she would not give him the desired information.

This seemed all the more remarkable since she had long been wax in his hands and hardly ever ventured to contradict him.

So he stopped urging the matter and decided not to miss a more favorable moment, which soon came.

One evening—during the second week in January—she seemed peculiarly preoccupied and absent-minded.

"What is it? What has gone wrong again?"

"Oh, people can torment you so," she replied.

"Who torments you?"

"They turn one inside out. They prowl about the most secret recesses. To have consideration— that doesn't exist for them."

"But who?"

"The teachers."

"And what do they want of you?"

She hesitated and swallowed hard.

"We are to write an essay on the subject of 'Profession of Faith.' In it I am to confess my religious convictions to them. I can't and won't do that. That seems like committing robbery against my soul."

"Why?" he said assuagingly. "Any one who amounts to anything must be willing to admit what he is. All great men have acknowledged their faith. Every idea, every doctrine is a confession; mine too, or ought to be."

"Ought to be?" she asked, surprised.

"Ought to be, or must be, either way," he replied, and swallowed the bitterness which arose.

"But to consign to paper everything you scarcely will admit to yourself, what I have not even confided to you and perhaps have to read to the class,—surely that should not be expected."

"Then you simply have to use a few phrases which are to be found in every catechism."

"I can't do that either. I don't make use of any phrases. All this is too holy for such uses."

"Holy is what you hold holy," he replied. "You are holy to me."

At this she took his hand from across the table, and kissed it. He jumped up, stood beside her, stroking her hair.

"Just stay as you are, and look elsewhere, then perhaps I can speak of it."

"I am waiting to hear," he replied.

"Well, then," she began, "it is written, 'God is love.' Then all love comes from him, not? The more fervently we love, the more we belong to him. But there are different kinds of love. There is sinful love too. From where does that originate, from the devil? That is nonsense. I don't believe in that. Well, then, if you cherish a sinful love, then either you have fallen from grace—but that is not necessary; one can be quite pious withal—or sinful love is also one of God's commandments; something he imposes upon us as a trial, or as a purge, isn't that so?"

"That might be," he assented.

"And so one has to strive," she continued, "to convert all the love within one into love of one's fellow man, for that is the highest. Then you become more nearly like God and rest like a child in his lap. Isn't that a thought to inspire happiness, and don't you feel something of a similar nature? Please say yes."

"In this moment I feel it," he said, in smiling solemnity.

Now she sought his gaze, her head on which his hand still rested, thrown back, her eyes, radiant with ecstasy, fixed upon him.

"Oh, that is good, then we are united as one in God."

"As one in God," he repeated, recalling that farewell hour in which that other, plighted to death, had united him too with her in such a mystic union, but here a young warm life blossomed towards him.

And then he kissed her, kissed her directly on the mouth, as one who comes into his own, that same mouth which on Christmas eve had lightly touched his as an augury of future blessings.

It was as though she had been felled by a blow. She crawled, she sank into a heap, her head almost touching her knees.

"Helena, come to!   Helena!"

She did not move.

"You should not have done it, just when you were thinking of Herma," he said to himself.

Then, as he gently stroked her head, she raised herself, threw her arms about his neck and pillowing her head on his neck, she lay as if sleeping, her long and deep warm breath over him.

It seemed as though a long painful tension had dissolved itself into a blessed tranquillity.

But he thought of Herma.

She had not communicated with him again.

Had she remained in her new home?   Or had she gone to the mountains?   Even in Pfeifferling's house no one had ever spoken of her again.

What had she said? "Once more I will write to you."

And when he had asked her when that would be, her answer had been, "At the proper time."

A painful premonition arose in him, that the time was near.

"As long as she is still on Earth, I belong to her," he thought.

Instead he was playing with this child.

But was it play?

Keeping holy, being worthy. He had not been chary with high-sounding promises before her or himself. Now she hung about his neck, and the rest would follow. Again, however, he pulled himself together. "Get up, dear," he said. "We must think of serious things. We have done no work to-day."

With wide, confused eyes, she looked at him. "Yes," she said obediently, "we have not done any work to-day."

But the work did not amount to much.

In sweet limpness, she sat seeking a support for her trembling limbs. Her glance hung on him and yet was turned inward as though searching for the undiscoverable. "United in God," he thought, in aching scorn. And then he bade her go home.

stopped in front of him, as he was going home. "Listen, colleague, I have something superfine that is about to take place to tell you about. The Junkers of the city and surrounding country have organized a new body calling itself, 'Prussia Casino,' and on the eighteenth are celebrating 'Coronation Day,' namely, the one of 1701. That something else happened in Versailles on that day, does not concern them. Splendid blockheads! There are unique figures among them, about which documents could be written. I have secured invitations for us and you've got to come along. No, no, you can't decline, and why should you? Looking on costs nothing, and experience knows no intellectual barriers. You will require full dress, white tie, and all your decorations. Have you any?"

Yes, these he had, he replied. The orders had once been conferred upon him by the titled father of his pupil, but he had never worn them.

"Very well, then, at quarter of six, you call for me. At six the feast starts and by eight, with the help of God, we'll all be drunk. Those fellows, though, can stand a lot. People like us will have to be careful."

At the appointed time, he was at Pfeifferling's. That gentleman was fairly covered with emblems. "But you, too, cut a fine figure, colleague. I had never heard anything of your court connections. Those will stand you in good stead to-day."

And then they started.

The organization had as yet no home of its own. The banquet hall of the hotel "Deutsches Haus" was brilliantly illuminated by hundreds of lights. The table in the form of a horseshoe completely filled it.

The President, a magnate, whose name had historic significance, had a high official at either side.

Many uniforms were in evidence, and many a full dress which did not deny its origin from Berlin or even London, but the rustic swallow tail predominated.

Some appeared to have celebrated previously, for on this or that shirt front there were suspicious-looking red wine spots.

Sieburth found his place card at one of the side wings as befitted his middle-class mediocrity.

Round about him were heads which appeared as though hewn by an ax out of hard wood. They were elongated, rust-brown with parted squarely trimmed beards, and one among them had grayish strands hanging to his massive shoulders.

He introduced himself to the right and left and to those on the opposite side of the table.

Titled, high-sounding names rattled and tumbled over him.

The caviar came, grayish black mounds, surrounded by glittering ice walls. A reddish blond Southern wine sought to warm the souls and yet formality prevailed. Even in drinking toasts, adherence to decorum and dignity prevailed. Even those who were on familiar terms indulged in stiff and formal gestures.

In the beginning Sieburth had no one to talk to. The men seemed kindly disposed towards him, for glasses were lifted also towards him, but they didn't quite venture to approach him.

Observingly, he noted the developing conversations, as for instance:

"My last team of four, yes, that I sold to Sicily."

"Good business?"

"Oh, it's more for prestige. I had to have the box-car they sent re-padded, and had to provide attendants. Then there was the commission for the Jew. Taking all that into consideration, the buttermilk eventually turns into curds."

"Well, there'll be bits of butter in it just the same."

"Only it's the other fellow who spreads it."

"An unfamiliar world," Sieburth thought.

"How is your game-preserve this year?"

"Not much. I just managed to keep the deer through the winter, but the fawns were nabbed by the foxes. I've taken on hazel-hens from Sweden, and have ordered pheasants. Well, we'll see."

"A foreign world," thought Sieburth.

His neighbor on the right, a rough-hewn clumsy

fellow with freshly powdered frost-bitten nose and clear hunter's gaze, at last turned to him.

"You're a professor,—what kind of a professor?"

"I teach philosophy."

"Honest-to-goodness philosophy? I thought that did not exist any more. I thought that species of humanity died out with our countryman, Immanuel Kant."

"There's some truth in that," replied Sieburth. "I and my kind are only the worms that feast on his corpse."

"Say, you," laughed his neighbor warningly. "Don't poke fun at us, we are simple men. What do we know of you heaven-gazers?"

The man with the Wotan's beard, who sat diagonally opposite him, bowed courteously in his direction. "Sieburth is your name if I heard correctly?" he asked with a light, gladsome, childish voice, which was hardly in keeping with the powerful exterior.

Sieburth confirmed the query.

"I have known of you for a long time. My nephew is a student here. Do you know what they call you?"

"Well?"

"The Mad Professor, they call you. I always imagined you must be some sort of queer creature and now I find in you a nice, modest young man who is entirely inoffensive. How did you get that reputation—are you at least a good drinker?"

"I fear I can't compete with you gentlemen."

"That would be a pity, but it remains to be found out. You know we are companions in misery. They used to call me 'Madcap Willy' long ago. Now I'm terribly sensible but to earn such a nickname isn't easy. One must have perpetrated lots of tricks. Once, when the Wartensteiners overlooked me at their Shrovetide Ball, for good reasons of course, I, in a rage, bought out a butcher shop and sent out invitations to all the dogs in town for breakfast, furnishing ivory cards, gold-lettered. Another time when gypsies were in town, I borrowed the clothes from one, blacked up—at that time I did not wear a beard—and went out fortune telling with the women. You have no idea all the things I told my friends,—and many a woman friend I took into my confidence. I made their hair stand on end, and not one recognized me. The worst of it was, I couldn't get rid of an itch for a long time. I almost emptied the old apothecary shop, and thought I'd have to make a trip to Persia for the genuine powder. Yes, indeed. And when I called for my bride to escort her to the altar, I rode right up the stairs to her virginal door on my horse. The parents screamed, 'It's a disgrace,' and threatened to call the marriage off, but the dear thing attired in veil and wreath got right on the saddle with me and we rode down again right into the throng. When one has had such an agreeable experience and one's wife afterward says, 'Now, Willy, that's enough,' then one stops it; then all that happened is like a myth out of a previous century,—but I'm only talking about myself. What foolish escapades can you boast of, fellow madman?"

For the moment Sieburth was relieved of the necessity of answering, for the presiding officer tapped on his glass as a signal for the first toast, which was in honor of the King.

"We are all good Germans," he said in the regimental tone which he had retained from his erstwhile Potsdam garrison. "It goes without saying that we are, but in our innermost beings we are even better Prussians. [Bravo!] The German Reich is a new structure which has still to achieve solidity. Prussia, however, is the *Rocher de bronze* on which the nations for many centuries have broken their teeth, and if Germany should ever fall to pieces, Prussia would continue to exist, and we, as vassals to the Prussian king, would gather about him, and shed our last drop of blood on the field of battle. [Wild applause.] I would like to meet the enemy that could defeat us. Let them come, all of them, even though they were as numerous as the grains of sand at the seashore. [Bravo!] There was one who deserved to be, but unfortunately was no Prussian, for he was born one and a half thousand years too soon. I refer to the Visigoth Alaric, who when threatened with the desperate battles of the Romans said, laughingly,

'The denser the grass, the easier the mowing,' and thus would we speak if our King needed us, and so to him, our Prussian King, we drink this toast."

Tempestuous cheers filled the hall. The band began to play, "I am a Prussian, do you know my colors?" and Sieburth, stirred by this mass enthusiasm, thought, "If this were a feast of Gothic warriors, their speeches and cheers would not be much different." Only that now there reigned peace and plenty, fragrant wine gleamed in crystal glasses, and jovial, obese figures were enjoying it.

A string of waiters now came and served ragout of turkey from shining silver platters.

Sieburth looked around for Pfeifferling, for in this sea of strange faces he longed for a familiar one, but he caught no glimpse of him.

His neighbor on the left, with whom there had been no interchange of civilities, now turned to him and asked to have the cruet stand handed to him. "I must lick a little salt, for I am not in the least thirsty," he said.

Sieburth did his bidding and looked at him.

He saw a glorious, hoary head, wide almond-shaped eyes, which were placed obliquely in relation to the narrow-bridged nose, a greenish gray mustache which fell in the shape of the letter S on the beaked chin. The neck skin was still firm but the forehead showed furrowed ridges.

He embodied a hero of German legend just as

the other over there represented an image of Wotan. "Blessed land," thought Sieburth, "where such types grow untended."

"Why do you look at me, Professor?" asked his neighbor. "Do you want to use me as an object of study?"

"I only took delight in observing your head," confessed Sieburth.

"Yes, head, head, of what use is a head if there's nothing in it, and the pockets even more so, if there's nothing in them. It is with me, dear man, as with the poet Shakespeare's King Lear,—I owned two fine estates, two beautiful daughters and two noble sons-in-law. You think, if you don't live with one you live with the other; both need your advice. And what is the final result,—that I can't live with either. Now I go from one to the other of my relatives like an old rogue who curries favors by teasing and card tricks. But I always make a wide circle around my former possessions. Still I'll always remain the old baron, even though I die like a beggar on the road."

Sieburth surveyed the speaker in astonishment. There was no sign of intoxication. Out of the sheer joy in honesty he revealed to the stranger the shame of his old age, which he doubtless hid timidly from his friends.

"I have lived among such people for years without realizing it," thought Sieburth.

The wine now began to make itself felt around him. The veining in the cheeks glowed, the eyes displayed twinkling lights, and a scream could be heard here and there above the babbling hubbub of voices.

Two speakers were still able to make themselves heard.

The one greeted the guests, the other thanked in their name. The latter, a representative of the Provincial Government, asked that the President be excused as he was unexpectedly called to Berlin and to his inexpressible sorrow was forced to absent himself to-day from this festivity.

"The high official has gone after a new honor," was the laughing comment, for the festivity of the Prussian Order was bound up with this coronation feast.

The reason for the general amusement penetrated to the speaking Privy Councilor, who smiled a crabbed smile tinged with humility, and poorly concealed his joy in emphasizing the small shortcomings of a superior; but on the whole he pretended ignorance.

The toasts to the hosts were heard only faintly.

Then the real jollification began.

Although the menu of many courses was by no means completed, any number of the slightly tipsy guests would no longer contain themselves in their seats. A general wandering, greeting and toasting began.

Behind Sieburth's King Lear, a young broad-shouldered Hun with true blue eyes, the color of the heavens, appeared and stretched both arms out to him invitingly.

"What, Father, you here too!"

"My dear fellow, my boy."

And patting each other's backs, they were clasped breast to breast.

But what they said to each other did not take long, and when the neighbor was again seated, he said in an eager manner to Sieburth, "That was one of the two scamps. The other I'll no doubt soon hug to my heart too. What does one not do for one's family?"

In the meantime one of those sitting opposite, a short, stocky, curly-bearded farmer, who up to now had been quietly eating, awoke to life, and with swinging gestures and emphatic tones, directed attention to himself.

"I only tell you one thing," he called across the table. "We landholders are much too modest. The good child who asks for nothing gets nothing. Therefore, cry, cry, cry again. What the others do, doesn't concern us. Let every one on earth look after his own interests. These new-fangled complaints of the poor and disinherited, and the fellows with the pretty phrases, when they start in with their—with their—what shall I say?"

"If I understand you aright," interjected Sieburth dryly, "you mean to say that there is no feeling so fell and low as fellow feeling."

An embarrassed expression appeared on the faces around the speaker who continued reflectively, "Even if not quite so drastic, there is some truth in it, for in looking out for myself I look out for others. My people enjoy good times. I've got all the women-folks on my side. When I go among my farm-hands I am, so to say, in the midst of my family. Look at me, strong stock, yes, and so I'll always have sturdy servants."

All laughed and one asked, "What does your pastor say to this infant industry?"

"As though I would ask his permission! Pastors, of all people! Well, yes, religion has to be,—naturally,—but to bow to God,—no, we don't do that by a long shot nor do we rinse our mouths with altar wine. On Good Friday—well, yes, perhaps to be an example to people, but there it stops. In my church I have a master choir in front of whom I had a red silk drapery hung. I can stand the jabbering for five minutes, and then I'm finished. Then it's a nap for me till the Amen is reached. But if any one would accuse me of not being a good Christian, I'd hand him one so that he'd spin around like a top;

then there'd be an awful stench, and then everything would be all right."

Again there was merry laughter; only the homeless baron seemed to feel ashamed.

"You'd better not listen to that gabber, Professor," he said.

"Why shouldn't he listen?" cried the berated one. "He is one of us, otherwise he wouldn't be sitting here. His name also appeared in the electoral manifesto of those Königsberg citizens, who made such fools of themselves. So he belongs doubly to us, though as far as politics is concerned, I say, it's a dirty business. To get oneself elected and go to Berlin, never, my friends. It smells of Jews there, even when you arrive at the station."

Noisy assent greeted him and he continued, "But we have people who want to eat at 'Dressel's' daily and that they call politics; others can't hold ink and others again when they see a footrest can't withstand the temptation of clambering up on it, and then they talk till their mouths have fringes and they choke on their own spittle. If I hear the word 'politics,' it's enough. Let Bismarck look out for that, I say. He understands his job and gets well paid for it, very nicely, I read. I wish I had as much."

"If I were you, I would not have so much confidence in Bismarck," said the man with the Wotan beard. "He has beaten us about the ears many a time."

"He has, he has, I know, but that was not serious, and in the meantime he has made up for that ten times over. No, even Bismarck can't afford to offend us and no one can. What would the King or, say, the Kaiser be without our support? We fight his battles, we hold office, attend to his elections. We oil his Jews, we put the bit into the mouths of his people, and should the Democrats but raise their heads—"

"They won't," all in the circle cried.

Only the man with the Wotan beard expressed some disbelief. "You underestimate the intellectual strength of the middle classes. Look at the city elections. Did any of us think in the fall that we would see such a whipping? Our Professor could sing a song about that, and you in particular, my friend, sputtered like the end of a tallow candle. Now for a change, let us listen to something worthwhile. Will you, Professor, give us your impression?"

They all agreed on this, and Sieburth, whether he would or no, was forced to speak. He began.

"On one point, I must agree with you, gentlemen. You need have no fear of Democracy. Although we read much in history of the power it has exerted, it has actually never existed and never will. It presupposes a sameness of viewpoint which it can never accomplish. Where we see her at the helm, it has only been a transition stage or, to be more exact, a preliminary to the formation of a new Aristocracy."

"Where is it to come from? How will it look? Are we to be exterminated?"

These were the questions pouring in on him.

"It is not easy to answer," he continued, "for what appears necessary to us, historically speaking, develops, if examined closely, out of the variegation of circumstance. In most cases war was responsible for the creation of Aristocrats. For example, the conquest of England by the Normans, about which we learned in school. A battle won, and to-day's Lordships were born, but there can be peaceful conquests as well. Imagine a people, by comparison degenerate, although richer in intelligence, richer in comprehension of the future, richer in adaptability, who are settling in Germany among us."

"Well, and we should allow that?" one cried.

"We would give them a wide berth and they'd soon go their way," another commented.

"Or who *have* settled," corrected Sieburth, "so that they cannot be kept out. In the beginning they were tolerated as harmless and useful, then as they developed strength, defamed and apparently scorned, they understood how to gradually make themselves indispensable. With sure instinct, they lean on every factor of power which is hostile or at least unfavorable to the ruling Aristocracy. They bring the catchword of their opponents into general usage, and create a new conscience for the masses. They reach

aroma of fresh Havanas encircled with blue clouds those who remained, while they were engaged in hot debates.

They went into a dim adjoining room where liqueurs stood on round tables. Waiters offered the coffee in a secretive manner. Its almost poisonous strength was denoted by a pungent sourish odor.

"Here he is, my dear Privy Councilor," said Pfeifferling, as he drew the man who had appeared as the representative of the President from a group who surrounded him, all of whom talked excitedly at the same time.

A small, stiff, typical bureaucrat he was, unaffected by the general loud humor resulting from drinking. "I am glad to meet you," he said, lightly giving Sieburth a thin, tired hand. "I am only here accidentally, for my official duties rarely bring me into contact with these rural gentlemen. Shall we be seated?"

They seated themselves at a small round table and the Privy Councilor continued in a cool, deliberate manner, "You know the President is a sort of intermediary between the University and the Ministry of Education. And I should say that to act as a sort of mediator in this instance is not quite my—my—duty. I must not assume that, but rather let us call it a privilege, so I would like to ask you, have you ever by any chance taken occasion to introduce yourself to the officials in the Ministry of Education?"

"On the contrary, I always avoided doing that," replied Sieburth.

"Yes, yes, well, yes, I can well understand your reasons and I'm far removed from disapproving of them. Disapprobation would be beyond my province."

"What may he want of me?" Sieburth asked himself.

"But as a fortunate coincidence has thrown us together socially, I would like to, quite privately, of course, give you this advice. When you are in Berlin again at some time taking a walk 'Unter den Linden,' do not pass the portal behind which certain authoritative officials make their headquarters. There is one in particular, the Assistant Minister Kürschner who is remarkably well informed on personalities and would, no doubt, be interested in you too if you gave him the opportunity of meeting you. Yes, I can even divulge to you that he wishes it. By the way, how do you like it here in this part of the country?"

"Very much, Privy Councilor."

"Well, you see, there are gentlemen who always want to be elsewhere, and if you can't spare them, places have to be created elsewhere and that causes disturbance. Isn't that so? And as I remarked before, I'm glad you like it here, and to repeat, I was extraordinarily glad to make your acquaintance."

With that he rose, registered another handshake

and then turned to a man who was lying in wait for him.

Pfeifferling, who, sucking his cigar, had listened quietly, nudged him with his elbow and said exuberantly, "You see, colleague, the scheme works. If you don't interfere, the whole faculty can stand on their heads, and everything will still turn out just as we wish. Good night, colleague."

Sieburth was alone.

As he felt even less at home in these surroundings than before, he knew nothing better to do than seek his way out.

The man with the Wotan's beard came towards him with a genial smile, and only now as he stood revealed before him in his splendid physique, Sieburth realized that he was the typical Grand Seignior.

"It is really nice, Professor, to see you again. You certainly threw a firebrand into our barn before. You should have seen the consternation after you left. Unfortunately, there is much of truth in what you said, but just the same you played the very deuce with us, and it seems to me one can be a 'mad fellow' without giving the dogs banquets and riding to a wedding up the stairs and getting lice from the gypsies, and assuredly your kind of madness is of more value. If sometime you would like to visit me, you would be granting my wife and myself a great favor. We have more than a shrug of the shoulders for the higher things, as you remarked before, but I believe we are starving without being aware of it."

His parting handshake hurt, but the hurt was gratifying.

"This world of the primitive is rich and wonderful," thought Sieburth, stepping into the street, "but what have I to do with it?" And was he to be tied to it for the rest of his life?

CHAPTER XXX

A LEGACY

"Davos, January 20, 188–

"My dear Friend,

"Now let us say good-by! Perhaps the time for it has not quite come. Who can know? But the thought that one day my hand will no longer be able to hold the pen and that I will have to take my leave of you without a farewell, torments me in the long fever-fraught nights.

"I often try to unravel the actual reason for our relationship but the further this narrow earthly existence recedes from me the less I seem to comprehend it. Sometimes I have a vague sense of predestination, but fate, natural necessity, destiny and urge of the soul—those are only words which clarify nothing.

"I cannot withhold from you the fact that you cause me much concern. You have been forced into a path which ends in darkness, and I seek and seek for a companion for you who would be a support to you in your wanderings, the support for which I was too weak.

"I confess, too, that in earlier days when my

238

wishes were still mortal, I was jealous of a certain woman whose name was often coupled with yours. Now I realize that I was wrong and in order to make restitution for this fault, I'll attempt to direct your future to the extent of which my strength will allow.

"One denies the dying nothing and so I beg you to go to Cilly Wendland and tell her that I sent you. I am writing her at the same time and am pleading your cause. I know that she was sincerely devoted to you and whatever may have come between you and caused you to separate, the wish of the departed will unite you, if such a union may still be consummated. I have not met her often, but whenever we met we gave each other a silent embrace for we knew or felt what we had in common.

"My dear friend, I would like to speak long and fully. My heart is full of you, and as concerns myself I feel I should like to pour everything out before you so that nothing remains in me that is not wholly yours; but after all, each one must carry his own burden, but it is hard to bear—so hard!

"Dear one, I grasp your white womanlike hand, which at first I so disliked, and cling to it tightly, and so you will be with me in my death's agony. Good-by!

"HERMA."

This letter, sealed, lay enclosed in another which read:

"My dear Professor,

"At the request of my dear patient who has since gone to God, I am to tell you how the end came.

"She died, endowed with the consolation of our holy religion, with faith in the mercy of our Lord and Redeemer and in the earnest belief that in the Hereafter she would be united with those she loved. In her last days she requested me to transmit many greetings which I herewith do in the performance of this duty. Her passing was not easy but she bore her suffering with fortitude, her gaze directed on the cross which I held before her and which received her last breath.

"God grant her Everlasting Peace. And to us, as well.

"Sister Erminolda."

This message penetrated to the very marrow of his being. He had not believed it possible for him to experience such deep emotion.

He raved about his room half the nights through; he talked with her, he wanted to be with her and say the things that had still been left unsaid. He felt a never-ending guilt as far as she was concerned, and there remained a never-ending quantity that wanted expiation.

Had he known her whereabouts, there might have been a thousand possibilities whereby he might have been spiritually close to her. Many a fear-filled hour he might have made more bearable. He could have dispelled much of the horror of loneliness.

He exaggerated his feeling of oneness with the poor departed to such an extent that only now he seemed to himself abandoned and lost.

Helena came and went at the usual hours but she meant little to him at this time. He considered himself unjust and ungrateful, but he could not conceal from himself the fact that at times she was irksome to him.

Had he been able to make a confidante of her, many things would have been easier. As things were, he saw her non-understanding and fearful gaze directed at him and exercised the greatest care to behave with perfect equanimity and not again to stray from the path of the helpful friend. Besides, it was essential that he give himself elbow room in order that he be worthy of the legacy which had entered his life as a sacred duty. He allowed a week to elapse and then wrote the following letter:

"DEAR MADAM,

"I take courage and address these lines to you because a dear departed friend requested that I should. As I understand it, you are already prepared for my knock at your door. If you should, willingly or unwillingly, be inclined to grant me the interview which was the wish of the one who has passed on, will you be good enough to send me your kind message? That the granting of this plea will be in response to any wish of mine will be far from my thoughts.

"In constant devotion,
"DR. SIEBURTH."

To which he received the following reply:

"MY DEAR PROFESSOR,

"Your dear departed friend who, I am proud to acknowledge, was also mine even though I never dared to express my feelings to her, honored me with a wish with which I must not hesitate to comply. I have, therefore, asked my parents to consent to your visiting me and will expect you to-morrow afternoon at four o'clock.

"In lasting esteem,
"CILLY WENDLAND."

The scornful laughter, which even in these days of agony of soul was ever ready to leap to his throat, rose victoriously within him.

Only gradually did he realize that the reply was more cordial than the message he had sent. Each word could have been examined under a microscope without finding in it a single cause for reproach.

At five o'clock his class on "The Contributions of Philosophy to the Religious Enlightenment of Mankind," which was a constant source of secret joy to him, began.

And this interview could easily result in the same thing. It would have to be over in an hour.

Undoubtedly the entire family had studied the lecture bulletin in order to set a time limit in advance.

But then he recalled the times he had roamed through the wooded shores with Cilly, as a friend and companion, when she took such a fervent interest in his work and brought her heart to him in the palms of her hands.

No, scorn had no place here—a gnashing of the teeth, perhaps, because of his forfeited happiness.

The dearly loved one who wanted to conjure it back even beyond the grave! . . .

The next afternoon, with a high hat and gloves, he went on his way to the house at which he often had been a welcome guest.

The best room—called "salon" here too, which the maid who received him made a point of emphasizing—opened out before him, and the steamy atmosphere created by the heating apparatus that had just been put into action, greeted him. Good oil paintings—a Knaus, an Oswald Achenbach that he had once admired—hung on the walls. Papa's big practice allowed of this otherwise unheard-of sumptuousness.

Brocaded easy-chairs and small gilt ones stood about and two freezing rubber trees, with drooping leathery leaves, stood in front of the windows.

Five minutes to wait—and then she appeared at the side door.

Her blondness was dimmed by the twilight, but her eyes looked as clear and as good as ever.

That her welcome smacked of embarrassment was not surprising for he, too, was almost abashed.

Her hand was stretched toward him and after a cursory grasp immediately withdrawn. Then she offered him a chair and sat stiffly on the formal sofa.

"I deeply regret that such a sad event brings us together."

He, too, regretted it deeply.

"Do you know any further details about the death of our friend?"

The "our" was so sharply emphasized that it sounded deliberate, but had she said "your" it might have conveyed an insinuation.

He told her what had been in the letter written by the nursing convent sister.

"It troubles me," he added, "that she should have been annoyed with this traditional farewell ceremonial. She considered herself a good Catholic, but she was religious after her own fashion."

"Aren't we all religious after our own fashion?" she replied. "I'm convinced that you are too."

These commonplaces annoyed him and he began to feel vindictive.

"The thing has presented a difficulty for me for some time past," he said, smilingly, "but now I've provided myself with a small house organ on which I sometimes play and which gently trains me to piety."

"Where did you get that?" she asked with interest.

"The teachers' seminary supplied me," he answered dryly.

"Oh!" she said, in wonderment, and because she did not want to seem inquisitive, she dropped the subject.

"How is your work progressing?" she asked instead. "Did you complete 'The Three Stages of Ethics'?"

"Every one, it seems," he said, "has a soft spot in his heart, and you have laid a kindly finger on mine."

"I'm glad of that," she said, it seemed to him with an air of aloofness.

"And like Minerva," he continued, "whom you always bring to my mind in my recollections, you immediately embark on the road to philosophy."

She smiled courteously and he continued: "Yes, 'The Three Stages of Ethics' has been completed and other things besides which, I hope, will also not fail to raise the desired storm of disapprobation."

Her eyes grew vacant with sadness.

"And you still hesitate about publishing them?"

"Business sense is the better half of science," he replied. "You will only find me in the market when I can dispose of my wares without loss."

Her sadness turned to amazement. Her eyes became cold and searching.

An indeterminate rage trembled within him.

"In the meantime you are consistently industrious?" she asked.

"You have to be," he answered, "if you don't want to lose entire control of your life. Only one's hands grow callous easily, and as a scholar, that is not confined to one's hands."

She winced a little and he enjoyed every drop of venom even if directed against himself.

She hesitated to continue. Evidently she was searching for a subject which would create less occasion for bitter retort.

"Have you been to the shore since we were at Rauschen together?" she asked.

"No," he answered, "that is the time during which one meets the fewest inhabitants of Königsberg in town and so I remain here as a recreation."

Now she knew of no other alternative.

"That was not friendly, Professor," she said openly, "not in regard to our good town, and I'm afraid also not towards me."

"Since I must reckon with being deprived of your friendliness for all time, my dear young lady, it does not matter about mine."

She was silent. Perhaps she was debating how best to discontinue the conversation when a saving thought came to her.

"Excuse me but it is getting dark," she said, rising. "I should like to send for a lamp."

He rose at the same time and she went to the center door to pull the tassel which formed the end of a beaded bell rope suspended from the ceiling.

The lamp must have been standing in readiness, for it was brought in immediately.

The silver blondness of her curly hair gleamed towards him as familiarly as in those other days and he recalled that moment when, on a sudden impulse, she had pulled out a few strands to tie up a bunch of flowers for him.

"It cannot go on like this," he thought in involuntary gratitude. "I must adopt a different attitude." And when they were seated again he began: "Your reproof before, my dear young lady, was entirely justified but it's been such a long time since we've seen each other that we couldn't quite get our bearings immediately. And in the meantime so high a wall has erected itself between us that I don't know whether it be advisable to stretch a hand over it."

"I believe that I stretched mine towards you," she replied.

"Forgive me if I was so blind as not to notice it."

"Would I have asked you to come here otherwise?"

"One always fulfills the wishes of the departed."

"But not if it means setting a trap for a former friend."

A short pause. Then he said slowly, "How is your esteemed mother?"

She was startled. Undoubtedly the question of whether or not he was to be welcomed by the mistress of the house had caused much discussion. To say nothing of the Privy Councilor, who was, of course, having his office hours at this time.

As long as the parents kept their distance, a resumption of friendly relations was out of the question.

"My mother greatly regrets her inability to make her appearance," she said, growing very pale. "She has not been well for some time and that is the reason we do nothing socially."

"Aha," he thought, "that means, you will never be invited again."

And his anger at being cast out raged in him more turbulently than ever.

But one thing seemed clear: This dear girl was still fond of him.

There she sat before him, lofty, pure, and soulful.

One redeeming word—and perhaps she would be his again.

Oh, no, not by a good deal. For she was surrounded on all sides by the whole coterie who were hostile to him and who stretched a thousand spears in his direction. She would have to be extracted from this atmosphere, and whether she would possess the courage to go with him was more than doubtful.

This hedging was senseless. She knew the object of his visit as well as he did, and for that reason, there were only two possibilities: either one spoke one's mind openly on the subject which, according to Herma's wish, should be the outcome of this meeting, or one took one's hat and went on one's way. He chose the latter.

Getting up, he said, "I am happy, my dear young lady, to be able to take your newly animated image with me. When I rearrange my intellectual rags, it will be a genuine stimulus to me to remember your kind interest."

She stood in the shadow away from the lamp. You could read nothing in her features, but her voice quivered faintly as she said, "May I convey a greeting to my fiancé from you?"

A shock went through him nevertheless.

"Conceited fool, you!" he cried to himself.

"Pardon me," he said, self-possessed. "I live so apart from your world that I had no inkling; otherwise, I would not have failed . . ."

"It isn't public yet," she interrupted.

"May I ask who . . ."

"It is Dr. Müller, an instructor in the University of Leipzig, a close colleague of yours."

"Oh, the one who wrote about . . ."

Müller, Müller, Müller. What was it that he had . . . Oh, yes! Correct!

CHAPTER XXXI

EVEN IDYLS GO UP IN FLAMES

IF Sieburth believed that this was a magic formula which would prevent Helena from coming, he was very much mistaken.

As she sat opposite him, he recognized immediately that something new of an even more depressing nature was about to crash about him.

Never before had she been able to summon the courage to ask him a question but to-day she ventured to break the silence.

"You have been so strange for some time now— so entirely detached—and to-day even more so than usual . . . please, tell me what is wrong."

A laughing refusal was his reply.

But she persisted in her demand.

"I know perfectly well that I can't be anything to you," she pleaded, "that I am a silly thing, that I— but perhaps it will be my luck to be able to do you some good."

"My dear child," he said, "we are here to teach and to learn. What goes beyond those limits is smugglers' booty. Let us keep to our program. That will be the best thing for both of us."

She resigned herself with a sigh.

And he threw himself so eagerly over her books that there was no possibility for any further digression.

But her concern held him as in a vise and her scrutinizing look did not leave his face—until finally he could no longer endure it.

"I see that you worry over me far too much," he said; "when you are more advanced in years, many troubles will come to you, too. For the time being, let your examinations suffice and don't ask me to load my troubles upon you, in addition. We'll stop for to-day."

She rose silently and gathered her notes and books together. She did not seem hurt, but fear dwelt in her eyes.

As she left, he kissed her on the forehead which she offered him obediently, and with that he considered her dismissed.

The night which followed these evening hours shaped up badly. One torment gave rise to another, self-reproach changed to defiance, and defiance changed to self-reproach.

Herma's legacy had terminated in desecration, her desire turned into ridicule. With a sure insight she had recognized the only way to reconciliation with the world about him and with himself. Now it all lay buried forever.

And in spite of everything, he had done the right thing. He had remained true to himself and the

"The door to the closet is closed and the door from it to my room too. And I've put out the lamp. And even if she came in, she would think I had gone to sleep. I always pass her bed and she never wakes up."

He looked at the clock. It pointed to three.

"Do you often work so late?"

"I've already told you: As long as I know you are up, I stay up too. I don't think I could go to sleep before, and I only pack up my books when I no longer hear a sound."

"But you will break down, my child, and when the examinations come, you will be so tired that you will fail."

"I'll never get tired as long as you are not tired."

"Then from now on, I will go to bed before twelve."

"That will be very good for your health and for mine too."

And saying that she even laughed.

"Is there any sense in sitting up so late?" he asked. "What, for example, did you do to-day?"

"To-day I didn't accomplish much—only listened at the wall, but now I feel myself growing very calm, for I see that you are calmer too."

"Yes," he said, "we won't think about it at all any more; otherwise it will come back again."

"But I can stay here with you a little while, can't I?"

"If there really is no danger as to your mother."

"No, no, really not; otherwise I would have— Oh, to-day, nothing really mattered. But mother won't wake up, really not."

With that she leaned back and blinked at him from beneath lowered lids.

"You are getting sleepy, child," he admonished her, "you had better go home."

"No, not go home," she pleaded.

"Then at least stretch yourself out."

"Yes, if I may!"

And she lifted the lower part of her body upon the sofa but as the robe had pushed itself up and bared feet and ankles up to the calf of the leg, she bashfully tried to pull down the hem. But she couldn't manage it and was about to get up and smooth down the misplaced folds.

"Don't go to so much trouble, child," he said, "for I know all about you."

All at once she was fully aroused. "You know all about me! What do you mean by that?" Bolt upright she sat staring at him with fear-filled eyes.

"Yes, indeed, you don't need to be so prudish."

And then he told her how he had come to ask her mother to wake him early (he had quickly thought of that excuse) and had seen her lying on that same robe without a chemise on.

"And I delighted in the sight, because you are so beautiful."

"How will she take it?" he wondered in agitated curiosity. She was not frightened, nor was she ashamed. She sat there motionless and only her expression changed. Fear changed to horror; out of horror grew pleading, and from the pleading developed a flame so tenderly wild, which seemed to transform her love and yielding to a positive longing so that he actually feared for her now.

"You shouldn't have done that," he said to himself; "in that way you may disturb the girl's peace of mind."

But it was done and could not be recalled, so nothing remained but to play the innocent or perhaps the esthete who finds woman and statue one and the same.

But she felt more honestly than he. She glided forward from her position on the sofa until her body sank to the floor in a kneeling position and then with a cry which was a sob and at the same time a sound of exultation, she buried her head in his lap.

He stroked the now entirely loosened strands of hair and thought at the same time, "Once another knelt before me like this."

Only that the other had begged to be spared and this one wanted to be taken.

But she would have to be spared just as his dead beloved had been at that time; otherwise her life would be blighted and he alone to blame.

"You must go, darling," he stressed.

But she did not move.

Only when he removed her head from his knees by force did she herself help him to get her to stand erect on her two feet.

And even now the strange, ghostlike expression that indicated the awakening of the woman in her, glowed from her eyes.

Placing his hand on her shoulder, he led her to the door. She dragged herself along like one mortally wounded. Then suddenly, with clicking teeth, she flung her lips on his and ran out of the room.

"I have started something pretty," he thought, looking after her retreating figure. She and Herma and Cilly turned in a mad whirl through his brain.

In that September night there had been three of them just as there had been to-day; only that Helena had stepped into Marion's place.

"This one, at least, will not try to ruin me," he compared, "but I, on the other hand, will bring her trouble."

No, that must not be!

"Rather than that, I would marry her." And with this sacrificial idea he went to rest.

The following evenings he conducted himself as quietly as a mouse and went to bed earlier to ensure her a complete rest.

With impatience, he awaited the day when, by agreement, she had been accustomed to come, but she stayed away and the next time too.

According to his calculations the examinations must have started. All the more urgent her need to come to him, for what had happened and what she could look forward to ought to be discussed.

Now and again he pressed his ear against the wall to listen for a sign of life from her. A clearing of the throat and a rustling was all that occasionally penetrated to him.

One evening he decided to give a signal of three knocks but there was no answer. The next evening it was the same.

Then he tried a more forceful measure; went out on the landing and laid siege to the door which led to the living room on the other side.

The keyhole shone brightly, but no matter how much he looked, he could not discover a trace of her.

"I'll have to risk it," he thought, and pushed the knob lightly.

The door yielded—the tumbling of a chair; a weary cry, and she stood before him, her cheeks red and with panting breath.

"Come," he said, retreating to his door, and she came. Robbed of every volition, like a sleep-walker, she walked behind him. She even forgot to close her door. He did it for her, jumping in front of her, and closed his own too.

There she stood, tall, taller than he, motionless in fright and surrender.

The red flowered robe fell in straight folds, her

chin was buried in a white woolen shawl and her hair streamed like rays over her breast.

"Why don't you come any more?"

"I can't."

"Why can't you?"

Then the flame which had terrified and yet made him happy gleamed again in her eyes, but no word passed her lips.

"I must speak to you—must know how everything is going with you. Can you meet me to-morrow afternoon at five at the Königstor?"

"Yes."

"Good night."

"Good night."

He drew her forehead down to his mouth and she was gone.

The opposite door closed almost noiselessly, then all was still.

The mother did not wake up to-day either.

The next afternoon he found her waiting in front of the dark arch of the gate.

Her everyday dress had grown too short for her and her hands stretched too far out of the sleeves of her coat. The fur cap covered the hair that curled on her forehead, and as on the day before the chin hid itself in the pathetic woolen shawl.

She greeted him with a faint smile. She seemed hurt and wounded and in urgent need of encouragement.

"How much time have you, dear?"

"As much as I want. Mother thinks that I'm with Irmela."

That was the friend at whose house the Circle was in the habit of meeting.

"Then we will take a long walk."

"If you like."

With that they walked along the walls towards the alder bush which was swinging its pale lavender catkins in the frosty wind.

But the frost could no longer do much damage. It caressed the cheeks as if it were glad that soon it would have to take its leave.

The blue snowy surfaces gleamed springlike and the gliding tomtits twittered their greetings to the spring.

Everything near and far was dipped in blue and where the trunk of a tree or a wall created a black background, the air wove a shimmering opalescent light which laid a soft coverlet over everything that had been dark or was a domicile of gloom.

Sieburth reached for Helena's hand and imbedded it in his arm.

"No one will see us here," he said. "Here we can walk like an engaged couple."

At which he was frightened. That had been almost too much.

"I need not ask you," he said, "why you don't

come any more. That you will tell me of your own accord."

"No, never, not ever!" she exclaimed.

"You *will* tell me, you can depend upon that. But before anything else, how are the examinations going?"

"We are in the midst of them," she replied, and the pride of making good shone from her sorrowful features.

"Things are going nicely then?"

"Better than I had ever expected. I know, too, that I have only you to thank for all of it."

"And you desert me already?"

She tore her hand out of the crook of his arm in distinct horror.

"How dare you say such a thing? If I didn't come, it was only because—because—"

"Well, then, why?"

"Because—because I wanted to concentrate my thoughts—I don't want to—to— Oh, there is so much that is strange in me—so much that is ugly. No, not ugly—but everything is difficult and every-thing is dangerous. And only the fact that you are calmer now acts as a balm to me. Oh, God, but that does me good!"

"And you will never come to me again?"

She was silent, and he waited for he did not want to urge her.

At last she began: "I reflected so much—if I should—or if I shouldn't, and then I reached the conclusion that I could come just once more . . . that shall be my reward if I pass my examinations— then I shall come to tell you about it for you must hear about it before any one else."

"Then I should have to lie in wait before the door of the school building," he joked, "and then, if your mother should come along—think of it!"

"You are to know about it before my mother does," she replied resolutely.

He asked her how that would be possible.

"It will be possible— Just you wait and see!"

And she remained firm on this point.

In the meantime they approached the upper lake which lay lost in its winter lifelessness, covered by a snowy blanket, except where on the other side a skating path had been swept, over which a swarm of ants were tumbling over each other.

Covered with snow and surrounded by yellowing reeds the bath houses, in which Helena and her companion once had sought refuge, rose before them.

"I must confess something to you," she said, not having taken her eyes off him in some time.

"Well, what?"

"A man—once—kissed me."

"Ah," he said in feigned severity.

"Yes,—and right over there."

She pointed at the dark wooden shacks on the

oblique roof of which a thawing snow crust glittered.

"And who—was it?"

"Must I tell?"

"No, you don't have to tell me anything."

"Yes, yes, yes—otherwise in the end you'll think it worse than it is. It was the young Cheruscan freshman who used to visit you sometimes three years ago and who—who—"

She hesitated. What had lately happened must remain a secret.

"Was his name Kühne?"

"Yes, Fritz Kühne, that was his name."

"Well, think of that!" And he whistled through his teeth.

"I'll tell you about it, no matter how ashamed I feel."

And then with long-winded veracity she told him how it all had happened.

"When yesterday you designated the same meeting place, I thought of it and made up my mind to tell you, and if you think ill of me now, it serves me right."

"If you want to dispose of this problem," he replied with relentless solemnity, "there is only one remedy."

"Well?" her eyes pleaded in fear.

"On the selfsame spot you must pass on to me what was given at that time to you."

She laughed jubilantly. She had not been prepared for such a mild punishment. And then she ran on ahead of him, across the pathless snowfield toward the wooden lattice work, to try whether or not it would open, for to climb over it as they had then, would have been beneath the dignity of both of them—but it was already open. In fact, it lay torn down by the winter's storms, stretched flat on the cloddy, frozen ground.

So she ran on immediately, around the pointed end, and when Sieburth caught up with her he found her on the snowy planks before a cabin door knocking against the wooden bolt which was frozen tight in the board wall.

"This is where it was," she called radiantly to Sieburth. "I remember it exactly," and she went on knocking but her soft hands proved powerless. Only when he used the iron top of his cane did the obstinate ice give way and let them step inside. It looked no different after three years had passed— not quite three years—but after all, who cared about a few months more or less? Only, when she threw herself on the board bench, it seemed much shorter than before, and it was not possible for the two of them to find room there.

"The best thing to do," said Sieburth, "is for you to get up again and then sit on my lap—only in that way will there be room for us both."

She was not in the least bashful and made herself comfortable on his knees. She threw her arms around his neck and wanted to nestle her head close to his but his hat and her cap interfered.

"We'll simply take them off," he said, and they did.

When she had hung both of them on the wooden hooks, they found that the door was still open, and this was also remedied—and now that she had returned to her resting place and lay happily close to his neck, there suddenly burst forth from her soul the long pent-up exultation expressing itself in the no longer stealthily guarded familiar pronoun, just as it had blossomed out of that Christmas joy at that time.

"And now you will always adhere to it?" he demanded.

"Always, always, always!" she promised.

And then came the kiss which was to be her punishment and which lasted so long that it very much resembled a reward.

"And when you two were sitting here together— close enough, I find it—what did you talk about the whole time?"

"About you," she replied without hesitating.

"Didn't you have a better subject?"

"No," she replied quite positively, "that was what I needed him for, only he misunderstood and thought that I meant himself."

"And what did you say about me?"

But now she did falter.

"I do believe I must no longer hide anything from you; even if it does sound shameless."

"Your conversation with him surely wasn't shameless."

"No, not that, really. But I was so inexperienced and didn't know what to do, and I told him about the things I heard through the wall."

"You noticed it already then?"

"Oh, it used to be too terrible, and now I am so proud and thankful that it has stopped, and that I am the reason—but I will always reproach myself for one thing—"

"And that is?"

"What do I give you in place of it—nothing, nothing at all! . . . Only you have always done the giving—brought me through my examinations—for they all assure me that my report will read 'good' . . . but you surely miss the small joys that those light-hearted girls brought to you."

"I miss nothing, my child, since I have you."

"But you do, you do. I am only nineteen but I am as experienced as a mature woman. You, and my worries over you, have opened my eyes. And I know perfectly well how men are, and what their needs are. . . . Oh, I would love to give you all that I have to offer, but there can never be anything between us."

"You are right on that score, my child."

"Oh, not on my account—it doesn't matter about

me—but I believe—I believe, if I place myself in your position—and I can very easily do that—you are not nearly as uncontrolled as you appear to be . . . you are quite conscientious, almost timid."

"How do you know that?"

"Well, could I have gone in and out otherwise, evenings and nights, and remained as I am? No, dear—dear—what shall I call you? I can't say professor any more and your first name—"

"Say friend—for I am that."

"Yes, you are that—and want to be—and if you would become anything else, you would regard it as guilt and would never forgive yourself. Perhaps it would be a form of guilt, but it would be mine."

"For heaven's sake," he thought, "it exists—such self-abandonment really exists! And I still hesitate to make her mine for life!"

But another thought said to him, "Don't confuse her. It is too soon for her, and you, too, must first reach your goal."

"Listen to me, child," he answered. "We have grown into one another and don't know ourselves how it happened. We want to give ourselves time. We shall be content with whatever happens, but to one thing we simply must adhere: You must not come to me any more."

"I will come," she said, and her eyes gleamed in steadfast resolution. "I will come once more. You are to be the first to hear the result—I told you that, and you must not forbid it to me. You must not deny me this one joy; otherwise, the whole examination won't mean anything to me."

"Very well," he said, "and if you want it, let it be so. And now let's go home."

She arose. The last faint twilight glow was reflected through the heart in the door.

Clinging tightly to him, she walked silently by his side and he thought of Herma, accounting to her, as it were, for what he was doing.

.   .   .   .

A week passed. The close of the semester came just at that time. Fully twenty students had remained with him until the very end, a result of which few teachers could boast.

On the last day Pfeifferling stopped him.

"You're making yourself damned scarce again, colleague," he called to him. "I believe you haven't once been a guest at my house since we were at dinner with that Junker crowd. But that has time. But get busy and make a trip to Berlin as that blockhead advised so strongly. The Ministry of Education have been looking for you with spyglasses for a long time."

Sieburth thanked him, laughingly, but took his time about making the trip. Helena's promised visit made his blood course hotly.

Whether she would come in the evening or at night had not been decided.

In order to be certain that he would be there, he never left his rooms after supper.

Nothing stirred on the other side of the wall. It almost seemed as if she had stopped her night work, but when once towards midnight he crept out into the hall, he saw the keyhole of her door gleaming as brightly as ever.

It was not easy to find out the day of the close of the examinations, for he did not even know the name of the institution she attended.

Well, then—wait!

And so another night arrived when he went reconnoitering and again saw the light through the keyhole.

As long as she worked, the examination was not yet over.

So towards twelve he went to bed with a book.

But his impatience had grown to such a degree that he could not concentrate.

He put out the lamp and allowed the moonlight which shone through the court window to throw its shadows over the wall and the bedclothes.

He must have fallen asleep and as he rose, in a half-dream, he thought he heard light steps pattering across the floor, in his study.

It was she! Yes, it was!

She stood in the doorway—a tall, slender figure in unbroken contour of line.

"Helena!"

She sank on the bed, bending over him.

"Is it over?"

"Yes, I've passed," she whispered, "with an average of 'good,' and you are really the first to know about it. I've fooled mother by telling her that the finish comes to-morrow; otherwise, I would have had no reason to sit up so late to-night."

"Well, then, I congratulate you."

"And I thank you a thousand, thousand times— oh, many thousands of times!"

Her mouth found his and would not relinquish it.

Then, when he wanted to put his arms around her, he discovered that she had nothing on whatever underneath her loose dress. Its buttons opened of their own accord and when she lifted herself up, he saw in happy astonishment the most beautiful body glistening like snow.

Touched by involuntary shame, she gathered the folds together over her breast, and threw herself over him again burying her face in the pillows close beside him.

"Helena, what are you doing?" he whispered.

And breathed into his ear he heard: "You said it had made you happy to see me—lying there—as you did, and I thought to myself, if it really makes him happy, he shall have it so again, and can have it as often as he likes."

His arms enfolded the glowing body beneath its covering and so they lay long, motionless.

"Listen," he said, softly, into her ear. "To-day, since you are mine, I will give you my confidence. You shall know what no one else on this earth knows. There was a woman I loved deeply. How much I loved her, I only realized after she was dead. I saw her only once during the last two years. How largely I am to blame for her mortal illness, I cannot know, but one thing I do know, I am not guiltless. In her life and mine, there was one hour during which she lay in my arms naked as you, but because she asked it, I let her go as she came. And I have not regretted it. Even on her deathbed, she wanted to think of me as being happy and sent me to one who seemed to be for me—and was perhaps really destined for me—but that is over forever. . . . You have taken her place. . . . You, to-day, seem as her legacy to me. Do you understand what that means?"

She did not answer. Her body was convulsed with suppressed sobs.

Then, when he was about to continue, he saw on the threshold of the door—where Helena had stood before—had a shadow remained there, was it a phantom of the night? No, in reality, there stood a woman's figure!

Suddenly he flew up—Helena right after him.

A cry—from the other side, as if it were an echo, a second cry!

And with that the phantom came to life. It approached with a wild leap clutching Helena's hair with one hand and dealing out blows with the other. With a clapping noise, they covered cheeks, brow and neck and every place that was exposed and within reach.

"You beast! You scum! You carrion! You whore!"

So rang and bellowed her disjointed lamentations. The jealousy of years was at last finding vent.

"Don't you think I know, you vile thing, that yesterday was the finish? It was in the newspaper. And when you lied and told me it would be to-morrow, I knew there was something behind it. And—and when I came in, you left your chemise lying there—you left everything lying there—you shameless beast!"

"Now, that's enough," said Sieburth, covering Helena who had fled back to the bed, with his arms. "I will not let you go on abusing the girl to whom I am engaged to be married."

Then the rage of the martyr turned vixen was let loose on him.

"You just keep perfectly quiet, you libertine, you debaucher of humanity. I could tell stories about you that would make the whole town shudder, about who has cried out here in other days, year in, year out, whom you've already outraged. . . . All those you have on your conscience. Oh, you, you, you! . . . And now in the end, to fall upon my own flesh and blood! What could be more shameless than that! Engaged! Ha, ha, ha! Engaged! You'd like to make it appear that, now that the knife is at your throat. Yes, indeed, that would suit you very nicely. But it will be nearly two years before she'll be of age, and until then, you can hang your-selves—both of you—next to each other! You can hang and I wouldn't even cut you down!"

So ranted this woman, who until this hour had nursed a faint hope in her breast, and Sieburth realized with a shock that he was helpless in her hands. The scandal with which she threatened him would undeniably cost him his neck even if he were exonerated in the main.

He felt as though he had a gag in his mouth, as if his arms and legs were tied with ropes.

And when he came out of this dim trancelike state to the full consciousness of his position, he found himself alone.

What now?

He got up, dressed himself and went out into the street, thinking that the March air would clarify his brain for necessary resolutions.

He wandered around the streets for hours. He tortured his brain but could find no way out. At the break of day, he returned to his rooms and threw himself on his bed fully dressed.

When he awoke from a sleep of utter exhaustion, it was close to eleven o'clock. His cold breakfast which the mother had brought in, in spite of every-thing, stood on the table of his study.

She must have come halfway to her senses, so he decided to go to her straight off and see whether he could persuade her to be somewhat more yielding.

When he entered, he found her sitting in front of the machine as usual, but her arms hung limp and her chin sagged on her highly upholstered bosom.

"I have something I want to talk to you about, Mrs. Schimmelpfennig."

"I thought as much," she said, penetrating him with a piercing look. "Please be seated."

She got up and dragged herself to the sofa—a shattered ruin, hardly to be called a woman.

He sat down and began. He spoke of the secret working hours, when Helena became dearer and dearer to him, and that he always regarded her as inviolable, as it was befitting for him to feel about his future fiancée. And then he asked for her hand with proper formality.

The furtive, bitter smile she assumed did not leave her face.

"Have you finished?" she asked.

"I'm waiting for your answer," he replied.

"And you shall have it. Helena leaves this house before the day is out. Where she goes, is none of your business, and you won't find it out. As to your proposal, I do this—"

And she spat.

"But should you attempt to find out where she is and to approach her again, I will go to the Dean and tell him what took place under my roof. I have threatened her with the same thing in case she should have a desire to write you letters. I'm sure she won't try it, and if you think that things will be different when she's of age, you're on the wrong track. . . . You can continue your diversions—but elsewhere. For that reason I—I should like to ask you—for when you moved here we decided on a three months' notice—to move. For a quarter of a year from to-day, everything can go on as before. You will find your rooms cleaned, your meals on the table. I will accept any messages for you, everything as before, but you will receive no answers from me to any unnecessary remarks. At what time do you wish your dinner to-day, Professor?"

Sieburth got up and went out of the door without bidding her the time of day. There was nothing to hope for here.

CHAPTER XXXII

THE REWARD

On a sunny day in the latter part of March, when the dirty snowy slush augured a beautiful spring, Sieburth arrived in Berlin and walked along "Unter den Linden."

He had not known of a better method of getting away from the torments of his home surroundings than to quickly pack his trunk, heed the advice of Pfeifferling and see for himself how correct was the information given him by the man from the Provincial Government.

There stood the Palace where the fate of all things intellectual in Prussia was decided.

A high-vaulted lobby, bronzed balustrades, and a marble group of the pious period of Schinkel's time.

"May I see Assistant Minister Kürschner?"

"Have you been summoned, or have you an appointment?"

"Unfortunately not."

"Then give me your card, and I will see."

With a commanding air, the corridor attendant, greedy for tips, studied his name and title and disappeared quickly behind the closed double door.

When he returned, there was a patronizing smile on his military face. That was not a bad sign.

"The Assistant Minister will see you."

Sieburth went in.

A large room, alabaster busts, flowered easy-chairs, a worn carpet, and behind the roomy desk a man with sparse hair and an air of cheerful and expansive dignity.

He had the appearance of an alcalde in a Spanish comedy.

As he arose a somewhat distended abdomen gradually came to view, such as Dr. Luther had developed; over it were stained coat lapels, and above it a black silk scarf from which, ensconced in a white rim of collar, rose a clean-shaven double chin and still farther up in the puffy epicure's face a pair of eyes from the reddened slits of which there radiated so much of laughing craftiness that Sieburth felt joyful and distressed in the same moment.

"He is not a man who is easily coped with," thought Sieburth, and on the other hand, his impression was, "He is easy to get along with."

"Aha," spoke a gurgling, oily voice, "are you stopping in too for once?"

"I did not know, your Excellency," he replied, "that in these sacred halls any one had taken notice of me, otherwise I would have presented myself long ago."

His Highmightiness chuckled.

"Be seated," he said, sitting down also. "There are men of science, and in fact of undisputed qualifications, who have their regular seats in my waiting room. When the swallows homeward fly, they are there, and when they return they are there again. That would not be necessary for them, for when one has arrived, my so-called omnipotence has nothing more to offer. There is a closed season even for decorations, but they're here just the same."

"I do not want to boast," replied Sieburth, involuntarily assuming a similar tone, "but the sweated toga has never driven me over the threshold of any haughty patron."

"Oh," said the other, with widening eyes. "What is that in the original?"

He reflected a little and then quoted, " 'Dum per limina te potentiorum sudatrix toga ventilat.' Yes, yes, he was a rascal, that Martial. He did not even spare his friend Juvenal, and they traced their origin to the same poison pits. So that's the sort of fellow you are! I don't want to anticipate Fate but it seems to me that under this sign we will reach an understanding."

Sieburth bowed.

"And—did you come with any particular wishes?"

"No others," he replied, "but those which are natural to my situation."

"Situation, situation," bantered the other. "Why

not rather say position than situation? Your position is clear; as to your situation, I'm not interested. The proverb says, 'As you make your bed, you lie upon it,' and your bedding is your affair."

"Oh, he's referring to my conduct," thought Sieburth.

But the laughter of the man was so broad and genial that one did not feel called upon to suspect any insinuation, and Sieburth's worry disappeared as it had come.

"I had a fuss with your Faculty on your account years ago when I brought you to Königsberg. I take it that you have been able, through your activities, to overcome this opposition in the meantime."

His look was watchful. A thousand to one, this question was put to ascertain how he would present his difference.

He answered carefully, "As to that, you are in a better position to know about these things than I am. If things were as you imagine, it seems to me I would have been proposed for the vacant chair long ago."

The Assistant Minister pouted reflectively.

"I usually have a good memory, particularly where I scent intrigue, but at the moment I really don't know the exact status. Give me until to-night and should you have nothing better to do—the ladies, of course, always take precedence—I hope you will give me the pleasure of entertaining you."

ince. Since the threats forced her to remain silent too, there seemed little hope that he would hear from her in the near future.

The longer he thought over the situation, the more hopeless it became.

Nevertheless, for to-day, the important thing was to assure his position and promotion. What would come later had to be left to the game of chance.

At the entrance to Potsdamerstrasse there was a popular wine house that was habitually frequented by scholars and higher officials.

Around white scoured tables were seated the regular guests, who had come there—and only there—for years when the gentle fetters of home life released them.

Sieburth presented himself five minutes before the appointed time as it would have been dangerous to keep the man waiting.

He arrived punctually, greeted people here and there, and as he joined the unknown young man a whispering arose, accompanied by knowing smiles which could be easily interpreted to mean, "Who is the unfortunate person he has by the collar to-day?"

"We will start with this tranquil spot," said the Assistant Minister, seating himself, "later we will see where our winged steps will carry us."

And then when the wine and menu cards were laid before him, he remarked, "You are my guest, of course, and I will charge your bill to the Prussian

State, for that State is willing to let the pursuit of learning cost it something. This has been the tradition ever since the time of the Humboldts."

A Franconian wine, which threatened to overheat the blood, was served in a pouch-shaped bottle.

"Have a care," Sieburth admonished himself, although he usually stood his ground at drinking parties.

"Here goes for a holiday feast then," said his patron, ordering snipe, preceded by brook trout, which were taken from the guests who had previously ordered them in order to facilitate service.

"Without pilfering, one can't make his way in this world," he said, justifying himself. "We learned that from Bismarck. The fun only starts with mischief. Don't you agree with me?"

"*Agent provocateur*," thought Sieburth, and smiled graciously.

"Well, now, in the meantime I have collected some information about you. One can't carry the biographies of all of you renowned people in one's mind. The students fifty years hence will have to see to that. As far as your Faculty is concerned, far be it from me to spoil your appetite. This Faculty of yours has been somewhat difficult to deal with for ages. There are some gentlemen among them who feel they have missed their vocation because barricades and scaffolds are no longer the vogue. If one is all set to demand freedom of thought, then it is a great catastrophe that freedom of thought already exists, for we actually do enjoy it in this Bismarckian State, at least so moderated that a place in the sun is still worth working for as a reward for supporting the State. You thought so too, did you not, Professor, yes?"

Sieburth felt the flush of shame rising to his cheeks.

Doubtless the concluding sentence referred to his activities in the recent elections, which were duly noted in higher quarters.

"If I don't strike the right way now," he thought, "then I am lost in his eyes, and also in my own."

And he replied, "The support of the State is a very important thing, particularly when you sit opposite the carver of your destiny, but I must disclaim it as personal motivating force even though I aimed to make myself useful at the recent elections."

The high official opened the cunning slits of eyes just as wide as he had in the morning when the words of Martial were unwittingly thrown at his head.

"Well, well, well," he said with a warning smile, pointing to the bottle, "we have hardly started."

"Even this wine will not bring confessions from me," replied Sieburth, delighted to again feel the sneering smile. "I only wanted to protect myself from the contempt which I felt approaching in my direction."

The Assistant Minister frowned.

"You don't quite understand me," he said. "Whoever serves the 'State Idea,' as we at any given time embody it, has every reason to count on our gratitude. Contempt may enter into it when one rewards the so-called 'non-gentlemen,' whom we unfortunately cannot spare either. But what has that got to do with our case? You allied yourself with the Government during the Reichstag elections, I hear. Your motives don't concern us, but if you would tell me privately, just to help along my knowledge of human nature, I would be deeply indebted to you."

"If I tell him the truth," thought Sieburth, "I deliver myself defenseless into his hands."

But the overweening superiority of the man challenged him.

And he replied, "Even at the danger of being considered supercilious, I will confess that what you regard as the prevailing embodiment of this 'State Idea,' I consider as being very incidental."

"Whew!" came a whistling tone.

"One can adhere to it out of many reasons, out of fear, out of a love for law and order, out of horror at the stupidity of the opponents, out of greed for personal advantage, and, last of all, out of convenience. I actually believe that we cannot estimate this factor highly enough in the maintenance of the State."

An expression of shrewd enlightenment came over the face of the man opposite.

"Think of that, and then you want to teach the Philosophy of the State."

"That was the occupation of the Hegelians," replied Sieburth, "and when I am once that far the technical jargon will conceal my ideas so effectively that every one can take from them what is right and proper for a future citizen of the State."

"And you believe therewith to draw forth the sympathetic enthusiasm which we desire to find in the cultured element of our Nation?"

That was putting the pistol at his breast. To gain time was now the paramount issue.

"May I first ask you, sympathetic enthusiasm for what?"

For the first time it seemed as though a shadow of embarrassment flitted over the Falstaffian features.

"Well, well, I should say for the aims the Government pursues at the moment."

"The aims of yesterday we well know, the 'Norddeutsche Allgemeine' reports those, but what in the way of aims the next sleepless night will bring to the 'All Powerful,' he does not yet know himself. And no teacher can obligate either himself or his pupils for such a contingency."

As he pronounced those sentences, he felt how much damage they might inflict on him; but the steps were taken and there was no turning back.

The good-humored discreetness had vanished out of the face of the man opposite, and he squinted at him sharply with a scrutinizing watchfulness Sieburth had observed before.

"You still have not confided in me, why you consider the basis of our social existence—for that is, after all, 'the idea of the State'—as incidental."

This was no longer a game of questions. This was an Inquisition of Life or Death.

In Sieburth the defiance grew to a self-destructive orgy. Future, advancement, and all the chairs of philosophy in the world, were at this moment not worth a penny.

And he replied, "One coincidence combining with a second creates eventually the third, which is the prevailing embodiment of the 'State Idea.' We serve it. Even as opponents, we are bound to serve it because it is, as you just remarked, the basis of our social—and not only our social—existence, but to take it seriously would be to attach too much importance to coincidence."

"So, so," said he, hunched up like a beast of prey ready to spring. "I was under the impression that you philosophers denied the existence of coincidence."

"Of course, we do. We deny every concept which simple men with normal intellects (*idiotai*, they were already called by the Greeks) find necessary. Besides, we exist for the purpose of throwing a teleo-

Martial threw a burning torch between, at other times Juvenal, and the running fire of Persius at times shone most glaringly.

The spirit of Montaigne also rose and Hume's shadowy form strode by unmolested. Ecclesiastes, too, of dubious sanctity, emerged smilingly from the depths and even Pelham, the hero of fiction, was there and contributed his quota. They would gladly have passed Schopenhauer by, because after all he was dogmatic, but that would not do. Too incisively his choleric insight had caught at the rotten foundations underlying the ostentatious compromises. By way of contrast, Hobbes sat safely enthroned on his far-seeing perch in the clouds; and in the end the old sophists triumphantly steered the race. An imperious journey it was through the sunny worlds of the great "Negation" where doubting constituted morality, and where the gambling-hell of life was forced to surrender its counters, which are not backed by gold, and amount to nothing but wretched bits carved from the bones of the dead.

The secret doctrine of Force, which is only at the command of the Elect, was touched upon fleetingly: "Might is right," beyond a doubt, but only when "right" becomes, with a threatening bloody fist, a bloody, godly "might"—and aristocracies and democracies found themselves in perfect accord in one ash-heap.

Freedom became the business of petty shopkeepers, intoxicated with progress, custom became petrified hypocritical egoism. And as for beauty! To what end did Voltaire say, "Le beau pour le crapaud c'est sa crapaude," if not to pass it by?

This was a different battle from the one he had thrashed out with the three scamps at the tavern.

They countered with brilliant flashes, and when they united they wrought havoc with the book-learning of the professional benefactors of mankind.

"But now we'll hold our breath for a moment," said the Assistant Minister, "that word of Juvenal's 'vitam impendere vero,' which Schopenhauer utilizes as a motto, may trouble us ever so much, yet I almost believe that the Truth, provided we really possess it, is nothing but a luxury, which permits of no husbandry. Truth is not productive, either for the individual or for the masses, and in the end nothing remains for us but the word of Persius—you are no doubt familiar with it. This quiet enjoyment, my laughter, which is valueless, I would not sell even for an Iliad. But is such laughter sufficient as the yield of a lifetime? I would gladly sacrifice the current embodiment of the 'State Idea,' from which we started out, and humanity is of fictitious value. If you say it is not worth while to raise one's little finger on its behalf, I reply, 'It's all the same to me.' But between the two there is something which is neither fiction nor perplexity. It calls itself,

'Fatherland.' How do you reconcile your laughter with that?"

Sieburth started. He knew well that on this rock every independent line of thought met shipwreck.

And the other continued: "You say nothing. I expected that. Had you been lying before Sedan on September second, eighteen-seventy, as I did, you would not only have sung the hymn, 'Now all thank God,' but you would have been a believer just like the Pomeranian peasant's son. Of what good is our skepticism or our power of thought if both are shattered by any mass spirit?"

Sieburth, in spite of his confusion, searched for further contentions.

"In the first place there is no question here of mass reaction," he said, "for behind it stands Homer's 'purple death,' to which even the strongest pays toll; and furthermore, skepticism would not be skepticism if it did not ultimately destroy itself. Every final argument is an abyss, and if we break our neck in it, it serves us right."

The Assistant Minister had grown serious and surveyed him with contracted eyes.

"Here is a tragedy," he said, "which I have read in your face for some time. You are no skeptic and no cynic. You are sick, intellectually sick, sick of life. The impulse of suffering has gotten into your blood, and poisoned it—but to the deuce to-day with all tragedy. Let us also forget all final analyses.

Let us leave to the Deity his hiding places, such as the spirit of the universe, timelessness and the like. Let us leave to humanity her most efficient panacea, which is mediocrity, and let us come then to another, which we have anxiously avoided hitherto, although it, if I'm not very much mistaken, has helped us both: it is called woman. Woman, the fixed pole in the swirl of diversions. Whoever might have listened to us to-night would have gathered the impression that we were two sexless beings."

With this sudden transition, every shadow was wiped away, and Sieburth said, laughing boisterously, "I have long since become a stranger here. Where does one get women here now?"

"Wait, now—not so fast, young man. I am fifty-eight, a married man, and too prominent a personality. I can't indulge in adventurous nightly expeditions, for to thus indulge I'd have to be a young lawyer or already in the Cabinet. But if, like sagacious men, we are willing to be spectators, then I could find this or that place where respectability is perverted into bacchanalianism. We can find bock-beer festivities, and similar frivolities and still better diversions. Frederick, the bill."

A few minutes later they walked in the night air toward the center of the city through some streets in which there were still crowds about.

Isolated girls, sweet loiterers, who were active competitors of the corner street-walkers, wandered from one shop window to another, where they dallied ostensibly out of curiosity, looking at the displays, but perfectly willing to answer and give information to any one who would appeal to them.

Sieburth, who did not let any one go by without passing judgment, said to himself, "Here I would have had better picking all these years."

"The world in terms of woman and thought"— here it had reached maturity.

"What is that, what is that?" he heard some one say next to him. "The world as what?"

Then he became aware of the fact that he had thought louder than he knew and laughingly he repeated his old familiar phrase.

"This parody is not so foolish at all," said the Assistant Minister. "One could pad out one's whole life with that."

"The deciphering of it, I leave to my 'boys,'" he replied.

"I'll have to invalidate your appointment after all," the Minister threatened, pinching his arm; "such instructors are dangerous to the State."

"I hardly think that I bring about worse consequences than the State itself which takes 'Woman and Drinking' under its wing."

The defender of the high moral code laughed lustily and acknowledged dire defeat.

And then they had arrived.

A tavern, apparently like others, two floors of it,

full to capacity, teeming with smoke and merriment.

A chorus of hallos greeted those who entered, accompanied by cries of welcome, and raised glasses.

"Good morning, here, shake hands, drink with us," sounded from every table, where men and women sat beside each other, if not on one another's laps. It almost seemed as if they had been anxiously expected.

The high official discarded all of his dignity. He shook hands, clapped shoulders, patted cheeks, and embraced two or three without asking much as to sex or age.

Sieburth tried to follow suit, but this mode of action was too strange to him and too surprising for him to be able to adapt himself to it so speedily.

On the upper story, which surrounded the lower like a broad gallery, was an empty table.

The neighbors to the right and left tried to fraternize; at least they wanted to be embraced, which was done without undue solemnity.

"Where are we anyway?" asked Sieburth. "I don't recognize my stiffly starched North Germans at all. Only in Cologne at Carnival time have I met with such an experience."

"This carnival lasts the whole year through," declared his guide. "We see by this how loosely the social forms fit the bourgeois, and with what alacrity they discard them. Along with it one drinks a bloating Moselle wine, one usually can't afford anything

watch out, you'll come to a bad end; I prophesy that."

"I'll take care, you may be sure of that," cried the Assistant Minister, "and you quit your babbling; otherwise, we'll send you right back."

And he lifted his glass toward the adjoining table where bows were heartily and courteously exchanged.

"Keep me just five more seconds," she begged, "until I know who you are. Are you a musician, are you a poet? No, I know what you are. You are a globe trotter, who chases from one country to another because he finds no redemption anywhere."

"Ahasuerus in a sleeping-car," said the Assistant Minister, laughing, "the latest romancing of a young girl's brain."

"Please, please, take me along," she begged further. "I will protect you, I will—" She made as though to put her arms around his neck.

"Stop," cried the now irate Assistant Minister. "Your five seconds are over. Make your bow and go home."

Without the slightest effort at resistance, she rose and quietly, with head thrown far back, went to her seat.

"Hysterical clairvoyance," said the Assistant Minister. "That particular tone was the missing one in the evening's music. Man, how rich you must be in joy and adventure!"

"If it were not for the 'bestia trionfante,'" said Sieburth, "which is always at one's neck."

The other started a little, but thought it best not to enlarge on that admission.

"I am just reminded of another word of Giordano Bruno," he replied; "love woman if you will, but don't forget to worship the Infinite; transposed into the language of to-night, don't forget to despise the Infinite."

Sieburth gathered himself together to contradict him, with respect not only to this last remark, but to everything that had preceded.

"We don't want to conceal from each other that what was talked of by us to-day was in great part only play and ecstasy."

"Are you already retracting, you harefoot?" scoffed the other.

"Not that," he replied. "The seriousness of our discussion may have been tempered by laughter, but just as I, in a few weeks, will analyze Platonic dialogue, you will to-morrow practice the Christian virtue of Maintaining the State, and you and I will feel that we're doing our duty."

The Assistant Minister made his pouting face. "Why, that's grist to my mill. We submit to a given order of things, no matter how unreasonable it may seem, but it doesn't even seem so. Order never is unreasonable, and when it gives way to a new order that also will seem full of contradictions, and yet will be no less reasonable than the old was. But hours such as we have lived through, have to be. Play and intoxication must be, so that the two arch enemies of human thought, Dogma and the Absolute, do not choke us. Leave that sweet stuff, dear friend, if you are satisfied, let us go."

Before they left, they did not neglect to say good-by ceremoniously to the table at the left. The adieus to the one on the right were more casual.

"Now just look at her," said the bridegroom, "she really worries me."

There sat the girl, with staring, dreamy eyes which hung spellbound on Sieburth—and she was motionless.

He stretched his hand out to her; she shook her head and continued to stare at him—as though she feared his touch.

And so she still sat, as Sieburth glanced at her once more from the door.

"Come to my office to-morrow at twelve," the Assistant Minister said in farewell. "Then we'll build the foundations of your future."

.   .   .   .

And now again he found himself opposite him. The flowered easy-chairs glowed in reflection of the forenoon's sun and the worn carpet showed up grayer the tracks of the men who had sat here with throbbing hearts.

The mighty one with his merry judicial face sat
enthroned in his leather desk chair. "Now let our
brains hum," he said, "and go valiantly at the business in hand. I must confess that my ignorance
yesterday morning concerning your 'situation,' as
you expressed yourself, was a pretty piece of acting.
I hope it was not badly done. . . . Just at present
we're taking a most decided interest in your case.
Your Faculty is in a tantrum over you. I intimated
that to you already last evening. Perhaps I have not
the right to show you their correspondence but I take
it that you will make no use of it."

And he handed Sieburth a bundle of documents
which the latter looked through with considerable
excitement.

Therein it appeared on black and white with what
energy and perseverance the Faculty had exerted
their influence against his appointment.

Time and time again since the demise of the great
Hegelian, the Ministry had brought his name under
consideration and there had always been objections,
and because an effective resistance was denied them,
they had begged to have the post held open.

They had been dignified in their grounds for
objection. There was not the slightest reproach in
reference to his private life and the success of his
teaching which, of course, could be proved by
statistics, was found to be appreciated without reser-
vation, but—they asserted—in a literary way he had

accomplished so little, and above all, the elementary training for the mathematical and natural sciences was lacking.

This they said about him who, in spite of his philological leanings, thought more clearly in terms of natural science than many who had for years hung about laboratories.

Nor did they fail to make counter proposals.

In his stead two others were named, who were as yet in the swaddling clothes of instructors, and one of them disclosed himself to be Cilly's fiancé. One could see "The Three Fates" at work at a distance of a hundred miles.

These two gentlemen then possessed the necessary qualifications which he lacked, he, who had a huge following among the students of *The Albertina* and who divested the good Hagemann of much of his popularity every term despite the fact that the latter's courses were very important for examinations.

But what hurt him most was that in the list of those who affixed their signature the name of his friend, Pfeifferling, also appeared. That he was in duty bound to sign, according to the rule that all decisions must be unanimous, had to serve as a justification, but it hurt nevertheless.

Thanking him, Sieburth laid the bundle of documents back on the table. "With all this my case seems to be closed," he said, with a shrug of the shoulders.

"I should say not," cried the other. "In spite of the objections of the Faculty we installed you as Assistant Professor—the devil only knows what those people had against you even then—and now we will appoint you regular Professor too. Yes, in confidence, I received a pretty stiff calling down from my Superior because it hasn't already been done."

Sieburth thought to himself, "The elections cannot be entirely responsible for these favors."

But already the solution of the riddle came. "And now one more question," continued the Assistant Minister, "which, with all due respect, I venture to ask you, 'From where do you have your court connections?'"

"Which court connections?"

"Now, now, cards on the table, if I may be so bold. A gentleman who stands very high interests himself mightily in you, and was already interested then. I thought yesterday you might mention something about this friendship, but you kept it to yourself. Well, now, out with it. What about this foster-brotherhood?"

"I can only think of one thing," replied Sieburth, and he told of the sickly prince, as whose friend and guide he had spent four years of his youth.

"And in such fine society you claim not to have learned to eat snipe," cried the other laughing. "But in this manner everything is cleared up. The

CHAPTER XXXIII

THE CHAIR OF KANT

I⊤ was the first Friday after the beginning of the new term.

The gong in the entrance hall struck six as Sieburth entered the University building in evening clothes and high hat.

The secretary awaited him at the foot of the stairs. He was notoriously gruff, disliked by professors and students alike, but of influence not to be underestimated. He also wore evening clothes and his shaggy-bearded head was set deep in the low collar from which his white tie protruded like a sailor's knot.

"Well, come along, Professor," he said with a sour smile. "The University Senate has been assembled for a long time and I've been waiting until I'm tired."

"I was asked to come at six o'clock," answered Sieburth.

"I know, I know," said the former, "but in cases like this one comes a little earlier."

With that he preceded him up the stairs and opened the door of the so-called instructors' room which spread itself before them, as they entered, bare and empty in the shadows of the late afternoon.

"Will you go and announce me?" asked Sieburth.

"Now, now, there's no such hurry as all that," he answered, "we'll have to wait until we're asked to appear."

Sieburth hung his overcoat on a hook on the wall, stood by the window and looked out at the budding green that was beginning to sparsely cover the bare branches.

"Well, now with God's help you've attained it," the voice of the secretary intoned behind him.

"Attained what?" said Sieburth, veering around sharply.

"Well,—the full professorship," answered the former, slightly embarrassed, "and that is no small matter when one isn't wanted by the Faculty."

"Mr. Gramatzki," said Sieburth, "I am not in the humor to carry on a confidential conversation with you."

"Now, now, now, don't get so easily ruffled," replied the former. "I mean it well with you. I always took your part when you were attacked from behind; besides which I am a man who is loyal to his king and know how to respect your attitude, so kindly apologize, Professor."

"There's really no occasion for an apology," said Sieburth, who realized that he had overshot the mark, "but if I have a friend in you, I'm very glad to know it." And he stretched out his hand to him,

"I should say you have a friend in me," he cried, laughing out loud. "Many's the anonymous letter I've dropped under the table! And now, in your new position, should you need advice, I believe I could be very useful to you."

"Good! Then tell me, what do I do when this solemn function is over?"

"Do you know, Professor—it might not be absolutely necessary since you have been here a few years and have the actual entrance formalities behind you, but I am revealing no secret when I tell you that you are not particularly pleasing to many members of the Faculty—but I always advise the gentlemen who are promoted to higher positions to hire a landaulet and make the rounds . . . whether you send in one or two cards is your affair, but I would not entirely ignore this courtesy."

Sieburth felt something like nausea taking possession of him. It was a new display of lack of character that was being expected of him. But no doubt the man was right; as it was essential to continue his existence in these surroundings, nothing could be neglected that would make conditions more bearable.

The hall door opened and a head protruded through the crack and disappeared so rapidly that Sieburth could not recognize to whom it belonged.

"That is for us," said the secretary and assumed a dignified posture.

Sieburth felt his heartbeat quicken, which seemed

senseless and humiliating to him. So after all there still were qualities in him that bowed before the world which he thoroughly despised.

One door slammed and then another and then the expanse of the senatorial chamber stretched before them—brightly illuminated, and within it a table in horseshoe form, around which sat a dark double row of humanity which seemed to unite at the window wall in a hazy gray cross-section.

In the center, in the seat of honor, sat his Magnificence.

And it was toward him that Sieburth was to steer.

A scraping, a rustling, a blustering. Every one rose in a body and stood at attention like soldiers, all of them staring at him.

He felt as if a turgid stream of intense hatred were corrodingly descending upon him like a wave.

And with knees that felt as if he were on stilts and projected as if by mechanical springs, he passed by dark shoulders, bald heads and shaggy manes in the direction of the Prorector who looked expectantly in his direction.

A jurist whom he hardly knew, lank and haggard, with gold spectacles and gray side-whiskers, in evening clothes like himself, adorned with the gold chain of his office, the circles and knots of which gleamed provocatively.

After a short bow he began consulting a yellow sheet which lay on the table. "I have the honor of reading an order of the Cabinet by which you, my dear associate, are appointed a regular professor in the Faculty of Philosophy at the Royal University of Albertus."

And he read. Read the mandate of the Minister of Education which was transmitted on a given date through the board of trustees to the University authorities.

His words dropped icily through the icy stillness.

Sieburth listened to him with tightly compressed lips. Since the reader kept his eyes glued on the paper, he did not need to look at his face, and he glanced sidelong at the rows of men.

Hatred! Hatred! Hatred! Hatred in the eyes that penetrated space, hatred about the lips that were convulsively tightened like his own, hatred in the posture of the heads which were tightly set in the napes of the necks,—heads of men revolting and revolted.

And no wonder! For was he not the unwelcome one, the one who was being thrust upon them, associated with them "par ordre de Mufti." What happened to-day to one of the Faculties could to-morrow become the fate of the other three, and for that reason they had united in defenseless and yet all the more revengeful opposition against him and his appointment.

That he had been installed in their midst at that former time no doubt looked like child's play to them to-day. The assistant professors did not count and the personal association had obliterated the discord until the break came which, gradually widening, had separated him from the others.

His eyes sought Pfeifferling. He had not forgiven him for the signature, to be sure, but he did want to know whether he had his support.

Yes, there he sat! A friendly glance could have put things right, but he too stared grimly into space, like all the others. No doubt the general bitterness had reached such a pass that he deemed it advisable not to go against the stream. For one second the thought rose in Sieburth: Throw the whole business at their feet and go your way! But he discarded it at once. He had reached the goal. The world should know it. What might happen later on, what probably was bound to happen later on, was optional with him. He would not hesitate to put even the most violent resolution into action. Not for nothing had he been called "The Mad Professor"!

The Prorector had finished reading. He dropped his papers and turned to make an impromptu address to the man standing before him.

He was at liberty to dispense with the customary oath, for Sieburth was already sworn when originally appointed. It was only his duty to remind him of that oath, and he acknowledged his colleague's vow as if it had been repeated that very day.

Sieburth bowed affirmatively. The Prorector's

chest rose and fell as he took a deep breath before continuing, and the links of his chain clinked slightly.

"And with this I have the honor of installing you in an office which is among the most honorable which the academic life of Germany affords. It is the chair of Kant in which from now on you will sit, and it is at the same time the chair of a man"—he pointed with his hand at the picture of the great Hegelian hanging on the long wall—"who was to most of us an object of reverence and love. If I ask you to follow the example of these two, I give expression to the wish that you may consecrate your life to this cause."

"His logic is not flawless," thought Sieburth.

"I ask you now to take the place assigned to you in the row of your Faculty, and—accept our greetings and congratulations."

The hands clasped each other—it felt like the glow of fraternalism and yet was only an empty formality.

With a hasty bow he went back the way he had come and looked about for the promised seat. No one helped him; no one beckoned to him and it was only when the secretary, who stood there as if he wielded sovereign authority, directed him that he found the place which was to be his from now on.

Three stiff bows to the right, to the left and to those opposite him and if possible even more stiffly reciprocated, and the reception was over. He sat staring at the wall. He saw nothing, he heard nothing—he had only one thought, "How can I get out of here?"

Then his glance fell on the picture of the great Hegelian who looked smilingly down at him with his sunny eyes.

What had been his farewell words? Often he had repeated them to himself. "To philosophize is to learn how to die. How little we philosophers would be worth if we did not understand this smallest of feats!"

And peace descended upon him. Calmly he allowed the business of petty things to glide past him.

Until suddenly there was a general moving of chairs, and the rising of those around him gave indication that the session was over.

This was the moment at which the new associate should have been welcomed by greetings and hand-shakes, but while groups were formed all around him, talking animatedly, he stood alone.

But only for a second. To put the fraternalism of his official brothers to the test could only provoke further trouble, so he went quickly to the door and disappeared into the instructors' room where his overcoat hung. There he stood by the window at which he had stood before and waited until the stream should have dispersed.

"In gratitude and adoration, Barrister Fritz Kühne, Dr. Jur."

Once before in his life he had been his "only one" and now he was again. If only that October evening when he too had stood against him, had not come between them.

At eleven o'clock the carriage came, a victoria, shining and roomy, like the ones the fraternities used for their pompous pageants.

To send in two cards—as though desiring association with the family—that was out of the question. Just an act of courtesy towards his colleagues, nothing more—anything more would have been presumption.

One stop—a second, a third.

Always the same waiting, the same murmuring in the interior of the apartment and ultimately the same answer:

"The Professor is not at home . . . the Professor regrets . . . the Privy Councilor is not receiving—" And so it went on.

Had he taken the precaution of being accompanied by a lackey, the edge would have been taken off the humiliation by the simple throwing in of the cards, but now it was necessary to empty the glass to its bitter dregs, for to stop in the middle of the expedition would have made him only more ridiculous.

His breast shrank convulsively.

What could be wrong with Her?

That she had not said.

"Now there's that worry," he thought, "on top of everything else which will torture me day and night and always."

But as to that he was mistaken. He was too occupied with himself and had too much confidence in Helena's youthful vitality for this to disturb him for any length of time.

Whatever had happened to her, she would be able to overcome it while he was being tormented by new difficulties that arose incessantly.

From this hour on, he was entirely alone.

Even though this woman had been ever so obdurate and embittered, still she represented some connection with the world and life, and at times something of a presentiment of better days and of future adjustment seemed to radiate from her.

Now even that was past.

The days went by, each one bringing a harbinger of spring and peering hopefully with a brightened gaze into the fully bared souls.

Only not into his.

Objectless, he ran around the country roads, half consciously nursing the hope of catching a fleeting breath of spring, but all that it had to give flitted past him like something foreign and hateful.

Again and again he found himself on the road

leading to the upper lake and the bathing pavilion where he had sat with Helena at the close of the winter. And his longing cried after her.

Now he would not have hesitated to take leave of his bachelordom. With burning desire, he pictured to himself the happiness of sheltering and protecting a softly yielding wife, but she to whom he fled in dreams was to be forever dead to him.

Almost as dead as that other with whose image that of this sweet child often merged itself.

Away then with everything calling itself Woman!

Back to the other side of the world in which Thought alone dominates.

The semester had begun. There was no further preparatory work to do. Besides the several-times conducted Kant lectures a course on "Phædo" was announced. Just why he had selected this, he was no longer able to say. Was it cowardice, a desire to commend himself as an up-and-doing schoolmaster? If it had to be Plato, one would better have selected "The Republic" or something else that offered the opportunity of striking the prevailing system in the back.

All of it was disgusting—all the more so now because it was no longer necessary to practice jugglery and no sycophant could harm him.

And yet—the change which was bound to take place could only come slowly and must be initiated with the utmost care. Years might pass before he dared appear on the scene with a new philosophy, assuming full responsibility for it.

How long must "The Three Stages of Ethics" and the "Natural History of Fundamental Problems," and with them, "The Salvation of Sophistry" be relegated to the prison of the cupboard before the intellectual nuptial flight could be made?

Any sudden reversal would be looked upon as a new crime. He could imagine them saying, "Until you were sure of a good berth, you were hypocritical and bowed before those high up, played up to them and tamely assented to everything, and only now you reveal yourself in your true colors."

If there were still anything left that hadn't been said in defamation of his character, this would complete his downfall.

And the worst of it was that the gentlemen of the Right party held him by the reins. To withdraw from their hold required arts which could only be carefully exercised and applied only at the right time and given opportunity.

He felt so completely encompassed, he who at last was free, that he felt constraint even in drawing a breath.

In the meantime the contact with his colleagues in the Assembly Room became more and more of a torment to him. Until the meeting of the University Senate he had simply stayed away, but he couldn't do this permanently and what had taken place at that time was repeated every day with variations.

Courteous coolness changed to icy snubbing. He became so much air to some. Others merely nodded their heads ever so slightly. No one held out a hand. And no one considered it necessary to remember his call, the return of which, as was to be expected, never took place.

Even Pfeifferling seemed at last to want to avoid him, which was small wonder, after that last meeting. If he on his side would not make an effort at reconciliation, that friendship, too, would come to an end.

And as for the lectures themselves!

True, the hall was filled, but there were few familiar faces. That in itself might not mean anything, for many went away for the summer, and besides almost all of his old pupils were familiar with the Kant lectures.

The "seminar" was naturally attended by a smaller group, for they were not drawn there by curiosity. But here, too, were mostly beginners who were thrilled by the magic name of "Plato."

There was no joy in either. Tiring objectivity on one hand, philological hair-splitting on the other.

It did not pay to lose one's morning sleep or one's afternoon walk on account of either.

No, nothing was worth while any more.

The goal had been reached—and now?

The world remained the same, the loneliness identical.

A shrug of the shoulders—and with that the matter was closed.

"I must look for another apartment," he said to himself each day, "so that the face of that woman will disappear out of my life forever."

But it seemed hard to give up the old accustomed rooms. He felt himself bound to them by thousandfold experiences. Here had originated everything to which value might be attached intellectually. In this sanctified spot, Herma had sat. Here happiness had been a guest in the shape of Helena's ethereal form.

No, not move! Remain there as long as he could and then, for his part, be put out.

Weary, weary!

In what moment, through what motive the thought of a voluntary death had first dawned upon him, he did not know. Perhaps lately, when in the Senate the recollection of the parting words of his predecessor had silenced the bitterness within him.

Although it almost seemed to him as if it had been with him always.

It fell from the tree of life like an overripe fruit.

Madness, of course! Hypochondria! Foolish trifling with an all-too-kind fate.

How many of them were there who had secured a full professorship at the age of thirty-five?

How many were in possession of a fortune, which, if not large, was at least sufficient to enable him to turn his back and shrug his shoulders in defiance of those self-appointed judges?

How many of them had in addition a powerful friend who, in case life became unbearable here, would, beyond a doubt, be prepared to secure him a more agreeable chair?

How many—the questions grew and widened and the answer was invariably, "Hardly any one has been so coddled by Fortune as you have been."

But in spite of everything, the weariness was there and would not be shaken out of his limbs.

Senseless was life—senseless the universe—more senseless than anything, work.

Therefore, if he left the world behind him, his work must go with him.

"Blotted from the tablets of Humanity," he had once said.

If only there had not been that loneliness, that cruel, choking loneliness!

Formerly, he had regarded it as a friend, amiable, rich in conception, laden with thought. Now it had become converted into a constantly watchful assassin.

Where to find a human being as a protection against it? one who would sit with him, who would talk to him, who would laugh away the horror in his soul?

Yes, there was one: That one from whom a kindly wish had flown to him.

Suppose he wrote to him, invited him to come and be a sort of companion to him.

But no. His image was too closely associated with that hour when, untrue to his ideas, untrue to his pride, untrue to his past, he had sat as a crony with shoemakers and tailors at the table of the unliberated and had to be reminded by the young dreamer of what he had formerly been.

The consciousness of that deflection gnawed at him like a growing canker.

Even though thousandfold feelings of hatred and rancor toward the party whose banner carriers appeared to have discarded him had driven him into the ranks of those who now had him by the throat, he had to admit that the desire for personal advancement had also played a part.

And even though this part may have been ever so minor, it was regarded as the only motive by the opposing party and considered a crime. There seemed no possibility of washing himself clean of that accusation. A climber he was—and a climber he would remain. The "pure ones" fairly shuddered at extending a hand to him. Were he to become the greatest thinker of all time, his human side remained besmirched even into the dim gray future.

And this sacrifice of character had been so futile.

So long as one saw such lilies with the waking eye, it was worth living, wasn't it? One needed only human contact. Where was one to get that?

Doubtless those three still sat, faithful to their beer, at the smoke-enshrouded table. After his return from Berlin he had not been with them.

Why not? That they had not sent him their good wishes rankled a little still, but the actual reason was a different one. Since his discussion with the Assistant Minister, the intellectual plane around which they revolved no longer appealed to him and he had lost the taste for its continuation, but now there was a dearth of companionship and it meant that one had to be satisfied with what was available.

And late one evening—around the middle of May —when in the brilliance of the northern light the nightingale's song of sobbing and jubilation welled, he, driven by fear, restrained by disgust, took his way to the tavern in which he had often caroused until early morning.

A hallo greeted him. The regular guests, whom he did not know, shouted a welcome, but the three seemed disgruntled.

"You've, no doubt, become too genteel," said the preacher Möwes, "to associate with such ordinary stuff as we."

And the candidate who had grown even broader and more bloated added, "He only runs around in a swallow-tail coat now to pay formal calls. And his twelve promised brides weep, for the professor's wife is not far in the offing."

The old schoolmaster was already drunk and his eyes were watery and he accompanied his remarks with a shaky slap of the hand. "Crawl under, man. The world bears you a grudge."

Sieburth twitched. He had again, in the prophetic instinct of his drunkenness, hit on the crucial point.

"Well, then, crawl under," he thought, and sat down in his old seat which was empty.

"Why didn't you congratulate me?" he asked.

"Why didn't you call for our congratulations?" asked the preacher Möwes in reply.

"He looks like the owl in the lard pot," laughed the candidate. "He's getting along too well for us."

"There wasn't much doing here without you," slobbered the intoxicated one. "Well, get on with your sage observations—slap them on the wall with a trowel. As long as they're damp one can peel them off."

"He only gives them out now for publication," scoffed the preacher; "paper has more patience than we."

"These, too, have become my enemies," thought Sieburth, "because they are infuriated over my rise."

"You literary scholar over there," he said to the old one, "do you know the Greek account about Diaphon, the envious one, who was sentenced to die

No, there was no one else.

As the night air made him calmer, the feeling of ingratitude took possession of him.

Those nights had *not* been wasted. On the contrary, they had helped to make of solitude the intimate friend which it had recently, under less favorable conditions, become to him. And they had lured many a thought from him or at least converted it into a useful form.

Be that as it may, he was through with the three of them and they deserved their rebuff.

But where was he to find human companionship now? Human beings, human beings!

They had become a scarce commodity in his existence.

There only remained the women one met accidentally and could address in the dark and take to one's rooms, as he had used to do before that dearly loved child had freed his life of that tribe.

Now there was no one who could listen through the wall. Why not indulge, then?

One evening as he was walking down the "Hinter-Tragheim" after theater-closing time, he saw a tall, gracefully rounded form walking ahead of him a little more slowly than was necessary.

Stepping up to her he doffed his hat and as she turned her face towards him, he saw that it was an old acquaintance, but it was impossible for him to place her for the moment.

She, herself, helped him out of the dilemma.

"Heavens! How nice! Why didn't you write to me any more? You were going to write me to the store and you didn't do it after all."

Yes, to be sure—one of the many, and a favorite one at that, for she had one of the most exquisite bodies upon which it had been his pleasure ever to have gazed; but later his evenings had been occupied with the two chorus girls and he had forgotten about her. She was manager of a millinery establishment—in her late twenties—living with her parents, and therefore of unimpeachable virtue—but available for these discreet and harmless little adventures.

Would she come with him? Certainly. She had time and would go gladly. She was so delighted that when she stepped into his study, she staged a regular reunion. She caressed the bust of Plato and found him to have been a fine-looking man, but the friend she had found again was also a handsome man—he unquestionably had nicer eyes.

"Undress yourself," said Sieburth.

She obeyed willingly, as women do who have no cause to withhold their bodily charms.

As she unfastened the gold buckle that held her collar in place, she said proudly, "I received this from you. Do you remember?"

He hardly remembered any more. He thought of the bracelet which he had given the locksmith's daughter and which had been the cause of all of his trouble.

"What a farce—this life!" he thought.

She continued her undressing. When only her chemise remained to be removed, she glanced toward the bedroom and saw that he was far behind her.

"I want to see you naked—here," he said.

That seemed strange to her and almost insulting, but as he insisted upon his wish, she dropped her last garment, cowering in the corner of the sofa.

"There Herma once sat," he thought, "and, how often, Helena."

"Herma—Helena! Herma—Helena!"

But she was beautiful! Lovelier, perhaps, than anything feminine charms had to offer.

"A fitting farewell," he thought, "this last view of womankind."

There was that farewell thought again which pursued him like a Fate by day and by night.

She was about to say something but he silenced her with a gesture.

"Don't speak." He asked, "Don't you see that I'm at devotion?"

That flattered her and she pressed her breasts forward a little so that she would look even handsomer.

He thought of the lily-bed. "As long as such things flourish on the earth—"

But even that no longer exerted a lure.

"Dress yourself, my child," he said, "I'm not in

a very happy frame of mind and would only depress you, too, if I kept you any longer."

He had thought she would feel hurt at being discarded, but without betraying any emotion she slipped the chemise over her head—then she got up, stepped up to him and caressed him.

Obviously, she wanted to console him.

He, sitting in his revolving chair, gazed up at her, wonderingly and gratefully.

The goodness of woman—that innate desire to dispense happiness, came to the foreground even here.

Only that it could no longer dole it out to him.

"What will I give her?" he thought, looking through his drawer, but all the stuff that was there from the past seemed inadequate.

He got the bronze Venus which he had brought with him from Italy, and treasured as his only antique, out of the closet.

"Here—your sister," he said, handing her the figurine. "Love it and cherish it."

She was thoroughly frightened.

"Is that genuine, 'cuivre poli'?" she asked.

"Even more genuine," he replied, "as genuine as your beauty and your goodness."

With that, he let her go. . . .

Attention!—Danger!—Mortal danger!

How to escape?

There were two ways.

Either to find Helena, careless as to consequences, or to go to Berlin to his new friend and say to him, "Help me, I can stand it no longer."

The second he discarded at once. The man had more important things to do than to listen to his pleas for help. The only reply he could give him would be, "Have patience until I can secure a place for you elsewhere," and years might elapse before that was accomplished.

Then there remained the first. That, of course, meant the bankruptcy of life. For no office could survive such a scandal. But suicide was also a life's bankruptcy.

No, it was not that, but rather fulfillment, elevation, and release. One needed only to disguise it in this manner, for, after all, everything was only a disguise.

However, it would be cowardly laxity to steal out of life without seeking an understanding with that dear child.

The next day he went to the post office to find out her mother's whereabouts. Where she was, the daughter would be, irrespective of the reasons for leaving the house and the town.

But they shrugged their shoulders. Mrs. Anna Schimmelpfennig, residing at such and such a place, had left a note stating that she was leaving for parts unknown; and would they keep any letters arriving for her until her return.

Then he went to the police station. There they knew nothing at all. She was not registered as having left and there was probably no registration elsewhere, else there would be official record of it. If he had no further means of tracing them, his efforts would be futile.

So he abandoned this idea too.

If he really wanted to bid life farewell, there were reasons lurking in the background which no tender feminine hands could wipe away as one dusted furniture.

Farewell! Farewell! Always and again that word crept out of the background.

Farewell from whom? There was no one left!

Yes, there was one left; God was still left. The God of his boyhood days. The God Herma had once visited so assiduously.

If only for that reason He deserved a farewell visit.

The next day was a Sunday. He wanted to wait for the hour of high Mass, and seated himself at his writing desk.

Pieces of paper with closely written memoranda lay scattered about on it. His own ideas and excerpts from other authors were jumbled together, disconnected and contradictory.

This he called work these days.

There was Seneca's aphorism, "Qui potest mori, non potest cogi."

And the troubled confession of Septimius Severus, "Omnia fui, et nihil expedit."

Then from Jhering's recently published work, "Teleology in Law," "Where life depends upon darkness the forcible introduction of light is a mortal offense."

Like the lash of a whip was this last merciless sentence, and it applied to almost every field of human endeavor.

But the wisdom of Protagoras, "There are two opposite definitions for everything," made him dubious. He had followed this theory in his trend of thought all too willingly and had on this account neglected the value of convictions. So he had passed by blindly the purport of life, which was subjective, for there was no other.

With all the greater joy he hailed the words of Pascal: "To joke at the expense of philosophy—is the true philosophy."

Often enough he had amused himself similarly, and much of what there was of his own authorship gave evidence of how he had been at odds with his own stock in trade.

"The more intensive the philosophic searching, the more it deserves the kick which unsophisticated thought gives it."

And: "With his vision, man builds the world, with his activity he seeks to establish a home there, and with his thought he again turns it into a mass of ruins."

And more of this kind of thing.

And then a thrust against the greatest of all masters whose chair he occupied: "Anything more absurd than Kant's remark about the two things that fill the being with ever-renewed reverence, the starry firmament above us and the moral law within us, does not exist in the history of thought. That the moral law is nothing more than the accidental precipitate of changing expedients most of us know but won't acknowledge, and the reverent awe at the starry firmament is only a disguised 'horror vacui.' 'Horror nihili,' it should be called. But every one lacks the courage to think this out."

It was a pity about that sentence because it dealt a vicious blow to the hypocrites who merely repeat what others have said. Nevertheless, away with it!

The hour of the errand had arrived. He laid the remaining papers aside and dressed himself in suitable attire.

Then he went to the Sackheim district to the Catholic church in front of which he had so often wanted to await Herma.

The dear, old fumes of incense. Childhood devotion, the glamour of fairy tales. The altar candles bore radiant wreaths. In front of the picture of Mary flowers were piled up.

Yes, that was it. The month of May—the month of Mary.

The priest stood before the high altar and knelt, and then sang this and that, and the congregation responded and the organ burst in with short interludes.

Such things existed. And they afforded people amusement.

Oh, not that! They were entirely serious about it. To them it was revelation. To those who knelt there philosophy counted as a superfluous thing. They were far wiser than he. They had their peace and their happiness. Not one of them thought of a voluntary death. True enough, they dared not.

Here again hung the avenging sword of the concept of duty and the rattle of the Postulates exceeded the organ's swelling tones. "You must live. You must live any dog's life. You must live even if the disgust with it suffocates you."

Not far from him waved a flag of yellowish crumpled silk. Three sweet women's forms were embroidered on it in pale lavender and reddish tones.

"Faith, love, hope," was written underneath in explanation. Oh, no, it ought to have read, "Believe in nothing, hope for nothing, love no one."

That was the motto of the strong.

"You are a fine hero," he thought. "You want to love no one and are sighing after two!"

Then he prayed. Prayed as follows: "Dear God,

thou proof of the poverty of the human brain, thou art necessary to it and therefore thou dost exist. Thou art, of course, not necessary to me, but thou wilt remain in the right, for as punishment I will soon cease to exist. That thou art almighty, the priests affirm, therefore in an enlightened moment, a disciple of Herbart said of thee—what was it he did say?—that it is one's duty to obey God means nothing else than that the wise man submits to superior power. But I am not wise for I am lacking in the necessary subservient spirit. At any rate, I'll do the handsome thing and expiate everything. I don't like unpaid debts.

"Was I selfish? I expiate.

"Was I exultant? I expiate.

"Was I frivolous? I expiate.

"Was I depraved? I expiate.

"Was I untrue to myself? I expiate.

"Or was I too little of all these things? I expiate that too.

"Now surely thou canst be satisfied, dear God."

With that, laughing aloud, he left the church. Those kneeling close to the door looked after him, startled.

This farewell had been a failure. Beyond a doubt. And he was ashamed of it.

How sadly he had been lacking in superiority! He should have been touched. He should have been pious. Had it been so, his capacity for enjoyment

value of which can only be found in the comprehension of its utter worthlessness."

The last clause contained a truth which could easily have been expanded. A whole system of ethics was bound up in it.

All the more foolish, what had gone before! Why should the belief in that fairy tale be an enormity and the belief in this reality not in the same category?

We are hounded from one lie to another so that at last we end up in the ruins of our existence.

"The Nuisance of Existence." How often he had juggled with these words!

Or should it perhaps have read, "The Nuisance of My Existence"?

Careful! Here was a repentant thought which was no less a nuisance.

But no matter where his strength had been spent, it had been spent, and the virginity of the soul which is the origin of all creative activity was gone.

Another, a greater one must come to wield the sword which sank from his hand, one who in a spark-flying combat would shower blows down upon the heads of the opponents, whereas he had only dealt laborious efforts into the air. One to whom the demonry, which he cowardly kept hidden in his brain and in the closet, would be a divine pleasure.

If he perished, this must also perish with him.

When the purple falls the ruler follows, or vice versa. It's all the same.

That was a blow of the fist directed against life which destroyed its values far more than mere dying.

Blotted from the tablets of humanity!

That's as it should be. That was worthy of him.

Make sure of it at once!

A clean sheet of paper. On it his last will: The small fortune, the library, the household effects were to go to Helena. The library she could sell, she could live among the furniture, and the fortune would be her dowry.

Her mother was to be considered, of course. But she would raise no objection. Poverty conquers even hatred.

And then came the principal thing: The destruction of his life's work.

Blotted from the tablets of humanity. Isn't that so?

He could have destroyed the manuscripts and the letters at the same time, but the gentlemen should know he had been no laggard.

"I insist that my remains may not be taken from these rooms until the various papers which at this time are in the two upper shelves of my closet have been burnt in the stove. As the executor of this will I appoint . . ."

Yes, but whom? There was only one available. The one who had sent him the good wishes.

But the letter containing his address was already in the stove.

He knelt on the plate in front of the stove, pulled out the balls of paper from among the winter ashes and searched until he found it.

Then he pushed everything back, added the pile of papers and lighted it.

While the flames licked at the tiles, he wrote further:

"The barrister, Fritz Kühne, Dr. Jur., living at Ober-Laak 23. I obligate him to withstand any attempt to interfere with the carrying out of these wishes in any manner which is lawful and proper."

What else?

Three farewell letters.

The first to Pfeifferling; just as the dying deer hides in the thicket, so the traces of his action had to be wiped away. He sent his so-called friend a polite farewell greeting giving as the reason for his voluntary death a species of hypochondria to whose growing tortures he did not feel himself equal.

The second to Fritz Kühne to inform him of his duties and also to tell him of the confidence reposed in him.

The third and last was to Helena. Few words, only: gratitude, love—thought of, to the last breath.

And that too was a lie. The last breath did not belong to her.

"How quickly one is through with life!" he thought.

He stepped to the window. The setting sun threw a glow on the rooftops. They lay there like floral decorations.

He thought of the lily bed. "I didn't take my leave of that," he thought, and asked himself whether he should go there once again.

But shrugging his shoulders, he put that sentimental notion from him.

Then he pulled Herma's letter out of his pocket, read it through once more, carefully, caressed it and then threw it with the rest, the remnants of which were still aglow.

Where was the revolver? It had not been used since the young crow had lost its life through it.

It was in the drawer of the writing desk hidden underneath the remaining trinkets. There were brooches, buckles, necklaces, and there was also a bracelet left. Everything for the "dozen brides" of whom none accompanied him into the universal bridal chamber.

He gathered the stuff together, swept it into the hollow of his hand and went with it to the court which was altogether empty of people. Making sure that no one saw him from the windows, he threw everything into the ash heap with a rapid movement. That was where it belonged.

Coming back, he examined the barrel of the revolver. There were still three cartridges left. They would suffice.

"Come, sweet death!" Not so stupid after all—that stupid hymn.

"Ah, I won't do it after all," he thought. . . .

CHAPTER XXXV

BLOTTED FROM THE TABLETS OF HUMANITY

WHEN Fritz Kühne, the lawyer, turned in at the Vorder-Rossgarten, he saw already at a distance that the street was filled with people.

As always at these imposing funerals, many people had gathered to gape in wonderment at the probable display of academic pomp.

Gradually gayly colored spots appeared in the dark crowd.

The student fraternities had for the most part marched up already, the color-bearing ones naturally in full regalia. The banners, guarded by the officers in four-seated carriages, were lifted haughtily above the many heads.

The Cheruskia was there too. Fritz greeted the colors which had once despotically crowded themselves between him and the world, with smiling reverence.

So great was the throng that policemen had to keep the space in front of the house of mourning cleared. Since he carried no academic card of identification, his progress was suddenly halted. Only when he could prove to the police lieutenant that an office had been accorded him by the dead man was he allowed to proceed.

He even received an armed escort of honor which piloted him up the steps.

The coffin stood in the hall. Probably the space in the study could not accommodate it and the guests as well.

Wreaths with colored streamers displaying gold inscriptions crowned the cover and leaned against the catafalque.

"From whom could they have come?" thought Fritz, for he knew in what loneliness the dead man had spent the last years.

The doors leading to his rooms, and the landlady's as well, were thrown wide open. Mourners gathered wherever there was room—even the steps leading to the upper floor were full of them.

Abruptly the secretary shoved his squarely built body from one knot of people to another to make room for the professors.

Several of them Fritz knew not merely by sight, for he had once attended their classes and had passed their examinations for his degree.

He did what bowing he needed to do and peered up over the heads close by in search of mother and daughter.

Back in the living room in the midst of the crowd stood Helena with vacant, lifeless eyes staring where there was nothing to see. He pushed through the crowd to her and offered her his hand. At first she looked at him as if he were an utter stranger, then she awakened slowly from her petrification.

"I have taken the manuscripts out of the closet and put them on the desk," she said as calmly and as casually as if they had discussed the matter for some time past, "but I have not lighted the stove because it is already too warm without it. As soon as the time for it comes, I will do it."

"I've been here twice," he explained softly, "but the place was always closed."

"We only arrived yesterday," she replied. "If we hadn't read the announcement in a newspaper, he would have been carried away without—without—"

Now she did falter while her lower jaw moved spasmodically, but by the next moment she had mastered her emotion.

"By the time we came everything had been arranged. The University authorities had attended to it all and the secretary told me about the terms of the will—he also told me what you have to do in connection with it."

"Where is your mother?" he asked.

The staring of her eyes asserted itself again.

"My mother? Oh, yes, my mother! She is sitting in the dark alcove. She's not in a very cheerful frame of mind—but shouldn't we do something about the papers? It seems to me that it's nearly time for it."

"I will make room for you," he said, and pushed ahead of her into the study.

That was emptier than he supposed it would be. Probably the great respect had kept out many. For there sat his Magnificence and the deans. Several of the closer associates also sat there. Of these, each had a stack of closely written sheets on his lap and read as eagerly as if the funeral services did not concern them in the least.

There, cowered together, sat Privy Councilor Auerbach, the great authority on the Roman world, and read and feverishly turned the pages and rocked his gray head to a beat which he alone heard. There sat Pfeifferling and stared wild-eyed at the sheet which he devoured greedily, from time to time emitting a grunt which was half aversion and half admiration.

There sat the dead man's colleague, Professor Hagemann, his cheeks splotched, his breath short, in his excitement crumpling the turned-down sheet and when a hand was free, pulling at his thin irregular beard. Not a sound issued from his lips but now and then he sent a shy glance at the circle as though he feared to be discovered in the commission of a dishonest act.

There one sat reading, there another. Privy Councilor Wendland sat there too, but he did not read. On the gray Apostle-like head which was sunk deep on his chest rested a grief, the manifestation of which seemed hardly to have been applicable only to the head for he had never been close to him. But of what was buried in the bosom of his family, no one had any idea.

In the human wall which had massed itself in the entrance to the study, there was commotion. The secretary, who up to now had preserved order, pushed his two arms forward forming a passageway by sheer force, and when he had accomplished this, a Catholic priest in full vestment followed by two choir boys appeared on the threshold.

The Prorector, who regarded himself as host and first mourner, arose and went towards him. A murmur of understanding, an extravagant handshake, and their two pairs of eyes, one astonished, the other impatient, turned to the readers.

"It is time, gentlemen," said his Magnificence in the hushed tone that the quiet of the house of mourning seemed to demand.

The readers heard the reminder for they looked up quickly, but then returned to their reading undisturbed.

Helena, in the meantime, was kneeling before the stove in order to light the fire and Fritz, who stood beside her, handed her the newspaper which she had laid there in preparation.

The priest, a stocky young man with a wise, all-seeing expression, looked at the face of the Prorector in amazement. The latter bent toward his ear to give him a whispered explanation, and then he raised his voice somewhat and again said, "It is time, gentlemen."

Then Auerbach rose, and, pressing a bundle of papers against his body, he said quite loudly, "Gentlemen, a crime is about to be perpetrated here."

Through the human wall in the hall there was another commotion. The Prorector put his forefinger to his mouth rebukingly and said in a low, commanding tone, "I ask you, gentlemen, to get closer together."

Finally the others also rose and laid the sheets back on the piles which covered the desk.

In their greed for destruction, the flames leaped high.

Fritz Kühne, who had observed every detail, went over to the group bunched together at the window.

Those out in the hall wanted to know what was the matter, but the secretary planted his broad-shouldered form at the beleaguered door to block the way.

"I beg my colleague, Professor Auerbach," the Prorector said in the accepted whispered tone, "to justify the remark he has just made, for I would be responsible for any crime committed here."

The old man's puny form shook. Spasmodically, he felt for his red-rimmed eyes behind his glasses. "I am not in this field," he answered just as softly, "but from what I can gather from what I have read, there are unusual, perhaps never-before-uttered thoughts being brought to light. To destroy these writings would surely mean the sustaining of a heavy loss to the world of knowledge. As for the rest, perhaps our colleague, Professor Hagemann, will be able to express himself with a greater degree of authority."

The Prorector looked over at Hagemann questioningly.

That massive frame of a man, who at all other times went in undaunted comfort on his pedantic way, was unable to find words in this sudden upheaval. He pulled at the stringy beard and at last stammered, "Gentlemen, after half an hour, I cannot give a professional verdict but this much I do know, that I have wronged this man, we all have wronged this man, for we thought he did no work and had nothing to publish and now we see a lifetime of work piled up—what its value is may be in doubt, but its destruction—in my opinion—should not be permitted."

The Prorector shrugged his shoulders adversely, and said, "I have the document with me which gives expression to his last wishes. Before the remains are carried from the house, the papers must be burnt. I know of nothing which will justify interference with these instructions, for as to the intellectual cloud"—here, he cast a furtive look at the priest who stood aside in dignified constraint, and lowered his voice even more—"which we reported to the Catholic parish in order to insure a burial with suitable church rites, privately none of us really believe in it."

Then Pfeifferling took up the discussion. "If it comes to that, Magnificence, I, in a measure, stood closest to the dead man. In fact, I have a farewell letter from him. And I can testify by oath, if necessary, that of late he has been, shall we say, peculiar. If we here agree, a clouded mind or impaired responsibility, or however else the law technically expresses it, could be established to the fullest satisfaction."

The University professors looked at each other approvingly, each one expecting to read the consent which in his heart he had already given, on the face of the other.

Fritz Kühne felt his heart pounding. There could be nothing bolder than for one as young and as callow as he felt himself to be, to stand in open opposition to these mighty and these famous men. But it had to be. The dead man himself had appointed him to carry out his will. With two resolute steps, he walked into the inner circle.

"I ask your pardon, gentlemen,"—a half-dozen pairs of indignant eyes were turned on the presumptuous youngster—"but I, too, am in possession of a document which justifies my interference. May I beg your Magnificence to examine it?" And he handed the Prorector the communication which he had guarded as a sacred relic. He read it carefully and handed it further.

Then he graciously gave Fritz Kühne his hand. "We know each other. There could be no doubt of your identity even though you had no letter. What have you to say to us?"

Fritz, who was fully conscious of the duty that had been imposed upon him, now felt completely free of any timidity.

"It goes without saying that what I am called upon to do tears my heart as it must every one's who understands the matter in hand, but I think we are dealing with a decision that is irrevocable. There can be no question of a mental disturbance. My departed teacher conducted his classes up to the last working day. I have made inquiries. Not one of his pupils noticed the slightest sign of mental confusion or turmoil of the soul. I believe that under these circumstances no one can undertake to commit the sin of interference with his last will."

An embarrassed silence ensued.

The priest, who had obviously tried to assume indifference to the proceedings, now considered that the moment had arrived when he should remind the learned gentlemen of his sacred function.

It was just the tiniest motion, a mild, almost help-of worshiping at the grave, of offering the heart-swelling devotion to which he could not give vent during empty ceremonials.

As he went through the latticed door, the gate keeper did not want to let him enter. It was too late and there were no longer any visitors inside.

But a bright thaler changed the situation. He might stay as long as he wished. He would find the gate open. A long path led through the labyrinth of shadowed graves. At last something colored and something white gleamed through the blue purpling night. And over the flower-bedecked sandy mound lay a woman's form fallen from a kneeling position, the face buried in the wreaths.

"Helena," the thought flashed through his brain.

He lifted her up. He shook her free of leaves and earth. He spoke to her with pleading words. And when even then her body still required support, he quickly got a bench from a neighboring grave.

Now she sat quietly hunched in the corner, stared tearlessly ahead of her and let him talk however he liked.

Involuntarily he referred to her mother.

Then she started up abruptly.

A look of horror glided past him into space.

"Have I hurt you?" he asked, frightened.

She was silent and stared.

"Has your mother hurt you?"

Again she was silent and stared.

"Do say something. It will do you good. It will lighten your heart."

Then she burst out: "My mother—yes, indeed, my mother. I could have saved him. I alone— but my mother forbade me. I had a presentiment about the whole thing. I cried for him day and night. But I dared not write to him—not even to tell him where I was, for she would plunge him into the misfortune she threatened—and so he remained in his solitude . . . and he only did it because he was so lonesome. If I had been with him he would be alive and everything would be all right."

Dismayed, he heard this confession which seemed an utter surrender. And beyond that he had a presentiment of destiny and consecration at which his soul bowed before her.

"I know—you always loved him," he said, remembering that far distant rejection.

She did not deny anything. "He wrote to you," she said, "but he also wrote to me."

She unbuttoned her blouse and handed him a letter. And when he hesitated to take it, she said, "Just read it, I have nothing to conceal."

The evening light still sufficed to decipher the words of his farewell.

"You are the only one on earth I am leaving behind. To me you are like my beloved, like my wife, and I love and honor you as such."

"Once, when I did not know my way in or out," he answered, "and in my anxiety, asked you what I could do, you gave me this reply: 'One must be good.' Do you remember?"

"Yes," she reflected, and nodded.

"That seemed silly to me at the time, but the longer I thought about it the more I found that there was no better recipe with which to get on in life."

"He was good," she sobbed, "and yet he perished."

"Dear Miss Helena," he replied, "we two will not solve the riddle as to the cause of his death. That is all too difficult and too confused for us. Perhaps later clarity will come to us—perhaps never. It is possible that his works might have revealed it—but they are gone."

"Aren't you making yourself any reproaches on that account?" she asked.

"No," he answered in a tone of conviction. "The departed must be able to depend upon those he trusts for the carrying out of his wishes. They are the part of him that still lives, and therefore we must feel no doubts or regrets—not you, nor I. And as comfort we must say to ourselves: 'The truth which they contained will come again.' Perhaps it is already here—only that we do not know it."

Again there was silence between them.

The twilight glowed darkly, throwing black, jagged, lattice-like shadows among the branches.

Somewhere a nightingale sang. Now and again from the far-off harbor a long-drawn-out, weary, ebbing whistle was heard.

"Oh, how secure we are here!" she whispered.

"And even so we shall have to go," he reminded her.

"Yes," she said, "and I will go home to my mother. She goes from one spell of crying into another. I will sit beside her and pet her, for one must be good, you said."

"No, you said that," he replied with a serious smile.

"But I did not act accordingly," she said, and rose.

She reeled a little, but then she straightened herself out and stood staunchly.

And while he carried the bench upon which she had been sitting back to its old place, she bent over the mound and replaced the wreaths which she had disturbed.

On one of the silk streamers which was luxuriantly spread above the others glowed the gold inscription in the twilight, "Our never-to-be-forgotten friend—Marion and Rudolf Follenius."

"That friendship, too, had dwindled away," she said, pointing down at it.

He laughed a short abrupt laugh, and replied, "It was probably worth just as much as those others, the proofs of which are lying about here. I fear if we do not keep faith with him, he will soon be forgotten." And as in parting a new paroxysm of weeping caused her to totter, he softly laid her arm in his and led her from the abode of ever-wakeful death back into the sleep-laden world.

END OF VOLUME II